Habit

Habit
Copyright © 2021 by Kassandra Dick
All rights reserved.

Published by Kindle Direct Publishing
First Canadian edition

No part of this book may be used or reproduced in any manner whatsoever
without the prior written permission of the author,
except in the case of brief quotations embodied in reviews.

ISBN 979-8-5989-0676-7

Cover by Joel Macleod, Dream State Design

Special Thanks

to Bert Van Cleemputte,
who gently reminds me that
Writing is Erasing.
To my Editor, Merielle Kazakoff,
who came into my life at the perfect time.

To my whole family, blood and soul,
you are the ones I think about late into the night.
To my twin flame, Connor Gray,
you are the one I call.
In loving devotion to my teachers,
this is not the book you deserve, but it's only my first.

Mike opened his eyes against the darkness. Far off, the heater pumped hot air into their stifling Vancouver apartment. Mike didn't know what woke him. He only knew he would not be going back to sleep. His body ached when he rolled over and his bladder almost gave out. His mouth was dry as he moved his tongue across furry teeth. He must've passed out before he could brush them.

There was a cough stuck in his throat. He tried to clear it softly, so not to wake his sleeping wife, but the sensation remained. Worse, the effort made his brain throb. Many mornings began like this, with the full bladder, the swollen skull, and the desire to exercise some demon from his throat. Mike crept out of bed and made his way through the night.

Blinking in the black hallway, he felt as if he was moving through liquid. The night-time fog still clung to him. The little workout timer that sat on their toilet stated that it was 5:04. Mike flicked on the light and felt instant regret. Lightning struck his eyeballs. At the same time, a slug of mucus edged its way up his throat. He closed the door behind him, took a piss, and began his ritual. The demon burned all the way up Mike's aching esophagus until he was able to expel it with one shot into the sink. Once Beelzebub was freed, Mike turned the tap on full, and blasted the red-brown bastard down the drain. *Fuck it*, he thought. *I'm quitting today.*

He squeezed some toothpaste out and began to scrub his mouth. In the mirror, he saw his thin brown hair get caught in the up breeze of the heater. He had a simple, toned-down version of the pompadour he'd seen on most men these days. He didn't like to have to style it every day, but he liked the look of it with the top slicked back like a greaser. Mike ran a hand through his hair. He rolled his eyes at himself and felt a pang in the inner muscles. Stretching his eyes wide, he saw they were bloodshot and tinted yellow. There were dark shadows underneath them too. Mike spat out the toothpaste, along with more tell-tale phlegm, and then he tried to smile at his reflection.

In the hallway, Felix, his wife's twelve-year-old cat and best friend, mewed and scratched at the door. Mike opened it and the grey tabby brushed past him and went straight to the litter box.

"You better not be taking a shit," said Mike, but Felix only blinked at him and rooted around in the gravel. Mike turned back to the mirror. If he tilted his head up towards the vanity lights, he wasn't that bad looking. His eyes, despite their haggard appearance, were a pleasant brown with gold rings around the outer circles. He was tall and wide in the shoulders. His body was not toned the way it had been in his twenties, but it was still strong from years of football, hockey and, of course, hauling patients in and out of ambulances.

He was mostly just out of shape; his pale stomach showed under his t-shirt as he stretched and yawned. He hiked the shirt up over his head, revealing a pair of large, lax pecks dotted here and there with round scars.

On his back were matching scars. Mike had blanked on where these marks came from; just some stupid drinking game involving cigarettes and college boys, he figured. He ran his fingers through his hair while narrowing his eyes and frowning slightly. *That's alright,* he thought, but then he looked down at his hand. There were mousy-brown hairs tangled in his fingers. He bent down to shake them into the garbage. As he stood up, Angie appeared in the mirror beside him.

"How're you feeling, Hon?" Her concern showed through her toothy smile. What she meant was, *I heard you coughing all night.*

"Fine," Mike replied, trying to sound fine—not wanting to alarm her or give her that casual false promise that he'd given so many times before. No. Mike was tired of talking about quitting. Tired of feeling like shit in the morning and shit at night. He felt like his life depended on giving up this vice, and there was no need to jinx it by saying so out loud.

Angie caught on that he wasn't telling her something. She wanted to press him, but she was nervous of the back and forth—nervous of being the nagging wife her first husband had always accused her of being. No. If Mike wanted to talk about his health, he could say so. She bent down to scratch Felix who now wound himself around her ankles. He purred loudly.

"Okay," she heard herself saying. Her green speckled eyes met Mike's in the mirror. She turned from him and examined herself, feigning care about a stray grey hair in her shoulder-length, blue-black braid. At 6'2", Angie was four inches taller than Mike, though she had a habit of stooping. Years of childhood bullying made her cautious of standing at her full height. Seated in her office or conference room, she was the picture of poise, but standing, she preferred to shrug and pop her hip out—anything to seem shorter than she was. In their cramped bathroom her stature was unmistakable, but she leaned over the sink and busied herself with a makeup bag, otherwise ignoring her reflection.

Mike could not help but steal glances at his wife as he took a capful of mouthwash and swished it through his teeth. She really was attractive apart from her lack of confidence. Mike didn't care about that though; it made her modest in his opinion. In public, he'd learned to ignore her twitchy eyes and compulsive smiling. In private, he never shouted or showed aggression. She was humble and charming and, most importantly, she was kind. Angie was a vegetarian. Mike wasn't. He sometimes wished she'd show him the same

Habit

kind of love she showered their cat with, but then again, Mike wasn't the affectionate sort.

Angie had anxiety, hand delivered with a bottle of benzodiazepines, by her first husband. Jackson Forcier gave Angela Dane many things after their wedding day, including broken bones and a busted nose. The nose had been reconstructed beautifully. Only the slight bump on her bridge and a tiny scar gave it away. Angie and Mike both had scars. They even shared a scar. Each had had their collarbones snapped at some point in their lives.

You would think she'd be able to hold her own—this tall, Amazonian woman—but Angie's gentle heart kept her from defending herself even when her life had depended on it.

Mike realized he'd been staring at the jagged pink scar that ran the length of Angie's cheek. Angie caught him with a look, but went back to her own reflection without comment. That scar was the last thing Jackson Motherfucking Forcier had gifted her. If Mike could have been there when it happened... Mike looked away. Violence. He saw so much of it in his line of work, or the results of it anyway. He pulled out a length of floss and set to scraping the crevices of his teeth. Angie was applying some cream under her eyes.

When she stood still like this, immune to the world around her, she was a painting of alabaster skin and raven hair. The little cracks at the corners of her mouth and eyes were testaments to a full smile. The little rolls under her full breasts were testaments to joy. As Mike slathered on some shaving cream, he found himself wondering how they must look together: he with his sunken eyes and permanent grimace, she with her incessant smiling and aversion to eye contact. To Mike, of course, Angie was beautiful and successful. She owned her own marketing firm that served local pharmacies, real estate agents, and contractors. *It's not that big of a deal*, she often said. Yet even though her business wasn't reaching multi-million dollar deals, she was still a big player compared to him, an overworked and underpaid paramedic.

Eternity passed them by with only the sound of Mike's razor, shucking the day-old hair off his face, along with the little puff-puffs of Angie's makeup brushes. How she managed to cover that scar still amazed Mike. It wasn't textured. Her doctor saved her from that fate. It was just pink, and it became pinker anytime she flushed. She was flushing now. That's how he knew she knew he was looking at her. Neither spoke. Even as he watched the process from the corner of his eye, Mike didn't quite understand what he was looking at. First one layer, then another, then another, then powder and the lightest blush. She was flawless.

Felix interrupted his thoughts with a respectful mewl.

"Be right there, Sweety," Angie chimed.

She would make a great mom. Mike let that thought pass, as he'd let it slip away ever since the day they'd stopped talking about a baby. Mike wouldn't mention her beauty, or her brains, or her motherly perfection. It would only upset her. He didn't know what to say that wouldn't upset her these days. He had to pull himself out of the ditch he'd been living in. Nothing he ever said felt real. He was on a conveyor belt and too often he'd agreed to try as soon as he was off the darts. He was supposed to quit before his 39th birthday, back in June.

Angie had set up their room with candles, soft music, and rose petals she'd painstakingly plucked and placed about the bed in a heart. Mike wasn't supposed to see the scene until after his birthday party. He'd run in for his keys when his father keeled over the barbecue, but he'd never even mentioned what he'd seen. It was too painful. Cleaning up the undisturbed flowers the next morning had been painful for Angie too, but she'd never mentioned trying again. A silent contract had been drawn up.

His father, Alan, had been his best friend and the loss sent Mike reeling into nicotine and drink. Now it was October and Mike had become a serial smoker and reclusive drunk, which was difficult considering his profession. He hadn't sunk so low as to carry a flask around, but he'd slip away to sneak a drag anytime he could. Sometimes his patients would smell it on him and either ask if he could stand a little farther back, or they'd ask if they could bum one. He'd been called into Peach's office three times since June too. The first was to instruct him that he'd been given a personal number to call to reach a therapist; Mike never called him. The second was to warn him that his late entrance every other morning had been noted. Even with the warning, he was only able to make it on time three out of four days. The third time was to kindly ask him to take a leave of absence and, as Peach had put it, *stop avoiding his therapist and start mourning properly.*

Today was the first day back, but nothing had changed over the week he'd spent *recuperating*. If anything he'd drank more and smoked twice as much. Apart from that, Mike remained a high-functioning addict, even if his liver did feel like it had been functioning at 40% since August.

Felix meowed a little more urgently now. They both looked. Mike smiled over to Angie, and Angie smiled down at the cat. When he looked back into his own reflection, he saw the razor pressed against the skin of his throat, Mike watched a dribble of blood roll off into the sink, and thought about his marriage dripping down the drain too.

Habit

Angie and Mike had been married for about a year. They were only in their late thirties—very late in Mike's case. Still, health problems weren't supposed to tear them apart for another ten years. Mike's late-night therapy sessions with the whiskey bottle and the little white quacks put him on the fast track towards—well, neither of them wanted to talk about the big C. This morning, it was too much for Mike to let go of both his vices though. He chose smoking because it felt easier than alcohol. He knew he'd have to cut back on that too if he really wanted to end this. Frankly, he had no motivation to quit even though he knew better than most people what was in store.

Meanwhile, Angie struggled with her thoughts on coming to terms with this new partner in her life. She remembered when they used to spend their late nights together. Now, all he wanted was to take a bottle out onto the balcony and sit there on his own. It was like he thought his dad was out there, smoking with him. Angie was determined not to leave Mike just because he was sad though. She'd promised herself that much. Hell, she'd stayed with Jackson five years after he turned mean. If she could stay for a monster, she could stay for a man who'd lost both his parents too young and who was only trying to find comfort, even if it had become Southern Comfort. Angie *was* going to see this marriage through. She just hoped he wouldn't smoke himself into an early grave. When it seemed like they would be in this hollow space in the bathroom forever, Angie put away her instruments. She observed herself and then Mike. He met her eyes in the mirror.

"Well, I'll see you this evening then," she mentioned. Mike deposited his whiskers into the sink and wiped his mouth. They kissed with a mediocre smacking sound. Then with half-smiles, they parted, each smelling the fading morning dew of the other and wondering what exactly was left for a couple once they'd come to this crossroads.

Mike dawdled away the rest of his morning, trying to keep himself barricaded indoors, not wanting to be tempted to buy a pack before work. He wound up settling for one shot of whiskey and then one more for the road. He was late to work again and Peach, his petite, strawberry-blonde supervisor, was pissed right off.

"You're a pain in my ass. You know that? Michael?" Mike looked up from the floor. "What if we had had a call? Tom and Sara have been waiting twenty minutes for you."

"Sorry, Peach." He was. "I've been sick all morning..." She eyed him. "But I'm okay now." Peach looked him up and down, reading the dark circles under his eyes like newsprint.

"Well, it's not much of an apology. I just hope you're actually taking your health seriously."

Mike nodded emphatically. Even when she was mad at him, he liked her. Since the day he'd set foot in her office four years ago, having transferred here from Prince Rupert, it was a crush that never seemed to stop crushing him. He liked her curvy body. He liked her no-nonsense attitude and her cursing. He liked her curly hair most of all. Peach had the bounciest hair he'd ever seen. Where Angie's were temporary and his mother's had been limp, freeze-dried curls, Peach's were perky and sun-kissed. She was also one of the most intelligent women Mike knew; the other being Angie, of course.

"Don't let this happen again," Peach was saying.

He nodded, but then shook his head.

"No, it won't."

After backing out of Peach's office, Mike clocked in then found the crew and muttered an apology to some of the others on duty that morning. Eric just shook his head and clapped Mike on the back. The newest member of the team assumed the only reason anyone could have for being late was because they were having some raunchy sex at home. Zane said nothing but handed an inspection sheet over to Mike. Tom and Sara were already ducking out of their uniforms when they saw him coming. Mike gave them a tired wave and found himself muttering more apologies. It was his first day back and already he'd pissed off half the team.

Then he felt a slap on his shoulder and Val was saying, "Welcome back." Mike smiled at his partner. The 53-year-old ex-soldier was 220 pounds of old-man muscle and divorcee practicality. Next to him, Mike felt like a freshman even though he'd been a paramedic for ten years and an EMT for four years before that.

"Thanks, Val. Good to see you."

"Ditto."

They puttered through the daily inspection. Mike was in no shape to make small talk and Val didn't press him. He appreciated how the older man knew his moods. They'd been partners on and off for four years now, and they had a clear sense of each other after thousands of hours of dealing with their patients' pain and suffering.

Mike's throat was still raw. He was itching for a cigarette, but he couldn't bear the guilt of lighting one up. He picked at an old scratch on his arm

Habit

instead, peeling off the dirty brown top layer—another bad habit for a man in his line of work. Unsurprisingly, the gash started to bead up with blood. Mike took an alcohol swab to it, swearing under his breath as if surprised by what he'd done. Twelve minutes later, a call came about an overdose some fifteen blocks away.

"You're on, rookie," called Val, tossing the keys to him. Mike smiled. He had only driven the vehicle every day of their partnership. Val was myopic but refused to wear his glasses so long as he could avoid it. Keying the ignition, Mike let out a sigh. He put on his cap, tossed the ambulance into gear, and began the day by scraping the right side of the vehicle against the garage panels.

"Fuck," Mike breathed.

Luckily, the sirens weren't on so only a few umbrellas outside turned to see what had happened. Luckier still, he hadn't busted the light or damaged the tire. There was just a perfect line of cat claws along the side door. Once he'd checked out the damage, Val shrugged and got back into the vehicle.

"Come on. They can put your head on the block once you're finished saving lives."

It was rainy season in Vancouver, though Mike couldn't really remember a season without rain in this city. He managed to avoid any further destruction, but the day fell down around them in wet, miserable drops. The overdose turned out to be a waste of time. The supposed victim either was only sleeping or he'd been frightened away when they arrived. The request for help had been made on an unregistered phone number; no one in the area could even point them in the right direction.

They went to three more calls before lunch. Then there was another overdose sometime around noon, and this one was real and frothing and fatal. Then a heart attack only an hour later, and less than an hour after that, someone was suffering unspeakable pain in their stomach, which was possibly appendicitis, though they wouldn't let Val or Mike near them for an assessment. The patient made a miraculous recovery when he found out that, no, they were not able to *just* give him something for the pain and, yes, he would have to be registered when they reached the hospital.

By the end of the twelve-hour shift, Mike felt like a bent-up cigarette. He hadn't had a single smoke out of guilt—plus he'd left the pack in the glove box of his Ford—so he was desperate to get into his truck and chain-smoke the whole way home. He said goodbye to Val and the others, including Tom and Sara who were ready to start their next night shift.

Mike liked Tom; he was the one who worked nights with him. He didn't know Sara all that well. She worked four days here and then the next four at another hospital in North Van. She was only about 22—a nice kid though, and noble as all hell. She was the kind of EMT who would stop at nothing to save people. This, while admirable, usually amounted to the expensive replacement of drugs and equipment without an increased survival rate. It was something Tom would need to train out of his protégé before she became a paramedic. Mike didn't want to chat with them. He was thirsty for more than the dust-encrusted hospital water. He changed out of his uniform and washed the day's memory off his hands.

Walking past Peach's office, he peered in. She sat behind two computer monitors and her hair was still in perfect ringlets even after a full day. Her skin was glowing, and not just because it was next to the screens. Peach, like Angie, was a strong, capable leader. Besides having to deal with all of the timetables and route schedules for employees, plus all the station's inventory, she was also responsible for complaints, wages, and all manner of disagreeable paperwork. Yet, she never complained except with sarcastic bouts of misanthropic cursing.

It was all of these qualities that had made him fall in love with her in this very office during his interview back before the dawn of time. In fact, when she'd presented him to Angie as a blind date two years ago, he'd been taken aback. Getting to know Angie had in many ways smoothed out this school-boy crush. Still, he often wondered what it would have been like to marry Peach, with her cool demeanour, her smooth, blushed cheeks like the fruit she was named for, and that mane of hair. Peach looked up and smiled, oblivious to how long he'd been standing there, or unfazed.

"Oh Michael, it's okay. You can go. I'll have the insurance papers for you tomorrow."

She turned back to her monitors.

Mike's memory lapsed. "The insurance papers?"

"Yes," Peach replied slowly, "for the incident with the wall this morning."

Mike flinched. "Right."

He questioned why she kept him on, unless she really did have feelings for him too; she probably only felt sorry for him. Ever since his father passed, he'd been pushing the limits of work ethic. Not only that, but concerned citizens were always phoning in with his ID number, either for his poor bedside manner or because he smelled of cigarettes.

"Right," he said again. God, he needed a drink. "Well, goodbye."

Peach caught the resignation in his voice and looked up again.

"Wait, Mike. Are you alright?" She didn't wait for an answer. "I worry about you. You know that don't you? I worry about Angie too. I haven't seen her in two weeks and I think she might be getting depressed from

Habit

worrying about you too. Both of you better show up for Thanksgiving, you understand." It wasn't a question. Peach was Angie's best friend. She was the one who caught the bouquet at their wedding. If nothing else, the fate of Peach's potential future husband rested in Mike's hands.

"Course we will." Mike didn't know what else to say, but that was the beauty of Peach; she never held a grudge and she never let a silence turn sour.

"Good. I'll see you tomorrow, Michael."

"Yeah, thanks. See you, Peach."

As soon as he was safe in his truck, Mike smacked open the glove box. His pack was there waiting for him. He fumbled to withdraw the last skinny wolf. *Well, if that's not a sign*, he thought, twirling the cigarette between his fingers the way his dad used to. He wasn't deep in thought the way his dad used to be. He was just trying to remember where his lighter was without having to pat himself down. Then he realized it was right beside his spare keys in the little dish that Angie kept in the hallway. It was a big-eyed fish that she made in her pottery class last year. Its bulgy stare still made him smile even when he'd forgotten his keys in its mouth day after day.

With the mystery solved, there really was no point in wishing he had some other form of fire. He'd lost his truck's old electric lighter, and he wasn't about to go buy a Bic just to light his last cigarette. After one longing look at the small white smoke, he sighed and slapped it back into the compartment.

The drive home felt like a loop for Mike. He tuned into some AC/DC on the radio and went over the trials of the day again. The routine in the bathroom with Angie, the lack of sleep, the lack of motivation and libido... Everything was normal, yet inside something seemed irreparable. It was as if Mike had read his obituary in the mucus this morning. Was this how people managed to quit? It felt anticlimactic.

His thoughts turned to Angie, who had the same dark circles under her eyes as he did, although she covered them up so well. He thought about whether this change would really be enough to salvage the feelings they'd had prior to his dad's death and his own health deteriorating. He had to do this. His sanity depended on it and so did his marriage. If he didn't quit right here, right now, this could be the real end.

He realized his fingers were twirling against his thigh. Alan Perry, his dad, used to have a trick where he could pass a lit cigarette between his fingers while holding a bottle of beer in the same hand. He had to quit once his arthritis had set in and he burned a strip across the back of his hand. Mike couldn't think about his father at all without flashing back to their last meal together. Val, Tom, and Peach were all there, plus the night shift sierra, Rita, and Angie's parents. They were throwing a barbecue in the park for Mike's 39th birthday. The day they planned to try for a baby.

Alan didn't look good. He hadn't looked good since his wife died in 1973, actually, and Mike always felt guilty that he chose to block out the memory of his late mother. Her death was part of the reason Mike didn't want to have kids. His dad just stood around at the barbecue staring at people, muttering under his breath. He had been muttering insults, Mike realized when he got up close. Alan was acting off ever since Mike picked him up. Then he threw up blood.

There was far too much blood intermixed with the chips and dip on the grass. What was worse, was that his father fell face first into it. If it had been a cartoon, maybe it might have been funny. In reality, it was the scariest thing Mike had even witnessed. Scarier than any emergency.

Mike wanted to drive his dad to the hospital, but he too was inebriated; that would have been the end of his career right there. But Val insisted on driving and Mike held his dad in the back seat. Mike wanted to help with his intake, but the emergency nurses pushed him out of the room. When Alan puked up more blood and lost consciousness, it was enough to sober Mike completely. That night, the doctors discovered the burst vein in his esophagus. The next day, the report came that he had class C cirrhosis. He was given a few months.

"No donor list." His famous last words.

Maybe two weeks after that, he had another hemorrhage in his sleep, this time in his brain. The stroke lasted well over twelve minutes, even with emergency intervention, and it cost his dad his life. Mike was there to see it happen, but once again he could do nothing to prevent it. Sometimes, the inability to save his old man hurt more than just losing him.

Tears started to blur Mike's vision. He veered off to the side of the road next to Livingstone Park. Closing his eyes, he could see his dad's yellow fingers still twirling an unlit cigarette, and sans bottle, even while he wore a hospital gown. Mike killed the engine and sat in darkness, trying to remember what his mother used to say about his dad while he was on the road and they were left behind at the farmhouse up north. Was he the gleeful, amusing friend that Mike remembered, or the "bastard" his mom used to scream he was whenever he left alone? Hell, his mom was worse. She'd called his dad all kinds of nasty things, but she was the one who decided to overdose and leave her husband and their fourteen-year-old son. Mike tried to remember a time when his mom didn't have her drug of choice warming up on a spoon—*fuck*. He broke the thought stream and wiped at his eyes.

Habit

Breathing out, Mike rolled down the window. The outside air was so frigid it made the tear streaks on his face sting. He heard conversation on the air and saw two figures walking along the path towards him. He wondered if the couple in the distance were smokers. If they had a lighter, then Mike's conscience could be clear. He would just ask for a light, smoke this final dart, and start fresh tomorrow. Maybe he would even forgo his ritual nightcap. They were within shouting distance now and Mike could see two small orange orbs at their fingertips. He made his move, finding the cigarette but dumping the contents of the glove box all over the passenger's seat in the hunt. Then he opened the truck door with what he hoped seemed like indifference instead of fiendish haste. He realized his seatbelt was still on right before he made a real fool of himself. With shrugged shoulders, Mike approached the pair.

"Scuse me," he called to them. They looked up with the butt of a joke between them, and Mike continued, "You gotta light?" The boy stepped forward and brandished his lighter, clearly not interested in getting too close to a stranger who had just been sitting there in a truck, in the darkness.

"Catch," he said, tossing the lighter from about ten feet away. Mike held out his hand nonchalantly and the lighter passed through his fingers and hit the ground. He retrieved it, fumbled to get his smoke lit, but the lighter was non-responsive. No matter how he shook it up, tilted his head, or spun around, Mike could not resuscitate. Finally, the girl approached with a laugh.

"Must be a dud," she said. "Take mine." Mike was grateful she didn't throw it. Her small hands were warm when he brushed them. As she handed him the lighter he could see the details of her face. She looked about sixteen; she had the same kind of heavy eyeliner and red lipstick that Angie wore in her old high school photos.

Mike struck the flint, thanked her, and the boyfriend interrupted, "Can I have my lighter back?" Mike tossed the empty lighter back without looking, hoping to catch him off guard, but of course boy wonder caught it like he'd been waiting all day for the throw. Mike returned the other lighter to the girl. She brushed his hand this time. Mike could have pulled her fingers in towards him, but he resisted the urge and dropped his hand to his side. He made eye contact only to realize she had been staring at him the whole time. Now she stood unmoving, even while her friend was heading off down the path.

"You don't look so good, Dude," she said with slipshod concern. Mike shifted on his feet. She probably saw the tear stains.

"Yeah well, getting old does that to you." His voice sounded gruff even to himself. He inhaled from his cigarette. After a day without nicotine, he felt buzzed from the hit. His throat was still raw, but he willed himself not to cough. He'd hate to really scare the kid.

The girl smiled, but the boyfriend called over his shoulder, "Smoking'll do that to you too." Mike glanced at the lit cigarette in the kid's fingers.

Without mentioning hypocrisy, Mike muttered, "I'm actually thinking of quitting tomorrow." The girl's face lit up.

She said, "You know, my grandpa quit smoking when he was 86. He still died of lung cancer, but it was pretty amazing." Mike wasn't really sure how to reply. He didn't have a chance to though because she kept talking. "I had one cousin who quit with Nicorette, another one who used those pills—you know, the ones that give you freaky nightmares?" She took a drag off her cigarette and continued, the smoke obscuring her voice, "Course, you could always try hypnotherapy." The other youth finally registered that his friend wasn't going to follow him, so he rejoined them.

The boy said, "What kind of therapy?"

"Hypnotherapy. I looked it up when my mom threatened to kick me out if I didn't quit. First they get you into a state of relaxation, then they make suggestions about things you already want to change. Like if you really want to quit smoking," she looked directly into Mike's eyes, "then your subconscious will open up and you'll be able to work towards your true desires." She took another drag, but found her dart was only half lit. She held it up and blew on the tip to keep the spark. Looking into the cherry of her cigarette, she said, "It's kind of spiritual if you think about it..."

The boy didn't let her finish that thought. He threw his butt to the ground and said, "That's stupid. My dad says you can only quit cold turkey, and everything else is just a suit of science." Mike smiled. He thought the kid was probably right, even if he didn't know what he was saying. For a minute they all stood around in the smoke clouds, the boy kicking rocks and the girl still staring—off in the distance, back to Mike, down at her cigarette. Finally, Mike realized his own cigarette was halfway through. He hastily bid the kids goodbye, hoping to savour the last few drags without these two.

"Good luck." It was the boy's sarcastic groan.

The girl said nothing, only waggled a goodbye with her fingers.

Once again in his cockpit, Mike inhaled the very last of his smoke. His throat burned fiercely and his eyes watered from the stray fumes. He closed his eyes, waiting for the pain to subside. Then he methodically double-checked every empty pack in his truck for one last cigarette. He ran his fingers along the inside of the boxes, trying to will one into being. Eventually he had to give up and go home.

Habit

Angie was passed out in bed when he got back. She must have taken one of her pills when she got home. Sometimes she did that when work was stressful. *Or when she's avoiding me.* He could hear her snoring while he fished around in the fridge for any dinner she might have prepared. Nothing but leftovers from the night before. That was fine. She worked hard too. He always liked it when she surprised him though.

Felix made an appearance while Mike was putting together a double Alabama Slammer, hold the orange juice. The cat sang for his supper even though Mike was sure Angie would have fed him before she went to bed. She never forgot about the cat.

"Come on, you deadbeat." Mike poured a handful of kibble into his dish while Felix wrapped himself around Mike's legs. He stared down at the silly cat, with his fluttering tail and his big ass.

"You're getting fat," Mike told him. Felix looked around, licking his chops. He looked to his left, then his right, and then he blinked up at Mike as if to ask, *Who exactly are you talking to?*

Mike couldn't sleep yet. He was still wired from being on for twelve hours. He slumped onto the couch, his drink in one hand and a mix and match meal in the other. He flipped absently through Netflix shows before landing on some kind of true crime series. Around midnight he retreated to the bedroom.

Angie's deep, peaceful inhales made Mike sigh in unison. He undressed and crawled in beside her, careful not to touch her, yet aching for her to wake up, roll over, and nudge herself into his outline. She always did that when she was sleeping naturally, but tonight she kept on snoring. She was deep in the realm of zolpidem. Mike lay stiffly on his back, breathing softly, until sleep overtook him.

At 6 a.m., the birds began their routine. Their voices mixed into the violent dream Mike was having about ramming his ambulance into a crowd of people. His breaks had failed and no matter how hard he held his foot down, the machine plowed on. Screams became chirps until finally his eyes were open and he was conscious enough to feel disturbed. He recalled his decision to quit smoking, just as the first craving of the morning set in. Mike braced himself to hold out for as long as he could. Slowly and carefully he rose from the bed. He peeked over at Angie, who was watching him with one eye open. Her hair covered most of her face, but he could see she was smiling that comfortable morning smile, like a reset button.

"Good morning, beautiful," he ventured. She buried her face under the covers, but he'd already seen that toothy grin. Not wanting to press his luck, he kissed her on the side of the head and left the room.

In their tiny apartment kitchen, Mike gargled salt water to try and kill whatever bacteria had taken residence in his dry mouth. Then he put on the coffee. Felix was chattering at the birds, so Mike let him out onto the balcony. He watched the cat pace back and forth. His little potbelly wobbled as he slunk to and fro along the barrier. Every now and then, Felix stuck his head between the bars to swipe at the pigeons flapping around on the building next to theirs. Mike didn't know if it was a desperation thing, or a lack of depth perception, but he shook his head. That cat was a few hairs short of a fur coat.

After clattering around in the kitchen, Mike found they had nothing for breakfast, so he attempted to cook oatmeal. Angie only liked the stone-cut kind that took twice as long to cook and never quite softened all the way through. He found a Ziploc bag of the stuff way in the back of the pantry. Mike chopped up a week-old apple from his lunch bag and added cinnamon and some ageless rocks of brown sugar. Then he sat with his coffee, waiting for Angie to emerge.

While listening to her sing in the shower, he realized he was thinking about buying a pack. He racked his brain to remember if there was a stray smoke in his coat pocket, or maybe in the truck somewhere. He had to shake himself free of the fruitless endeavour. There was not a single cigarette left and he knew it. For a moment, he wondered if this was going to be the end after all. He was already looking at the clock to see if he'd have time to make it to the gas station before work. If Angie sat down with him right now, everything would work perfectly.

Fifteen minutes later, Angie entered. She spied the food on the table and smiled at him. She wanted to fix her coffee first, so with her back to Mike, she chatted to him as she found the soy milk and the sugar.

Habit

"I thought I heard you rummaging around," she said. "Thanks for breakfast, Hon. Are you excited for the weekend? Only one more shift. Maybe we should go out tonight. There's a blues band playing…" She turned and Mike knew too late that he was scowling, still thinking about how to get his paws on another smoke.

"What's wrong?" Angie asked, sitting down close to him.

"No, it's nothing." Mike hurried to smile. He awkwardly served their oatmeal, but he could feel Angie's uncertainty. So, he kissed her on the cheek. "Hey, it's all good, Ange. I was just lost in thought."

She smiled meekly and dug into the cold oats. "So?" she asked after a moment. "You wanna go to that show tonight or what?"

"Sure, Hon. I'm off at seven. Why don't I pick you up?"

"Oh, I'll have to ask my father."

By the time Mike ran downstairs, called Angie to throw him his keys, and got through the traffic, he was two minutes late to work. He hadn't forgotten about the craving. It was burning a hole in his mind. Every time he passed another driver on the road with a smoke in their hands or smelled tobacco off of a passerby, he felt another pang, like a hunger pain, but in the back of his throat. Work began with a longing look at the smoking area, where Peach's nighttime counterpart, Rita, was passing one last puff with some other administrators before heading home for the day. She waved to Mike. He gave her a limp hand raise in response but kept on track to the EMS headquarters. He wanted to cave in so badly, but he was not going to upset Peach again by arriving late *and* smelling like cigarettes.

The morning went as well as it could. Mike managed to stay alert and keep his mind occupied through several routine emergencies. Around eleven, a call came in about an accident at the intersection of Hastings and Main.

The radio crackled and a familiar voice reported, "Two pedestrians, a four-year-old female casualty, and her twenty-something mother, in critical condition. No pulse, no breathing. I'm on the line with a woman giving CPR."

Mike and Val were already in their vehicle. Mike checked behind him, then backed out of the parking stall and flipped on the sirens in one smooth motion. There was rain as per the usual, enough to obscure Mike's view. After fighting residual traffic towards the accident, They were the first ones on the scene.

Citizens had barricaded the intersection as best as they could with their cars. A Ford F-150, black like Mike's but with a lift kit, was propped up on a bent park bench. The hood was dented. The woman who'd dented it was lying prone on the ground a few metres away. Her ankles were the only part of her still on the sidewalk. The rest of her sprawled out on the road. She was plump, but her body looked deflated by the impact and the rain and the way her chest was being compressed again and again by a frantic woman. Mike heard her counting, which was good. Another pale-faced woman held a floral scarf up to the victim's head. Beneath the silk was a mess of blood and hair. A crowd had gathered.

What must have been the driver of the Ford was crouching on the curb on the other side of the truck. He was a big, flabby, brown guy with his fat hands pressed to his ears. He rocked himself back and forth on his heels, staring underneath his vehicle. Mike followed his line of sight and at first saw only the coat. Then, the child's sundress. The little girl was still beneath the back tire.

Mike was already there, removing the coat carefully and checking her for signs of life. Better that he saw the kid rather than Val. His partner moved through the bystanders with the stretcher in tow, calling for them to step back. The woman giving CPR said in a panicked voice, "I don't think I can save her. I couldn't save her baby and now—I don't think I can save her."

Val put on his gloves and said shortly, "It's alright. You're doing what you can." He motioned to the scarf and added, "Good thinking. You can keep pressure on that wound, but we're here now. You're okay."

Mike covered the girl again. When he looked under the huge truck and met the driver's troubled eyes, he shook his head. Something inside the big man snapped and he made a sound like a dying bird. He dropped from his perch on the sidewalk and just rolled to his back on the wet pavement, pounding the palms of his hands against his forehead. Mike looked down but told himself he didn't have time to comfort the guy. He turned his back to him and joined Val by the mother. Val took over compressions, lucky his would-be assistant could hold a C-spine.

"Mike, you're on air. Let's go."

Mike already had the oxygen bag in his hands.

Chaos swirled around the figures on the ground. The rain would not let up and there was a rivulet flowing under the mother's back. They had to move her into the ambulance and dry her off. As they were lifting her onto the stretcher, Mike and Val both saw just how much blood she'd lost. They shared a grim look. The water running into the sewer was not ruddy, but crimson. It had seeped onto her shoulder, turning her yellow jersey burgundy. While they hurried out of the rain, Val kept a rhythm. Mike popped the gurney carefully into place, cut away the woman's bright clothing, and applied the AED pads. The dripping scarf revealed a leaking four-inch head wound that depressed, when Mike applied gauze, like a soft

Habit

boiled egg. Her right shoulder was dislocated. The radial bone of the same arm gleamed up at Mike through the skin.

"How the fuck did he not see them?" Val was asking. So he had noticed the vibrant flower dress under the vehicle, Mike realized.

Mike had no comment. The AED's robotic voice warned them to stand clear. The gauze he had been holding was soaked through. He took the opportunity to open another pad.

"Shock advised."

Val pressed the button and the woman's chest jerked.

"Shock delivered. Scanning. Do not touch the patient."

Some people stood around looking in through the back door. Mike closed it grudgingly. He wasn't claustrophobic, but the light helped them both.

"Begin CPR."

Val did, and a sweet, sweet melody declared an approaching fire truck.

The real heroes, thought Mike, thanking his lucky stars he wouldn't have to retrieve the kid. They carried on with their procedure, knowing all the while that too much blood had poured out at her temple. Too much had been left to spread out in the flood of rain. Val continued compressions, but the patient wasn't responding. Not even close. Whatever signal the AED had felt, it was long gone now. Still, Mike intubated. They had to get moving. He was just excited to drive them to the emerg when he met four reds at the back door. They took one grim look in and their eyes confirmed what both Val and Mike had known when they started. She'd been dead since her head made contact with the truck. Her head wound stopped bleeding. Her heart never beat again. Val covered her with a sheet.

Stepping out, Mike took in the rest of the scene. Firefighters were assembled behind the truck where one of them was jacking up the tire. Police were taking statements and helping with crowd control. One officer was trying to talk to the driver, but he seemed incoherent. No other ambulance had arrived, so Mike went over to assess him.

He had a nasty gash across his forehead. Though, Mike felt it was from falling to the pavement, not bashing into his padded steering wheel. The blood was smeared where he'd tried to rub it out of his eyes. He was clearly still dealing with the shock of killing a child (and not knowing if the mother survived), so the cops settled him down in the back of their cruiser, away from the judgment and the rage of bystanders. The back was cramped when Mike squeezed in to talk to him. Even though they were in an SUV, Mike felt like he was sitting in the big guy's lap. He didn't bother to close the door, and started off with some background questions.

The guy grabbed Mike's arm and gaped at him with huge, deranged eyes. "I'm going to hell. I'm going to fucking hell." His jowls swung with every syllable. "I didn't mean to do it. You gotta believe me. I lost control. I just fucking lost control."

"Calm down," said Mike coldly, but this only made the guy pop and cry uncontrollably. Mike could find no other words. He shouldn't have responded like that. Val was so much better at this kind of thing. Mike cleaned the head wound, but it took a long time for the big guy to stop bawling. He never really stopped trembling. The crocodile tears made Mike uncomfortable. He said, calmly this time, "I need you to tell me your name."

"It's—Chris. Oh, fucking Jesus Christ." He grabbed at his face. Mike was sure he was trying to hide from some onslaught of images. He thought about sedating Chris, but the police knocked at the window. They wanted to take him in.

"He should be checked out at the hospital first," Mike told them. They agreed, and Mike explained to Chris what was going to happen. His huge body went rigid when he heard he had to ride in the back of the cruiser and not the ambulance. Mike could see that he wanted to beg to be taken in the bus, but then it was like the image of the woman he'd be riding with made him go limp. Chris wasn't willing to move on his own, so Mike had to pull the seatbelt over and buckle him in. Once he was secure, Mike slipped out without another word. He told himself he had to hurry back to Val.

Val was in the back of the ambulance, zipping closed a white bag, which was okay. Chris's truck was now lifted off the little girl and it was better if Val wasn't out here. Mike's eyes were drawn again and again back to the pink roses on her sundress. He didn't stay to see the rest. He joined Val in the cockpit and headed silently back to the hospital. The cruiser with Chris followed.

Mike kept an eye on Val beside him.

Val caught his look and said, "Don't worry. I'll pull through."

The truth was that Val had lost his own daughter while he was on tour as an army medic. She had leukemia, but Val couldn't leave the service to come home during her treatments. *Wouldn't*, claimed Silvie, his wife. Silvie left six months after the funeral. The funny thing was Val never returned for duty after their daughter was gone. Mike sometimes looked at Val and tried to know what it would have been like to trade places with his dad—or his mom for that matter. What did it mean to lose your child? Losing both parents was bad enough, but it felt like the lesser evil. Every now and then, Mike checked to see if he could spot Chris in his side-view mirror. The

Habit

colossal man looked like a stuffed bear behind the much tinier officer seated in front of him.

The rain never let up that day. It kept reminding them how this city by the sea was meant to drown and drown. By 7 p.m., Mike was suffering, but it wasn't necessarily the accident that had done him in. He'd seen plenty more like that. It was the combination of a high-stress job and the absence of any vice whatsoever to help him keep it all together. When Peach called him into her office and asked him about his day, he blanked. She was handing him the insurance forms from yesterday's mishap. Mike blasted back to the pink roses then to the feeling of that cooked-egg skull.

"It wasn't great," he said without malice or irony. He took the papers and signed them, but decided against talking further about the incident with Peach. She knew all the gruesome details from their report anyway. Instead, he told her with what he hoped sounded like optimism, that he hadn't had a cigarette all day and he felt better than ever. Only half of that was a lie. He had a blinding migraine and felt like he might be coming down with tuberculosis. Peach sensed his discomfort but left him to it.

"Looks to me like you need a good night out," she said. It took a moment for Mike to understand that it wasn't an invitation. She meant a night out with Angie. She thumbed through the insurance pages. When she was sure he'd dotted his i's and crossed his t's, they said goodbye and Peach reminded him for the fifteenth time about Thanksgiving dinner.

Mike drove home in a daze. It had been dark for two hours before he was finished work and now the city lights poured down onto the windshield in an incomprehensible dance to the tune of *All of My Love*. Traffic was travelling at approximately 10 kilometres an hour. Mike's phone rang and Zeppelin penetrated Zeppelin with a weird echoing effect. He stared at the phone, but let it go to voicemail, remembering instantaneously about his promise to take Angie out. The truck's clock was an indifferent green, showing 8:26. So this wasn't traffic. It was another accident. Who would be on site tonight? Probably the twins, Brenda and Pat. They were usually in this neighbourhood.

Mike checked his phone and sure enough, there was a message from Angie. He typed out a quick apology and sent a blurry picture of the rows of taillights. She sent back a photo of the red dress she was wearing. It was a layered little number, low-cut to show off her assets. It was just long enough not to be trashy on someone as tall as Angie, but not long enough to be modest.

Mike had to slam on the brakes to keep from colliding with the car in front of him. The photo was enough to send him racing, though that meant little in this traffic. Alongside his craving for Angie was his usual desire for a smoke on the way home. A car pulled up next to him with someone smoking out the passenger-side. It was too much to handle.

Mike rolled down his window and called out, "Can I bum a smoke?"

The passenger, amused by the novelty of the situation, tossed one into Mike's hands just as the light turned green again. Mike twiddled the cigarette in his fingers while admiring it, then regretting, yet applauding, his audacity. He absently grabbed the lighter from the centre console and wondered, *Was that actually there the whole time?* Before he could chastise himself, he had it lit and he was inhaling the calm. *Ahh.*

All around him, red, yellow, and orange reflected off of the pavement and off the other cars. Pedestrians were invisible under their colourful umbrellas. Through the wet glass, they appeared like beach balls bobbing in and out of dark waters. Mike took another puff, swirling the fumes out through his nostrils and taking in the lazy change of traffic lights, the drudging movement of passersby. His guilt turned to secret pleasure. The Ford was a speakeasy for a brief moment of nicotine-induced high. Mike could have smoked a thousand cigarettes and driven all night, like his father had in his long-haul days.

The reverie was over before it began. His apartment building reared its ugly pink head. Mike parked underground and dashed upstairs to find Angie lounging in the living room with Felix on her lap. Mike drank her in; she had on that flowy little red dress, cut strategically at the side, to unveil one long leg. She was sitting sideways in her favourite chair, with ankle-high boots on. She could have been straight out of Hustler; the sleek black hair, evening eyes, and the low, low reveal. She eyed him coyly and smiled at what she saw.

"Sorry I'm late, Mama," said Mike, trying to sound in control of himself. Angie let him linger when he kissed her. Then she caught a whiff and realized that Mike had not quit as she'd hoped. In fact, she was certain he'd been smoking right up to the ride home from work. His eyes were tinged yellow and his lips were dry when he kissed her. She didn't say anything though, determined not to ruin a good night with confrontation.

Once he'd showered and become somewhat presentable in a salmon shirt and black jeans, they made their way out into the rain with one umbrella between them. Angie held Mike's arm and he guided them through the dark streets. The rain let up somewhere between their building and Gastown. Now, the overcast sky was underlit by the city below. They passed coffee shops and markets, which were closed and barred. They bowed their heads to the homeless couple who were camped in their usual spot in the middle of the sidewalk, along with their four dogs. Sometimes Mike would hand them a fiver, but tonight the onus was off. They were all asleep, even the dogs.

Near Cordova, more people appeared in doorways and crosswalks, some in dresses and silk shirts, others in ripped jeans and fishnets. The night brought all manner of party goers into the street to mingle and smoke before returning to their appointed destinations. Tonight, Mike and Angie were not even the oldest folks on the block, as several middle-aged groups were scuttling around.

Just outside the blues can, they had to walk through a makeshift smoke pit. Mike held his breath, suddenly certain that if he drank even a single beer, he would be out here within minutes. The chemical reaction between the first taste of booze and first puff of smoke was like clockwork. Angie sensed him stiffen. She had hoped that since he hadn't smoked on the way over, there might be some chance he would spare her the long awkward moments alone while he shot the shit with strangers outside. Now, she wasn't sure if he had just finished his pack and was hoping to score another, or if he was thinking about bumming smokes all night instead.

"Come on." She shook Mike out of his stupor. "I want to get a good spot."

They scurried past the enormous doorman, who nodded without really looking their way. Inside the orange-tinted pub, the opening band was already wailing. The bar was only half-full, so their amps were turned down, but that didn't stop the singer from bursting a vein in his neck yelling into the microphone. He was an older guy, probably trying to relive the days when he could really croon. Now his voice was shot, but he just kept on howling. *Sometimes I feel like I was blind before I met you. You let me down when you left me in the dark.*

"Oh," said Angie into Mike's ear. "At least the guitarist is good." He was. He was playing a polished red Gibson and laying down some pretty smooth licks, matching every other broken note from the singer with a warm and eloquent line. Angie felt a tingle down her spine just listening to him. She slipped into a booth along the back wall and Mike set off to retrieve their drinks.

The bartender was a slender twenty-something with bleached hair and tattoos that had more personality than she did. She would have been cute without the septum ring that almost perched atop her upper lip and the Monroe piercing that stuck a quarter inch out of her face. Mike smiled at her, but her face had about as much expression as a piece of toast.

Looking away from him and out into the crowd, she stated, "What can I get for you."

"Two Heinekens, please."

"Eighteen dollars."

Mike whistled as he took out a $20. "Steep."

When the beers were delivered, the girl took his money without response. She held out his change, still avoiding his gaze. Something deep inside Mike sprang up. It made him want to grab her and shake her, make her look at him, make her look into his eyes. Instead, he took the beers from off the counter and left her standing with the toonie in her hand.

"Thanks," He thought he heard her grumble above the money hitting the jar.

Angie seemed to be enjoying herself; she was staring at the guitar player, which was fair. He was handsome, and younger than the singer, still silver though. He wore his hair short on the sides and long on the top like Mike's. It was slicked back like Mike's too, but a few strands had loosened themselves to hang demurely over one eye. His bare arms were tattooed. The tendons in his forearms breathed with each passing sweep.

"What a babe," remarked Mike.

Angie's grin spread across her face. "You like him too, hey?"

Mike sat down at her side so they could watch the show together.

"Oh yeah." He slid her beer over to her and wrapped his other arm around her shoulders. "I'll bet he's got a cute butt too."

Throughout the night, the music grew louder, the crowd grew thicker, and the bartender grew more sullen. Mike desperately wanted to sneak out for a smoke but realized the very notion of that was an oxymoron. Angie would be left alone, and she only had about a five-minute comfort zone, after which her anxiety would follow him back to the table. So, gripping his beer like an idol, Mike stayed pure, drawn tense under the escape plans that kept springing in his mind.

There were two more bands, but only the headliners were of any merit and so they watched them for a long time. They were younger and more versatile. They played a mix of blues and rock that had the whole place stirring. There were couples on the dance floor at all stages of incapacitation. Angie desperately wanted to dance, but she could tell Mike was in no mood. He was wound taut, more so each time he brought them another round.

He hadn't slipped outside at all as far as she could tell, so she was thinking to ask him if he'd forgotten his pack but thought better of it. Why jinx it? What really worried her was his silence. It reminded her of his father. Alan used to be a ball at parties—until he wasn't. Then he'd just stare and stare and make quiet, cruel remarks until people finally left him alone. Mike was never so intense. He had been the one who could snap his dad out of it.

Habit

Now, he just kept staring at people, saying nothing. The resemblance was unnerving.

Mike was eyeing all the smokers and damning himself for it. What was this urge to inhale, this black void that could only be filled with a toxin? It was eating at the back of Mike's throat, making him drink more than usual, which made him crave it more than usual. In turn, he was oblivious to his wife and his surroundings. He was like a hound on a fox's scent, intent on hunting down just one cigarette. Just one puff. He could easily be outside for a breath and then back by Angie's side before she'd even miss him.

"I can't take this anymore," said Angie. Mike recoiled. He'd forgotten to say anything to her at all since their last round of drinks and now his beer was nearly empty.

He asked with some difficulty, knowing full well what the answer would be, "What is it?"

"How can you sit there, glaring at people all night, not saying a word?" Softly, she continued, "You look like you want to kill somebody." Angie was already pulling her purse over her shoulder. Mike wanted to change her mind, but at the same time he felt he would be safer at home without all the temptation. He considered his options and decided the best thing to do was come clean.

"Look Ange, I haven't been feeling myself lately. I've been trying to quit smoking, you know, but this place is a freaking opium den. I do need to get out of here."

Angie was looking through him. She smiled a little. "Thank you Mikey, I'm glad you were honest about your feelings. Jesus, I was starting to think you were angry at me for dragging you out here!"

They gathered themselves and stood, instantly realizing they'd both had too much to drink. They smiled guilty smiles and leaned into each other for support. Angie giggled. She held Mike and carefully navigated the crowded room. Just on the other side of the door, they walked through a noxious cloud of smoke and Mike had to actually squint his eyes. That's when he heard something he thought he'd never hear again.

"Ya, hypnosis, man. I quit for two months after a few sessions." A jittery little man was chattering up to his tall, avian friend. The image was of a black bird towering over a chipmunk. The skinny dude looked Angie up and down. Mike met his wandering eyes and the guy turned back to his friend.

The tall one said, "Well how come you're smoking again?"

"Oh man, don't give me that shit. You know I lost my fucking job. I'm living at my sister's. She's got three crazy kids. I'm just trying to stay sane 'til things pick up again." Mike didn't notice that his pace had slowed once he was beside the pair. He wasn't really listening to the words, only the idea. He'd gone his whole life without hearing of hypnotherapy and now it was on his radar twice in one week. Angie was slightly ahead of him, trying to avoid the two men. She tugged at his arm.

A few metres away, she asked, "So, would you try something like that?"

Mike was still in his head, reliving his encounter with the teenagers the night before. "Like what?"

"Hypnotherapy. I had an aunt who got rid of night terrors with hypnosis. I didn't know you could use it to cure addictions." Mike looked up and down the street. His first instinct was to say no, to say he didn't believe in that stuff; it was just *a suit of science*, he thought ruefully. At the same time, he could feel the itch in his throat, the ache in his eyes, and the hammer on his brain. He wasn't naive enough to think he'd been doing well on his own.

Crumpled fast food wrappings rolled around at their ankles. Some stragglers still held onto their highs, babbling to each other as they hobbled down the middle of the road. The air was cold and moist, the rain was finished for now, but dawn threatened to reveal the state of this city.

"Yeah… I guess. I mean, it couldn't hurt." Mike could feel the smile spreading on Angie's face. So, he'd finally made someone smile on this miserable day. Mike held open the apartment door for his wife. It felt good to leave the grubby world behind. He couldn't help himself from squeezing Angie's ass as she passed by. Her little giggle let him know it was the right move. How long had it been since he'd made the right move? She led him straight through the house, into their bedroom. Mike had to brush the cat off of the bed and toe him outside, but then he laid Angie down on the comforter.

With half-closed eyes, he kissed her neck, her mouth. He lingered there until he felt the heat. Then Angie's deft hands were unbuckling his pants. She slipped her hand around him. For a few moments they lay there, her working him to the point that he had to lean into her just to stay afloat. How long had it been? It felt like months since Mike had even had the energy to make love. He remembered guiltily that he'd once promised her they'd try for a baby.

He opened his eyes. Angie's were shut tight. No. Not yet. Not tonight. They breathed into each other, trying to get closer than humanly possible. He had her laid out on the bed and now he knelt down before her. When Mike couldn't wait any longer he pressed his wife's dress up to reveal black lace underneath. Like an animal, he ripped this away from her. He heard the tear too late.

Habit

"Hey!" Angie smacked Mike's hand away. "Those are coming out of your salary!" She gave his forehead a nudge with the tips of her toes and smiled wryly. Drunk and wilful, Mike pulled Angie's leg around him and brought her to the edge of her seat. Then her sighs were music in his ears. It was maddening to keep rhythm and try to make her sing at the same time.

A few minutes later, Angie was biting his neck trying to wake him. He'd fallen asleep just like that, on top of her and smiling. The cat had crept back into the room at some point. He lay purring somewhere above their heads.

Angie whispered, "You're out of shape, old man," and Mike could only watch her walk away.

One thing to be said of Angie, when she set her mind to a task, she delivered. Whether it was the CEO in her, or she'd merely met the end of her rope, she went ahead and booked Mike for a hypnotherapy session at 3 p.m. that Monday, and she had already spread the word to her friends about his "rehab."

"Don't call it that, I'm not a drug addict."

"Don't be so sensitive," Angie replied, stroking Felix, who purred in her lap. "Peach says she's rooting for you. Oh, and she invited us over for Thanksgiving."

Again.

"I'm so excited to meet Collin."

"Who's Collin?"

Angie had her fists up near her chin like a schoolgirl with a secret. "Her new beau."

"*Peach* has a boyfriend?" Mike scoffed.

"What's that supposed to mean?" Angie's fists were on her hips then.

"Oh, I mean... I guess I've always just thought of her as an independent woman."

Angie rolled her eyes. "Are you saying I'm not an independent woman?"

Mike shut up.

Saturday's hangover never seemed to quit and perhaps his morning beer hadn't helped. Angie bought groceries and made omelettes. Then they spent the entire afternoon and evening in each other's arms on the couch while two seasons of The Walking Dead marched across the TV. After making some lazy, sloppy love, they ate a late dinner and passed out. Sunday, they splurged and went out for supper.

It was another trying evening. The couple at the table next to theirs were smokers. They went out every twenty minutes or so and returned smelling like tobacco and tar. *They're the real addicts.* Mike looked down to see Angie stroking his hand, trying to coax him back from his thoughts.

"I really don't know how that smell can make you want to smoke," Angie whispered behind her glass of wine. "It makes me want to throw up."

When Mike was finished his steak and Angie had packed up some of her lasagne, they walked back to their apartment. Wrapped up in one another on the couch, they watched the news until there was a story about a missing woman somewhere in Surrey. That kind of thing always upset Angie, so she got up for a drink of water. Mike listened to the report on low volume. He wanted to know the details just in case she turned up on his shift. It wasn't impossible.

Habit

Mike had been on duty in Prince Rupert and found a missing woman—and it was part of the reason he transferred down south. Not that he really expected the city to be safer than the woods, just that he was less likely to trip over a body while looking for his patient in the dark.

The report ended and Mike flipped on Netflix while Angie curled up across his lap. The night swam by in a mix of more zombies and more cravings. Mike daydreamed about sneaking out to the corner store to buy a pack, but he felt Angie's breath on his arm and he held out a little longer. He only vaguely heard his wife's reminder about the session tomorrow before he conked out on the couch.

On Monday, Mike would begin his night shifts. He didn't hear Angie leave for work in the morning. However, bless her heart, Angie really did not want to find out he'd missed his 3 p.m. appointment, so she called him at noon to remind him about it. After that, Mike was wide awake, with his bladder and his cat betraying him completely. Felix whined for Mike to fill his dish, but it was only half-empty so he ignored him. He spent the next few minutes coughing something like a leech out of his throat, then he scrolled the internet. He'd tried to eat a deli-meat sandwich at some point but couldn't stop stressing about the session. He didn't want to be put under. He didn't want to give up control.

The countdown put him on edge. What exactly did he hope to achieve here? He didn't think he could side-step withdrawal with an hour away in semi-consciousness while someone spoke nice words in his ear. Maybe it wouldn't work because he was beyond repair. He had actually tried that god-awful gum back when Angie came into his life, and the patch, and those crappy vaporizers too. Anything in an attempt to quell the cravings. Once his dad was gone, remedy had been out of the question. Maybe he really did need something more extreme now.

The time was upon him and Mike looked down into Felix's yellow eyes as he put on his coat.

"Well?"

Felix meowed.

"I'm not getting out of this," *and I'm not getting emphysema either.*

Felix yawned.

In his truck, headed to the clinic, he'd absently found a stick of gum in his glove box. He hadn't been searching for a smoke. Mike chewed the gum like it was the only food he'd tasted in days. He arrived at the clinic and steeled himself.

The waiting room smelled of citrus and something sharp. *Ginger*, thought Mike. There were pictures of people on beaches, on mountains, on long dirt roads, all smiling. The pictures had italic captions like: All who wander are not lost, or, Photographs fade, but memories are forever. *Not in the age of digital cameras and Alzheimer's*, thought Mike.

Still, the images had their effect and Mike felt a little calmer as he approached the front desk. That was until he had time to soak in the receptionist. She was a gorgeous woman with layers of flowy blonde hair spilling over her shoulders. Her supple smile looked as if it never left her lips. Her eyes were turned to the computer, but the glow of the screen through her designer glasses made them seem an otherworldly blue. She wore a v-neck that nestled between her small breasts, and her jewelled necklace only accentuated the reveal. When she smiled in his direction, Mike's heart went for a jog.

"Hello," she said, her voice softer than he'd expected.

"Hi." Mike thought his own voice sounded like a teenager's.

"You must be Mr. Perry." Her voice was as smooth as whipped cream. "Welcome. My name is Tamara. I have a few waivers for you to sign. We should go over them together." *Tamara*, Mike was committed to remembering that name. He felt a strange urge to get to know her outside of this place. *The fuck am I thinking?* He didn't want to get to *know* her...

He looked away from two slowly lifting breasts, realizing he'd been staring all the while that she was running her manicured finger down the sheet. He had to grapple with the wish to look again but was aware of how thin the piece of paper was between Tamara and himself. From then on, he looked only at the bold print on the white page. He dared not glance up at her face or down that plunging v-neck. She finished speaking, and after a respectful moment pretending to scan through the fine print on his own, Mike consented. His signature shot across the bottom of the page and Tamara smiled at him again. Mike smiled back, showing—he hoped—no hint of how much closer he felt to her in that moment.

She gestured to a door on her right. "Please go right in. Dr. Tehrani will be with you shortly."

Safe inside the small room, Mike took a moment to orient himself. Across from him, a high bookshelf stood between two windows with their grape-green drapes drawn closed. The bookshelf was overflowing with books on the top three shelves and leather binders on the bottom two. There were a few austere pieces of furniture, including a rosewood desk perpendicular to the window. It was almost as wide as the room. Behind it sat an old, black, straight-backed chair. There was also a velvety green armchair that looked at least a hundred years old. Its oiled legs shone darkly in the translucent light through the drapes. It must have been reupholstered through the years, but

Habit

the tarnished brass buttons holding the cloth in place looked straight out of the Edwardian era. Naturally, there was also a couch.

The couch sat opposite the desk. Mike took an instinctive step towards it. It was the same shade of green as the chair. It was the sort of love seat with no back, and just one slanted arm. It looked lavish underneath a huge impressionist painting of a lake and mountain scene. Throw pillows of various sizes were lined across it. Mike settled himself on the end nearest the exit. He turned and noticed a reasonable number of certificates hiking up over the door frame. Mike leaned forward to read the diplomas.

There were a few from the Canadian Institute of Hypnotherapy and several from UBC's Department of Psychology. It appeared Dr. Tehrani was a shrink after all. He wasn't sure whether that soothed him or made him more nervous.

His mother had seen her share of shrinks while he was still in grade school. No diagnosis was ever shared with Mike, apart from her rampant drug abuse, but he'd found out from the psychologists much later on that forcing your son to sleep outside so you could get high and have sex with different men was not the behaviour of a healthy woman.

With a shudder, Mike remembered a certain house call made right after she'd died. Mike had never enjoyed the company of shrinks back then, since most of them had gone to school around the time that *Sybil* came out. Reports were everywhere about bogus repressed memories and multiple personality disorders. The doctor asked him all sorts of awkward questions. When Mike revealed the extent to which she'd pummelled and neglected him, the therapist asked, "And did she ever *try* anything with you?"

"Like what?"

"You know, did she ever touch you or make you touch her?"

Mike shivered with the memory. The door opened in front of him and in stepped a distinguished-looking man with smooth olive skin and an impeccably manicured beard. Mike stood respectfully. The doctor smiled. He was taller than Mike by a head and he wore a blue silk shirt under a tailored grey vest and matching slacks.

"Welcome, Mr. Perry. I'm Dr. Tehrani."

His voice was deep and resounding. If Mike had to choose who had the better vocals—this guy or Tamara—it would be a toss up. The psychologist extended his hand and Mike shook it. There was confidence and competence in that handshake, enough to peel away the corners of Mike's last thought.

Mike smiled a little. "Hello."

Dr. Tehrani's eyes glinted behind rectangular glasses. They were the strange kind of grey that looked green one moment and blue the next. He wore half glasses that gave him a professor's appearance. It was difficult to gauge his age; he had to be in his forties, but the imperceptible fine lines on his face might have added up to fifty or more. He was in good shape. Mike could sense this much in the handshake and by the way he carried himself across the room. His salted black hair was tied into a tight bun and when he turned, his smile was no longer visible past his moustache, but Mike could see it in his eyes. Tehrani gestured for Mike to sit and then lowered himself into his armchair.

"Now, I understand you were sent here by your wife."

"In a sense," said Mike quietly.

"Yes," came the knowing reply. "Amazing how they always have such peculiar ideas about our health, hmm?" Dr. Tehrani chuckled. "They know what's best for us before we do. Please, get comfortable."

"Sure," replied Mike, setting the smaller pillows aside and settling on the couch.

"I'm sure you have some questions for me before we begin?"

"Uh…" Mike dropped his hands to his thighs. "Like what?"

Tehrani didn't miss a beat. "Well, I guess you've heard some weird reports about hypnosis? Right. Well, it's not the stage show people always expect. I'm not going to take you anywhere you don't want to go, and I'm not going to mess with your head." Dr. Tehrani leaned back in the chair and continued, "That being said, it's normal for unpleasant things to come up during or even after a treatment."

"Okay," said Mike noncommittally. He wondered, W*hat kinds of unpleasant things?*

On cue, Tehrani said, "You may experience upsetting memories, thoughts, and emotions, but it's all part of the process. Addiction," he expressed the generality of the word with a wave of his hand, "is fuelled by all sorts of disturbances to our psyche."

Mike nodded slowly.

"My job," continued the doctor, "is to flush out those disturbances, so you can learn to deal with them up front."

Mike remained silent. After a moment, Tehrani straightened and took up his writing materials from the desk. He looked very much like a shrink then.

"You'll be fairly conscious the whole time. Only, it's not the same sensation you're used to where you can quickly shift focus from one thought to the next. It's a lot like the space between being awake and being asleep. It's very comfortable, and we are all very open to suggestions in this space. Does that make sense?"

Habit

"Yeah," said Mike hesitantly. "Actually, it reminds me of when Angie starts sleep talking and I...well sometimes I like to mess with her, you know? Reply to the crazy things she says."

Dr. Tehrani cocked his head back and chuckled. "You've got it." He took a moment to observe Mike before finally asking, "Now, I understand you want to quit smoking, is that correct?"

"Yes."

Dr. Tehrani made a note on the page before continuing, "And what do you think will be the biggest change for you once you've quit?"

Mike had to think for a moment, about his health, his career, about Angie.

"I guess my relationship will change."

"Ah, and you are looking to rekindle things?"

"Yes."

"How long have you been together?"

"Four years—no just two, I guess."

"I see. And has your relationship with—Angie, is it? Has it been strained because of the smoking?"

"Yes. No, wait. Only since my dad died."

"I'm sorry to hear about your father. When did he pass?"

"Four months ago."

"Oh yes, that's still quite fresh. It must be very difficult for you and your family. Are you close with your mother, Mr. Perry?"

"My mother...died when I was fourteen."

"Oh, I'm very sorry to hear."

Mike shook his head. His mouth was turned down, but he was trying for indifference.

Tehrani waited for him to go on.

"She...was an addict. A real one. I mean, I guess it runs in the family. When she overdosed, my father... Well, I guess that's when his drinking really began...and my smoking."

A solemn moment passed between the hands of the clock.

"Do you sometimes blame your mom for what happened to you and your dad?"

Mike was taken aback. He was going to say no; he didn't want to think about his mother having that kind of power, but immediately his answer came out in a hiss.

"Yes."

Tehrani set down his notebook and pen. He held his hands open on the arms of the chair like he was cupping water.

"We never know the impact we can have on people, do we? We never really know the impact other people are going to have on us."

Mike knuckled his eyes but stayed quiet.

"The good news is, you're here now. Have you ever undergone this kind of treatment before?"

Mike shrugged. "I went through therapy when my mom died. I don't remember being put into a trance or anything."

"No, hypnosis is still emerging. Even if you were exposed to it, you might not remember. Now, I think I understand what it meant to lose your dad, Mr. Perry. I lost mine when I was about your age, of cancer. But what about your mom? Are you okay to talk about that?"

"Yeah, it's fine." Mike was preoccupied with whatever was still caught in his eye. "Uh, as soon as I found her, I called 911. That was kind of the moment I wanted to be a paramedic. After seeing the man try to revive her, I just knew I could handle being the first on the scene. My dad moved us out of the farmhouse after that though. He couldn't watch TV in the room where she died. He found a little apartment and got a job in town so he wouldn't be away from me anymore."

"He was away a lot when you were little?"

"Always. He drove a rig, then he was a heavy mechanic in Fort Mac."

"So, after your mom passed, you two grew close?"

"Yeah." Mike smiled to himself. "Those were good times. He coached my hockey team."

"It's good that you have those happy memories, Mike. Hold onto them, especially when you think about how much you miss him." Mike laid his head back on the pillow. Tehrani asked, "Have you experienced any other symptoms since your father's death? Depression, fatigue, pain or migraines, lack of interest and libido?"

Mike checked off a mental list. "All of the above, I guess." He thought about his weekend with Angie. There was no lack of sex drive there, but actually, he couldn't remember the last time they'd made love before Friday night, probably June.

"And how would you describe yourself before your father's passing? Before the addiction came up for you?"

Mike hesitated. "I guess I was happier, healthier, for sure. Maybe stronger?"

"Okay, and so from these sessions, you would like to return to those states of mind?"

"Right."

"And you'd probably like to find peace, with your dad for sure, maybe also with your mom?" Mike stalled before nodding. Of course, letting go of his dad was exactly what he wanted, but he wasn't ready to dig up his mom just to rebury her. She could stay right where she was.

"Okay, Mr. Perry. And are you willing to make this change of mind?"

Mike cleared his throat. "I mean…I hope so."

"I think you are. And I think you know you are too. You have to be willing to revert back to your old self, the one who allowed you to feel those three things you mentioned. And you have to be willing to open up a bit, even if it's uncomfortable. I'm not going to take you anywhere you don't want to go, but if you need somewhere to go with everything that's happened to you, this is the place to do it."

Mike analyzed that statement over the sound of a swinging pendulum. He blinked over at the clock as if it would have the appropriate answer for him. The clock looked a bit stuffy in the otherwise elegant room. It looked very much like the cartoon clock from some Disney movie. It also looked familiar. He watched it pass its golden yo-yo from hand to hand before, finally, he agreed. "Okay."

"That's great. That's a good place to start. Now you have an idea of your purpose for all of this." The praise was subtle and the proffer simple. When the doctor's smile fell on him, Mike felt a sort of wave, warm and not unpleasant, roll over him. He was sweating, yet he felt okay. Yes, rest settled on his chest when he met the doctor's eyes.

"Alright, let's begin." Dr. Tehrani dimmed the lights. "Please, lie back and make yourself comfortable. Good. Now I'd like you to close your eyes and breathe naturally for a few moments."

Mike rested his hands on his belly and felt it rise and fall. He was tempted to try and lengthen his breaths, but Tehrani repeated, "Just breathing normally.

"As you do, you become increasingly aware of your own relaxation. You are increasingly aware of the comfort of the couch, the warmth of your body, the calming clock."

The ticking was audible, but it seemed to Mike to appear somewhere far in the back of his mind. He was centred on the disembodied voice. It was like listening to God, or at least the man who played him.

"With every second passing, you feel more relaxed. So relaxed that your hands fall open." Mike hadn't noticed that his hands were tense across his belly. They unfurled. The clock continued to sound.

"Become so relaxed that your jaw unclenches."

It did.

"You no longer notice any itching or aching. Total ease...total ease to the point that you are no longer aware of any body sensation at all. Only the ticking of the clock and the sound of my voice." Every syllable of that voice melded into Mike. He was not even surprised to realize that the doctor was right. He couldn't feel anything, not even the steady rise and fall of his chest. Where normally there was a twang in his lower back and a pinched nerve in his left buttock, he felt...nothing.

"Perfect relaxation. You are so relaxed that you begin to sink into the couch." It happened just as he said it. Mike felt his body merge into the soft fabric. It was like he could have been a dust mote pressed against the green cushions rather than a body at all.

"That's right." The voice felt larger than life. "I want you to imagine you're at a time where you still felt like your old self." Mike thought for a moment about who he was before his father died. He remembered smiling a lot back then.

"See that this is available to you. This well-being is still within you. You are allowed to feel okay again. Think even farther back, to a time just before your first cigarette."

The first time he'd stolen a smoke from his mother's pack was when he was fourteen. It was very near the time that she died. He was getting back at her for hitting him in front of his friend, so he decided to steal not one cigarette, but the whole pack.

"Go even farther back," said Tehrani. "Back before you ever thought about smoking." Mike might have been ten or eleven before he'd first been curious. "The very smell of it bothers you. The very taste of a cigarette nauseates you." Mike considered these words. They had been true at one point in his life. He could almost smell the ancient fumes on his own shirt. Dr. Tehrani responded to a sharp inhale from his patient and said, "No. There is no cigarette smoke here right now." He said it with such finality that the scent retreated.

Habit

"You have only the sounds of my voice and the vision of your mind's eye. You also have the complete rest that still envelops you...Now, think back to a place you visited at this age where you were perfectly at ease with your surroundings, maybe you are in nature or on a vacation."

Mike was about eleven when he built himself a fort out in the middle of the woods. He'd taken pride in that place, actually, and painted it with camo-green and brown paint. That—was where he went when his mother kicked him out of the house. Dr. Tehrani noticed Mike's eye twitch.

"This is a safe place for you, Mike. This is a place where you can lie down and relax. No fear of intrusion. Wherever you are right now, go ahead and lie down. You are calm and safe. It's the most peaceful place you could imagine. Go there in your head." Mike did. In his mind, he laid down on a little cot and he remembered he'd sometimes see his patients in that fort, like a field hospital. His friends would come over and he'd pretend to brace their broken bones or pile their intestines back inside them. Other times, it was a lab where he'd dissect them and switch their brains with the brains of monkeys. He'd always wanted to be a doctor. *A doctor*. Maybe that's what was happening; he'd reached his midlife crisis and now here he was smoking himself into oblivion to avoid beginning a future he actually cared about. Maybe it was about trying for a kid of his own.

Tehrani's resonant voice came back into focus. "Look around and imagine this beautiful place... Imagine this wonderful place that you have always enjoyed visiting, a space for you to be at peace and at ease with life. Now, Mr. Perry. Now you smell something foul." It came on like a tidal wave of vodka and cigarettes. Mike assumed he knew the doctor's next instructions. He was half-right.

"This place is completely filled with the stench of cigarettes."

Mike was well aware of his body's sudden tension.

"That's right...it *is* horrible. There is a lit cigarette in your hand. Smell it now?" Mike could sense the smoke wafting into his nose. It reminded him that his fort had caught fire just before he left the farm for good.

The smell in Dr. Tehrani's room was overwhelming. Mike coughed once. He wanted to open his eyes, but that powerful voice just said, "You don't need to see it. You can smell it. It ruins everything. It fills your nostrils and it makes you sick. But it doesn't have to. You don't need to smoke. Not now. Not ever. The very idea that you like to smoke is only a memory. You used to smoke with your father, but now your father doesn't need to smoke either. You're both free. I'm going to count to three and I want you to drop the cigarette...."

At the bottom of the countdown, Mike's hand twitched.

"Now that you chose to relinquish it, the smell is fading. The smell is fading. It's gone... This is your true self. It doesn't want to smoke at all. It wants to remember what life was like before cigarettes. You want to remember what life was like. You want to remember way back when you were still a kid, still happy, healthy and strong. Those things are available to you when you start to remember what life was like. You remember that cigarettes have always nauseated you. They have always made you sick. You don't have to be sick anymore."

Mike listened to the words, and memories flashed behind his eyes. Passing the puck around with his dad, kissing a girl behind the school, bringing home a tiny kitten; he really had been missing the healthy part of himself.

"In a moment I'm going to help you come back to the surface with this newfound wellness. You will feel a renewed purpose. You are going to reignite your passion. You understand that this meeting was not just about quitting smoking, it is about opening to your life. Start to come back into your body. Feel your skin... Feel your chest rise and fall... Feel your eyes behind their lids... When I snap my fingers, you will be fully awake, and in your own time you can sit up on the couch."

The snap reverberated through Mike's brain. His eyes opened slowly, painfully. It felt like breaking through old scar tissue. It took a moment for him to process what he'd been through. Getting back his childhood hadn't been a priority, but he never realized how much he needed that slideshow. He sat up slowly, aware of the psychologist's eyes on him. When he turned to face Tehrani, Mike forced himself to smile.

"How are you feeling, Mr. Perry?"

"I feel—okay," but the word was hollow. "It's hard to tell."

"Yes, there is a sort of limbo period just after a session, but I'm not going to lie and say your smoking days are over. After the initial excitement, there can be a period of intense emotions: anxiety, tension, distress. You can expect to need at least two, if not three, more sessions with me before you see any lasting progress, but I recommend coming back for as long as you think it helps. Are you alright with checking back here sometime next week?"

"Yeah...for sure."

"I'm glad to hear that. I can see that you are taking nicely to the suggestions. You can book an appointment with Tamara on your way out."

Tehrani stood and held out his hand. Mike shook it with new vigour. He couldn't believe so much had been illuminated in the hour he'd been lying there, but he still needed time to process what limited memories he had. How had he missed all these cues? The lack of initiative, the lack of motivation, the lack of will all connected to his addiction, which of course was connected to his past.

In the waiting room, the ginger smelled spicier now. The lime smelled sweeter. Tamara looked up and seemed to be wearing her sultry smile just for Mike. Her cheeks had a glow to them and Mike could almost smell her hair from across the desk. He leaned in closer, forgetting himself for a moment, but backed off smoothly when her eyes met his inquiringly. Mike pretended to need a pen.

"How was your session?" asked Tamara, handing him one. Whether she'd noticed him getting too close, he didn't want to know.

"Thanks. It was...transformative," stated Mike. He thought about how strange that sounded and he had to laugh. "Say, what's the number for this place?" He made as if to write on his hand, but Tamara only slipped him a grape-green business card.

"Would you like to pay for your first session now, or receive a bill once your treatment is complete?"

"Uh..." Mike looked around as if consulting a crowd. "Actually, why don't you bill me at the end, Sweetheart?" His tongue caught in his teeth. Never in his life had he called a strange woman *Sweetheart*. It was something gross he remembered his father doing. Tamara didn't seem to notice. Either that or she was used to it.

"Is there anything else I can do for you?"

He'd been standing in front of her desk for some time.

"No, no, that's great. Oh, I need another appointment for next week."

"How does Monday at three again work for you?" God, but her voice was like honey.

"That's perfect. Thanks again, *Tamara*."

Mike spun around and exited, fitting the business card into his wallet as he left. When he pulled open the door to his truck, he caught whiff of a gut-retching odour. He was disgusted by the overflowing ashtray, the mud-tracked packs of cigarettes on the floor, not to mention all the random wrappers and fast food memorabilia. He checked his watch and it was only twenty to five. He still had two hours to get to work; plenty of time to clean this rat-hole he'd been living in.

He pulled into a self-serve car wash and set to work. Using the dozens of sticky loonies and toonies at his disposal, Mike vacuumed, dusted, and scrubbed the Ford clean. He disposed of butts and ashes. He dove behind the seats and retrieved whatever had died back there. He even found another four working lighters strewn throughout the space. When the deed was done, he checked his phone. It was 6:26.

Angie had messaged him nearly an hour ago. Dinner was served—if he was hungry before work. She'd sent a smiley face. Mike texted back that he was sorry to miss it, but he had to head to work now. Almost immediately, she responded by asking how the session went. Breathing in the slightly damp, but soapy smell of the vehicle, Mike decided not to reply just yet. He wanted to find out for himself first.

He drove away without turning on the radio. Instead, he let the silence carry him back to his youth. He remembered his high school days when it was just him and his dad in Prince Rupert. Beyond that was still a blur. As a young child, he'd lived in semi-isolation with his mom, Carrie. Things had been fine, he thought, until he was about four. That was when his dad started long-haul driving across the province. His dad returned from trips only once or twice a week. His mom would clean the house up real nice. She'd scrub Mike until he was red and then stuff him full of food and send him off to bed right before his dad stepped through the door.

After age ten, Mike lived with his mom in total isolation. Alan Perry found work in Fort Mac and only returned home once every two months. Mike built his fort as an escape, but his mom made him sleep out there. He remembered that and the parties. There were roaring bikes pulling up to the house every day of the week. Mike vaguely remembered trying to make it through grade school during all of this. Mainly, he remembered getting into trouble. He flashed back to the scars on his chest. They hadn't been from some stupid drunken game...

A shot of red in front of his truck smashed Mike into the present moment. He braked hard and watched the little girl in the red raincoat scamper on, oblivious to the moment that could have ended her life. Mike's heart was pounding against his rib cage. *Fucking kid*, he thought before he could stop himself. The driver behind him honked, and he had to just carry on like he hadn't almost destroyed somebody's future.

He was nearing the hospital and still his thoughts were well in the past. Searching now for the years leading up to his mother's death, he remembered her addiction. He remembered her hiding it so well from his dad and thinking she'd hid it from him too. He remembered the night he had confronted her about the needles. That was the first time she'd hit him hard enough to throw him to the ground. That day he learned what blood tasted like and she whispered down to him, "If you say anything to your dad, or to anyone, I will fuck you up." He was five years old.

Mike gasped with a sudden flood of ice-cold memories. He really had spent more freezing nights in his fort than in his own bed, not for the fun and thrill, but so his mom could party undisturbed. He wiggled his toes, recalling the frostbite he'd received at the tender age of ten. It had turned the toes on both his feet hard and white and then puffed them up to the size of sausages when he'd finally been allowed to go inside to get ready for school. He told the nurse he'd been sleeping in his fort all weekend and she laughed, saying he was a real Kit Carson. Mike learned to wear his father's wool socks after that.

Turning in at the staff parking lot, Mike felt a mix of exhilaration and despair. Exactly how many painful memories was he going to recall tonight? Hypnotherapy was turning out to be a little too much like the psychoanalysis Mike had been submitted to after his mother got herself killed. He parked his truck, yanked out his keys, and practically dove outside into the chill. There was a break in the rain now, but the dark air still smelled menacingly moist.

The sun had already thrown in the towel, leaving the parking lot to the spooky glow of electric lights. The effect was one of contrast and confusion. The soft yellow streetlamps should have felt calm and warm, but the white hospital spotlights made him feel like a mark in a prison movie. Mike breathed in the humid air. Then, he turned up the collar of his jacket and escaped the glassy eyes overhead. For the first time in his career, Mike was early to work.

Habit

Night shifts were not the same as day shifts. Not in the slightest. At night, you came to expect the kinds of calls that would make anybody on a nine to five lose their $30 lunches. When the police were called to domestic disputes or robberies or drug induced car accidents, there was usually a victim requiring immediate attention, so an ambulance was called simultaneously. Val never worked nights, and neither did Peach. They were senior enough to choose their hours and so Mike waved to Rita in the head office and read on the board that he'd be paired with Tom as usual.

Tall, slender, outspoken Tom was originally from Saskatoon. But his dark features and angular face made him more of a New York type. He was the one who once told Mike how his own mother had tried to scare the queer out of him. She sent Tom to one of those crazy Christian camps where all the kids dress like convicts and they don't let you call home. That was why Tom ran away one summer and wound up working as a waiter—no, he'd said waitress—at a club on Davie street. Thinking back on this, Mike suddenly felt ashamed for being so sensitive. Like Mike, Tom had escaped a pretty fucked-up childhood just to get here. Like Mike should, Tom had let his mother's memory fade to grey and now he focused solely on saving lives.

Mike smiled at Tom. Tom smirked back at him. Tom had wavy, jet-black hair that never seemed to get in his eyes or even fall out of place. Though during triage, he tied it back with a pink tie that Mike was fairly certain was the same pink tie he'd seen for four years. Mike liked working with him almost as much as he liked Val. He supposed they related to each other because of their pasts, or rather Mike related with Tom's past. Mike had never spoken about his own mother, not even to Angie, he realized.

They settled into a rhythm once the calls began, trading driving, trading lead. Most notably that night were two rather unsettling domestic calls. Shortly after 2 a.m., at the first house, a shaky little redhead wearing one gold hoop earring was vehemently denying there was any problem at all. Mike, Tom, and the two cops on site could clearly see her split, purple lip and the torn and bleeding lobe where her other earring had ripped out. When asked about her wounds, she said she tripped and hit her face on the corner of the coffee table. She said she didn't even have a boyfriend, and her *fucking* neighbours only heard her screaming from all the pain.

"My hoop must've torn out when I lifted my head off the table."

The officer questioned her about that. "It takes force to rip an earring out. You would have had to lift your head pretty quickly after just having banged it on the table. Must have been painful—"

"—No shit it was painful." She stopped talking after that. She let Mike tend to her at least, but was tense and refused to go to the hospital. Tom grabbed her an ice pack for her mouth.

While Mike was cleaning the wound on her ear, and the others had stepped away, he asked her quietly, "So where is the guy, really?"

She pulled away and stared at him, the ice pack slowly coming away from her mouth. Then she checked on the two cops before glancing away and replacing the ice pack without a word.

"It's okay," said Mike. "I'm not going to say anything. I just want to know he's not hiding out somewhere, waiting to jump me." The ice pack came away again.

"He's not like that," she said coldly but quietly. With one more glance to the cops, she scowled at Mike. She must've made up her mind that he wasn't a threat because she continued. "He's either at a buddy's house or he's hanging out in the pub. But he's waiting 'til the cops leave. And look, he's just going to hit me again if he finds out I talked to these assholes, so don't tell them okay? I don't need a fucking hero. I just need a new boyfriend."

"So, he is hiding out somewhere."

There were tears in her angry eyes when she pointed them at Mike.

"Sorry, but you're right. You do need to get out of here."

She didn't reply, only looked far off in the distance. Mike finished patching the lobe even though he told her again that she'd be better off getting stitches. She shook her head and went back into the house.

Once she was out of sight, Mike said to the cops, "The guy is close by, waiting to see the back of your cruiser." The officers thanked him, even though they all knew there wasn't much they could do now that the girl had stuck to her story. They left the scene a minute later and Mike and Tom headed to the hospital empty-handed.

As soon as the bus's doors were closed, Tom said, "That girl needs to get a new boyfriend."

"Funny, she said the same thing."

Habit

"Yeah? And I bet she'll complain about him to everybody she knows except the people who could actually help her get out of that mess." Mike wasn't sure what to say to that.

Getting out wasn't always as cut and dry as people thought. He recalled running away from his own abuse during one particularly blurring arctic winter when his mom hadn't had a single sober night in twenty. His dad wasn't due back from the rig for another two weeks, but Mike couldn't stand getting kicked around any longer. He couldn't sleep another night outside and he couldn't live on nothing the way his mom seemed to. But the cops had brought him right back home as soon as they picked him up off the highway. He kept thinking about the threats his mom had made and the ones she'd carried out. So, when he refused to tell the cops why he ran away, they said he ought to be grateful that he even had a mom. Was that the night she broke his collarbone?

"Mike?"

Mike realized that that was not the first time Tom had called his name. He tried to recall the question he'd been asked. Something about girlfriends.

"No, I've never hit anyone. I'd lose my shit before I'd lift a hand to Angie."

"Well, aren't you a saint," replied Tom. "I've definitely cuffed a couple of my boyfriends, but as the saying goes..." He smiled sleazily at Mike. "They had it coming."

"Uh-huh. And, uh, is that why you're single again?" asked Mike.

Tom glowered open-mouthed at him.

Dispatch called them before they reached the hospital and asked if they could turn around and head back out since they weren't transporting anyone.

"Sure," responded Mike in the radio. "Where to?"

The female operator gave them the address and Mike typed it into their GPS. Tom flicked on the sirens and u-turned at the next light. As they drove, the operator relayed the details of the situation. "One known female victim, Greta Freeman, aged 34, and one apprehended male, Ferraro Freeman, 39, cuts and bruises to his knuckles and his face. No real damage, and you're not to go near the guy. He is violent and extremely dangerous. Greta, his wife, is unconscious but breathing. Stable, as far as the police can tell. She has a crushed rib cage though, a dislocated right shoulder too, and severe wounds to her face and skull."

"There are multiple animal casualties," stated the operator.

Tom waited until she was finished and said to Mike, "That's a first."

The front yard of the quiet suburban home was as inconspicuous as could be. In the porch light, they could see a little fountain in the shape of a miniature wishing well. It gulped merrily among some clean flower beds just waiting for the spring. There was a tidy apple tree still bearing a few withered fruits. A welcome mat lay dormant on the porch, all scrawled with swirling cursive letters, Home Sweet Home. Classic. Quaint. That's why the shape protruding through the broken window was so unnerving. It was dark, rectangular, and heavy. That's all Mike could tell. The shear curtains had followed it through the glass and hung over it as if it were an art piece about to be revealed.

There was one police cruiser in the driveway, lights whirling, but siren off. The perp was in the backseat, staring quietly. He was a huge guy, all bulky shoulders and no neck, stretching the silk of his expensive suit. As they skirted alongside the vehicle, Mike thought he could see blood on the silk, but it was too dark to tell. The man caught his eye. At that moment, a screen door slammed. Mike looked away. An officer came out from the side entrance and walked around to them. He held up a hand. He was a short, older guy with a crew cut of greying hair and an unassuming moustache. His eyes were dark and intelligent. He ushered Mike and Tom away from the car.

"I wanted to give you guys fair warning," he said. "This isn't your average domestic violence case. He must have had a psychotic break because this guy was..." He glanced over to the man in the back of his vehicle and said through his teeth, "Sinister." He pointed with his thumb to the shape trapped in the heavy curtains behind him. "That was the bird's cage. I haven't seen the bird yet, but I found the dog...and the cat."

"And the wife," muttered Tom, and the cop narrowed his eyes but nodded.

"Yeah...Greta is not looking good at all. Let's just get her on the stretcher and get you two out of this hellhole. Okay?" They followed the officer in, Mike at the head of the gurney, Tom pushing it. In the dim hallway, Mike lost his footing on a slippery patch leading out of the bathroom. He caught

Habit

himself on the gurney and managed to stay upright. The yellow light spilling in from the living room revealed a red smear under his feet.

Hellhole.

It was the only word for what lay in front of them. It was a tripwire. Mike looked around and there it was, that word waiting for him to trigger. He could smell it in the foul air. It was written in the crimson splatters on the walls. Its red lettering spread across the hardwood. The room was chaos. Pictures had been punched out, their splintered glass still dangling like loosened teeth. The furniture had been bashed against walls. The skeleton heaps of chairs and coffee tables littered the living room and the kitchen, from what Mike could see. Feathers were strewn across the floor; big blue feathers with red-tipped quills. *Macaw,* thought Mike distantly.

The huge birdcage gagged the smashed window. The love seat was on its back, like it had been knocked out—like it had fought and lost. What lay over the upturned base didn't register at first. Its back was bent the wrong way and it looked like a stuffed toy tossed absently over the edge. It was the rear end of a white cat. What lay in front of their feet did register. It registered as an immediate threat and Mike's pulse spiked. He started to sweat. His vision blurred. His brain tried to censor him from seeing the other half of the cat that had been separated and now lay sprawled across the floor.

The cat could not have been split any more evenly. This fact attracted Mike's attention, perhaps a means of distracting himself from what he was looking at. The cat...could not have been...split more evenly. But it had been walked through, or something had been dragged through it. The intestines were scrawled out like a message. *Hellhole.*

Mike's blood pressure plummeted. He swayed but managed to stay on his feet by leaning on the stretcher. When he lowered his gaze, he saw the other officer. She was a pale, bright-eyed woman with lips pressed into a thin line. She wore her black hair tied in a tight bun. She'd be pretty in any other circumstance, but she was sitting at the edge of the larger couch with her hand over gauze on the back of the unconscious woman's head. The woman was flung belly down, but her bloodied face poked out of the pillows.

Mike shivered. The sudden image of his own mother flopped on the couch made him light-headed again. He looked away, back to the officer. She was staring at a fixed point where the ceiling met the opposite wall. He could see how determined she was not to look at anything else in the room. Mike couldn't help but stare at everything around him. His eyes travelled over the scene for a second time. *A second time.* A prickle of sweat made him shiver as the whole scene seemed to be playing in his mind like deja vu. Like speaking the same words as another person at a crowded party. A jinx. *Am I living or reliving this?* Mike's breathing became shallow. He felt giddy.

Tom was asking the officers' names as he approached the woman. It was Amanda who held the woman's gauze to her head, and Ben who was crouching down on his other side. Mike was still staring. Still giddy. Tom assessed the damage to the woman's skull, her arm, and her chest. He made small talk to try and snap both Mike and Amanda out of their stupors. The officer smiled very faintly and murmured something, but she wouldn't look down. Mike stared and stared. And then another image struck him.

When he'd brought home a feeble kitten he'd found out in the cold, his mother had first been so sweet. She cleaned the kitten's filthy body, warmed up milk in one of Mike's ancient baby bottles, and even made up a little bed beside her own so she could feed the kitten at night. Mike had watched the two of them sleeping. So peaceful, so loving. The kindness lasted two weeks. He woke up one morning and there just was no more kitten. He knew better than to ask what his mother had done. He only remembered the dark stain on the beige carpet.

"Mike. The stretcher." Tom repeated, urgency in his voice this time.

Mike partially resurfaced. He walked the piece of equipment over to Tom's side, narrowly avoiding the mess on the floor, but not because he had tried to avoid it, only because his stride brought him past it without his consciousness kicking in. The stretcher ran right through the gore. Amanda cringed at the sound. Mike didn't even process what he'd done. He was just suddenly aware of being beside Tom. He blinked. Tom exchanged a look with Ben. Mike looked down at the unconscious woman, unable to blink away the afterimage of his mother.

The four of them carefully rolled the woman onto the board. She woke up long enough to cry out from the pain. Then she passed out again. Tom reassessed her breathing and tilted her head back before strapping her down. Then Ben moved the couch out of the way so that they wouldn't have to walk back through the dead cat. The vibration, however, disturbed the thing on the love seat and its limbs swung inertly and it fell. It looked very much like a stuffed animal—like some kid had just chucked it over the edge. Mike started to smirk but caught himself.

Habit

The female officer must have seen the cat drop and had enough. She dashed ahead of the stretcher and out the front door. Tom and Mike wheeled out silently behind her. Something inside Mike wanted to look behind him, but he caught the eye of the older officer and turned to the front. They passed through the blood by the bathroom again. Mike could see, through the crack in the door, a huge black paw.

Once outside the house, Mike was troubled again by the quietly gulping fountain, the tidy tree, and the peaceful front garden. Tom called out to Amanda, who was doubled over at the hedge. She gave him a weak thumbs down. Mike looked over his shoulder at Freeman in the back of the cruiser. The man stared back. His expression was cold resignation. Like he was saying, I know how it looks, and that is exactly how it happened.

Another cruiser pulled in beside the ambulance. Two older cops, out of uniform, exited the vehicle. Mike nodded to them and looked back at Freeman. He looked larger than he had before. Too large for the backseat. He was hunched over, just watching them load his wife into the back of the ambulance.

Mike looked away. He set to cleaning the blood off the back wheel of the gurney and then he climbed in beside the wife, feeling oddly like the husband was staring a knife into his back. He caught one last glance of the broken window with the cage hidden behind the curtains. As the gap between the ambulance doors closed, Mike thought he saw something blue lying on the neatly trimmed lawn.

Tom took a moment to exchange words with the four cops. He also triple-checked that Amanda was okay to carry on. She was white as a ghost, but she nodded with meagre enthusiasm and her partner with the moustache clasped her shoulder gently.

Once Tom was out of earshot, Amanda Reid turned to her partner and said, "That one guy was acting weird. Looking around like he was soaking it all in."

"I didn't notice," replied Ben Harly.

"You know I saw him hiding a smile while we were in there?"

"Holy mother of God," Tom exclaimed, climbing into the driver's seat. His voice was muffled by the panelling that separated the cab from the back, but Mike could still hear him well enough. Mike looked down at the woman to see if she'd responded to his voice. Her face came into focus in the vehicle's lights. It was a Rorschach of purples and reds. There was a wad of gauze taped to the back of her head, but it was bleeding through. She couldn't open either of her eyes; they were swollen, closed and puffy. Mike was fairly certain she was awake though. He could see some movement behind her lids. Mike opened a sterile pad to add to her head wound and taped it in place. She flinched.

"Ma'am, can you hear me?" asked Mike. She moaned and her fingers stirred against the straps around her hip. Mike checked to make sure the C-collar was keeping her neck secure. He decided to loosen the hip restraints minutely, mindful of her injured shoulder. Her hand patted the air again. She seemed to be reaching out. Mike saw her eyebrows furrow. She wanted to hold his hand. He drew his hand close, their fingers almost grazing. She was trying to open her eyes, trying to see him. Her fingers were still trying to reach him. Mike thought about his mother's hand dangling off the edge of the couch and drew back.

He said, "I need to insert an IV so it's easier for the doctors to give you some pain killers at the hospital."

She didn't answer, but her hand went still and when he took her wrist, she didn't pull back.

"You should probably give her something now, Mike."

Mike watched her face for expression when he inserted the needle. Even past the swelling, he saw her wince.

"Not a bad idea." Mike taped down the IV. "Ma'am can you make some noise if you can hear me?"

She moaned.

"Are you allergic to any medications? Any narcotics that you know of? Make noise if you are."

She was quiet.

"Make noise if you have been given fentanyl before."

She tried to say "yes," but it came out in a gasp.

"Okay, and keep your head steady, just make noise if you have no reaction."

Habit

"No."

Mike retrieved a bottle of fentanyl. He glanced at her body and guessed her to be about 120 lbs. Measuring out 75 mcg, he injected the dose slowly into her catheter. Mike worked to clean the woman up as best as he could. He had to check her teeth. She'd lost the front two and the lateral incisors looked loose.

"Did we find her teeth?" he asked Tom.

"Yes, Mike. Like Ben said, they're in the sandwich bag in her pocket."

Her mouth was still bleeding, so Mike stuffed gauze carefully into the sockets where her teeth had been. He asked her absently for her history, for any information at all, but of course, she couldn't really speak. Mike realized that he'd missed her name. He asked her for it, but she only moaned in response. Mike brushed away a strand of hair from her swollen face. She was lovely under all of this ugliness. Like her husband, she had on formal attire. Her dress was ruined, but once must have been dazzling with its gold thread and shimmering Swarovski crystals. The slit down the side of her dress had been ripped open up to her waist. She wore nothing underneath.

"It's Greta Freeman," called Tom from the front.

"Hmm?"

"Her name. Jesus, Mike. You really are somewhere else tonight, aren't you?"

Mike had no words. He felt uneasy about the whole event. This was normal, but he also felt unnerved by the sudden spawn of old memories. He'd always been able to close himself off to that kind of thing. If he couldn't get a grip, he wouldn't be able to work. He hoped this was the extent of the unpleasantries Dr. Tehrani had mentioned.

"It was the cat," he said simply, so not to leave Tom hanging again.

Tom looked over his shoulder, but he couldn't see Mike past the panelling. "Me too, man. Me too. It's too bad Greta can't tell us what went down back there..." Mike looked down at Greta, her hands had stilled. She seemed more comfortable with the narcotics in her system, but her eyebrows were knitted tight and tears streamed down through the creases in her tumid face. She was so tiny beneath the swelling. She looked smaller still, wrapped up on the stretcher designed to carry someone up to seven hundred pounds.

At the hospital, Greta was fully conscious, unable to speak, but able to tap out her answers to the doctor's questions. One tap for yes, two for no. Mike and Tom delivered her to the emergency nurses and went back to their vehicle. It was 3:54 in the morning. *Nothing good ever happens after 4 in the morning*, Mike's dad used to say. But they had another three hours to go. For the first time in a while, Mike thought about smoking. It was an honest craving. What he'd just been through was enough to drive any man to need a fix. He tried to remember if Tom was a smoker. He wasn't. Rita was though.

Mike crossed to her office and found she was already out. There was only one smoking area on the grounds and so he found her in the little fenced-off area. There were a few patients floating around in their hospital gowns and pyjama pants. One was in a wheelchair, others were standing beside their IV drips, all clutching smokes like little lanterns against the mist. Mike became aware of the rain. It was hazy, just wet enough to put out a dart, he supposed. Everyone had their hands held over their cigarettes, trying to keep them safe.

Rita was standing a little apart from the others. She caught sight of Mike and hailed him over. Rita was a skinny, pleasant woman in her late sixties, who'd lost four premature babies and promised herself that she would never try again. In the strange conflicting light above the parking lot, Mike saw the sad smile Rita always held and he wondered how often she thought about her past. He wondered if he had been the one to die, whether his mother would mourn him. He had never mourned for her.

Rita spotted him. "Hey, Mike. How's your night going?" She took a long drag on her smoke while she listened. Mike was not about to unload that last call on her around these innocent bystanders so he said, "Same laundry, different pile."

"I hear you." She took another inhale and pointed to his pocket with her cigarette. "Are you smoking?"

Mike considered the question. "Well, actually, I'm out...and I'm supposed to be quitting anyways...but I..."

Rita held up a hand. "Say no more." She had been an EMT for twelve years before moving into the management realm, so she knew how to read between the lines. She had also been trying to quit smoking for as long as he had known her, but life kept getting in the way. She pulled out her pack and handed him a crisp, white cigarette. The mist immediately began to dampen it, so Mike accepted the gift quickly and held out his face so Rita could light

Habit

it for him. In the moment that Rita's flame lit up her face, Mike almost dropped the smoke.

It was his mother's gaunt and hollow visage staring back at him. Mike inhaled too quickly and began to choke. Hunched over, he had to use gravity to cough. His wheezes came out as little clouds of grey that churned up the fog in the air. There was no end to it either. Some of the patients grew restless and started to back away. Rita put the flat of her hand against Mike's back and gave him three smart smacks. He hacked up a ball of phlegm that must have been all the way back in his lungs. It flew out of him and landed with a wet slap on the blacktop.

"Well..." said Rita. "You lost your smoke somewhere in all that racket, but something tells me I shouldn't give you another one."

"No," Mike agreed. "I'd better get back on the wagon."

He slunk back to the hospital, his throat ablaze and his heart beating a battle drum. It took him a solid five minutes to recuperate. For the rest of the night, Mike and Tom passed the time with paperwork and conversation devoid of anything to do with the last few hours of their lives. They rode out to two more calls before dawn: one overdose, one car wreck, both fatalities.

When his shift ended, the sun was only just deciding to give this planet one more try. It was rising slowly, cautiously, to the east. Mike drove home in silence, too exhausted to recall anything more from his past, too shell-shocked to think about the night's fresh horrors. He let out a deep breath when he finally reached his apartment building. Standing outside his truck for a moment, he tried to clear his mind. He wanted to focus on Angie. He wanted to really be with her. He wanted to make love to her, but that was beside the point. He wanted to tell her how he'd been changed from the inside out, how everything was going to be different now. It had to be. He was not going to wind up violent, or alone.

On his way up the stairs, he was thinking about how much Greta must have loved those animals. He wondered if that had been what drove her husband into that rage. Did the cat shit on the carpet? Did the bird ruin some electrical wires? A mental image stung his eyes and he stopped mid-flight.

It was the kitten; a tabby, grey like Felix... Something sticking out of its spine. It made him queasy. Mike had to stop and grab the handrail to steady himself. *What the fuck was that?* He was almost on his floor, but he needed to steel his mind. *It's normal for unpleasant things to come up.* He could call Tehrani and ask about it. He'd sound crazy for sure.

Hi Doc, I've been thinking about this horrible incident with a skewered cat...it's like a memory, but I can't really place it. Oh, and I've been seeing my mother's face everywhere. It could have something to do with this slaughterhouse I walked into tonight. That was not something Mike wanted to deal with, not after what he'd just witnessed. It was normal for anyone to have caustic images dance through their head after a thing like that. For now, all that Mike wanted was to get to the safety of the apartment.

Angie was in her favourite chair, eating a hurried breakfast with the TV on. The news was playing. The search was expanding for the missing college student from Burnaby. Angie was concentrating on the screen. Her brows had a neat little crease between them. Mike liked to watch her like this. Her focus was palpable. It didn't last long though. She turned, saw him and smiled a wide girlish grin.

She jumped up and hugged Mike fiercely.

"How'd it go, baby?" He felt her breasts against his collarbone. It was a comfortable feeling.

"Alright I guess."

"And...did the rehab work?"

"Nothing's concrete yet." Mike set down his keys in the little fish dish. "Tehrani says I need to come back for a few more sessions before anything sticks."

"That's fair," replied Angie, taking her dishes to the kitchen sink. "But how was your first night towards recovery?"

Mike winced at the question. He remembered learning that the best way to recover after traumatic runs was to talk about them, but he wasn't about to spill his guts right before Angie left for work.

"It was okay."

The words were a plea that Angie was familiar with. They meant, *I don't want to talk about it.* Peach once said that the last thing an emergency worker wants is to unload. Usually, they want to process whatever happened before giving you the PG-13 version. Peach also said that if men like Mike didn't talk to someone about their work, they'd explode. Against her better

Habit

judgment, Angie decided to leave him for now, and Mike hit the shower after she went to work and then fell into bed without the thought of food. The day turned out to be sunny. The first sunny day in a long time. Bird song brought Felix to the window to chirp and chatter. Traffic made its usual cacophony. Mike slept mightily through it all, not even rising for the bathroom.

When he finally awoke late in the day, he blinked in the fluorescent lights. He must've left them on, but only noticed them now that the sun was out of frame and the sky was dark again. He could hear Angie in the kitchen. He lifted his head and called out to her.

"Come and eat," came the reply. Mike wiped the drool off of his face. He rose like the dead out of an open grave. He took a piss and washed his hands. The little clock on the toilet read 5:47. Mike dragged himself into the kitchen. He wrapped himself around his wife, melding into her every curve, swaying drunkenly.

"Mmmm." Angie nuzzled him with her cheek.

Mike sat down on the couch and Angie placed a plate of food in front of him, stealing a green bean off his plate and flopping herself onto the seat beside him. Out past their balcony, the rain picked up wherever it had left off.

"So how was your night really?" asked Angie. A pang ricocheted through Mike's stomach. Sleep had helped him forget what he'd seen. He kept his face neutral.

"It was okay. We had a couple of nasty house calls." Mike replied, stuffing a mouthful of food into his face to avoid telling her about the dog or, god-forbid, about the cat. Mike glanced guiltily over at Felix, who was stretched out on the carpet at that very moment. He looked too much like the split cat. Mike froze.

"You work tonight too?"

Mike didn't respond. *Had Freeman ripped that thing apart with his bare hands?*

"Honey? You work tonight?"

Mike nodded; his mouth still full. He began to chew again.

"And tomorrow?"

Mike swallowed. "For the next three nights."

"Weird you didn't get much of a break in between. Do you have the long weekend off?"

"Mhmm. Peach planned it so Val and I could make dinner Monday night."

A half hour passed by with idle conversation before Mike had to leave. He kissed his wife goodbye, grabbed a fresh uniform, and went out into the drizzling evening. Again, he arrived to work ten minutes to seven. Again, he waved to Rita. Again, he met Tom at their assigned vehicle. It was the one Mike had scratched up last week. He stared at the injured side. Tom made some joke about not letting him behind the wheel. Mike admitted that he wouldn't mind that at all, actually.

Habit

The night went by without a hitch. For the second shift in a row, Mike was able to quell his cravings. Unfortunately, each time he overcame the void, it was only because he'd seen a flash of a dead cat, or his mother's limp form. Mike still had cravings. He just couldn't stomach following through with them. Was this the great trick—associate smoking with misery? Mike hoped this wasn't the long-term result. He couldn't deny it was effective.

Mainly, he was in a zone of hyper-focus, an attempt to avoid any and all disturbing images in his peripheries. Due to this cycle of craving, flashbacks, and subsequent nausea, Mike never got a handle on the timeline. There were distress calls to answer, injuries to assess, distorted faces in different degrees of pain and anguish to be compartmentalized and then forgotten. Then there was sleep.

Once, he had a delicious dream about Peach spreading her legs for him on her desk. He woke up around noon with an inglorious stiffy he had to shame himself out of. The rest of the week was just solid, uninterrupted day-time nothingness, out of which Mike would groggily tear himself the following evening. He ate at some points during the day and then the whole process repeated itself. Night shifts.

On Thursday evening, Mike was sitting beside Tom in the hospital parking lot, when he caught sight of Greta Freeman. She was being wheeled out of the building by an elderly gentleman. The man's face was strained and severe. He looked like he was rolling her out to a funeral instead of taking her home, which was understandable. Probably, he was her father. Probably, he was one who had to sort out the mess at her home. Their future was full of uncertainties, but it contained even more blistering certainties. Probably, they'd both need to give testimony at her husband's trial.

Through the windshield of the ambulance, Mike could tell Greta's swelling had gone down and her face was mottled with purple and green bruises. Her arm was in a sling and she still wore the neck brace. Her brown hair was messy, but clean. There was a bandage across the back of her head where the wound had been cleaned and stitched.

"At least she made it out alive," said Tom, following Mike's gaze. "Could've been a lot worse."

Mike didn't say anything. He just nodded, his eyes on the pair.

Tom said, "I hope that son of a bitch gets thirty years."

Mike was too tired to know what he hoped. He guessed he should hope for swift justice. That's what he wanted for most of the victims he treated. He felt like some good had been done since the police knew exactly what had happened *and* her assailant was in custody. Her home would be cleared of bodies and debris, or she'd move into her parents' place and never set foot in that hellhole again.

Mike thought back to the other call they'd responded to, with the woman feigning a self-inflicted injury just to shield her attacker. There was something wrong with these women. Who would stick around to find themselves beaten and their pets destroyed? Then again, hadn't Freeman suffered psychosis? That's what the cop had said. It was a psychotic break. What sort of justice could you dole out when the problem wasn't malicious intent, but mental health?

Mike thought about his mother. She'd been sick for as long as he knew her. His dad never told him about her past and she never offered anything up. She'd found Alan when she was young and for a while he was her salvation. Mike's birth was supposedly a happy occasion for both of them, but her trauma raked its nails down her back. She screamed herself out of nightmares every night. Then she found drugs. Then the drugs killed her. At fourteen years old, Mike had had to call 911 and find the words for what he was looking at.

His mom was lying on her back on the couch, as if she'd fallen asleep just like that. Her head on the couch's arm, her legs stretched across the three seats, she was sinking into the cushions and might have been comfortable too. The smell was what struck Mike. It hit him in a rush of hot sick and excrement. He wouldn't have even looked at her otherwise. He was so used to her passing out.

Her eyes were wide open and her mouth was slack. One hand still clutched her shirt as if she'd suffered a coronary. The other arm hung over the side of the couch. She still had the needle in. It dangled at an awkward angle like an elephantine mosquito stuck in her arm. The cops said that was unusual. Usually, a person had enough time to set down their instruments, maybe enjoy the rush for a while before the drug overtook them.

Mike snapped back to the present moment. He was driving to another call. Tom had flipped on the sirens at some point and locked their target into the GPS. Dawn was teasing them with a grey light. Mike was aware of that much, but he had driven through the night in a kind of a coma. Now he was aware of Tom chatting about something trivial. No, not quite. He was asking Mike something about his dreams.

"Dreams?" asked Mike.

"Yeah, you know," teased Tom, "the movies that play out in your head at night?"

Mike didn't bite.

Tom rolled his eyes. "Mine have been terrifying. I've seen Greta Freeman's face every time I close my eyes. It's fucking workplace trauma. I'm thinking about calling the hotline right after this shift."

"Good. It's important to talk about it." Mike heard the aloofness in his own voice. Over the blaring sirens, his words fell flat.

Tom searched his face for any sarcasm, but Mike was far away again. *He's been off in goddamn Lala Land all week.*

"Yeah, Mike. It *is* important to talk," he pressed. Mike glanced at Tom. His meaning registered in his expression, and Mike sighed.

"I guess that night kicked the wind out of me too. I have a cat at home, you know."

"And a wife," mentioned Tom.

"Yeah. Of course. You know...if anything happened to Angie..." He had no words. Would he die if she died? The correct answer was yes, but the reality was no. He would not actually perish after learning of his own Juliet's demise. He'd be distraught. No doubt. Defeated probably. He wouldn't descend into her tomb after her. Tom didn't catch on to these thoughts. He just nodded, understanding that if anything happened to Angie, Mike would be at a loss for more than just words.

"Well, we know it doesn't get any better than this," Tom said solemnly. "Just two guys saving the night, slamming the door in Death's face."

Mike looked out the window. The sirens wailed on.

The call turned out to be a suspected stroke. The victim's daughter, a middle-aged woman, was waiting for them at the front door. She wasn't distraught, but she waved them over and rushed them into the house. They wheeled in the stretcher, but of course the patient was in an upstairs bedroom. So, Tom and Mike hauled the stair chair up as fast as they could, following the daughter. Another woman in her twenties was seated by her granddad on the floor beside his bed.

She was a slender, long-limbed beauty, who shared her mother's high cheekbones and thin brows. Her shoulder-length chestnut hair was in a ponytail that leaned to the left and looked slept on. She wore lacy shorts and a pink, nearly translucent blouse that Mike couldn't help but notice. Her breasts were small and round. He kept his eyes firmly off of them, but it still took a moment to even notice the old guy propped up beside her. She got to her feet and said, "I've been trying to keep him conscious. I didn't know what else to do."

"That's good," said Tom, a little winded from the stairs. "We'll take it from here." Art Miller was slumped forward, leaning on the bed where he had fallen. His right arm was in his lap. His left arm lagged to the side. His right leg was bent, his left leg dragged out in front of him. Mike approached and saw the obvious sag of the left side of his face. The guy could barely keep his eyes open.

"Hi, sir," Tom said, "we're here to help. We need to get you up onto this chair. Is that alright?" The man mumbled something incomprehensible and made as if to rise, or maybe to bat away a fly. His movements were as inscrutable as his speech. Mike caught him and held him up under his armpits. Tom moved to his paralyzed side and together, they maneuvered him into the chair, strapped him in, and then made the perilous journey back down the stairs. All the while, they answered the daughter's questions as best as they could. They asked her to ride in the back with the old guy, so Mike could ask her questions in turn. She told them she couldn't. She wanted to drive her own vehicle over.

"Ma'am, we'll need a lot more information about your father before we get to the hospital," Tom said urgently.

The middle-aged woman waved him away. "Tiffany knows everything. She'll ride with you."

In the back of the ambulance, Mike asked after the senior's medical history and took notes. He checked the man's breathing and his blood pressure. He applied oxygen. The granddaughter watched him all the while, with panicked eyes. Only when Mike inserted the catheter needle did she tense up and look away. Her neat little frown turned to fear. Mike caught sight of those small, round breasts rising and falling rapidly. He wanted to reach out to touch her hand. She looked up and saw him staring.

It's okay, he wanted to say. "Does he take any medication?"

"Ramipril, 5mg."

She didn't move away, but she shivered, and no wonder—she wasn't wearing any clothes. Mike kept his eyes averted from then on. He had to keep prepping her granddad before they hit the hospital.

In his mind though, he pictured drawing her near. He felt an urge to take a woman in the back of the ambulance. Surprisingly, the thought had never occurred to him before. Guilt swept over the fantasy, leaving it with a greasy film.

"Grab yourself a heated blanket out of the oven to your right."

She did, and they both breathed a little easier once she was folded comfortably in the grey wool.

"Thanks."

Mike tried to focus on his work. He took a blood sugar sample; it was normal. He imagined what Tiffany would look like naked on the stretcher. He shoved the image away as he hooked Art up to the ECG to check his heart. He shot a shamed look at the old guy, angry that he couldn't stop envisioning his granddaughter in all manner of vulnerable positions.

Mike willed himself to stay on track, asking Tiffany more about her granddad, and taking more notes. This worked right up until he realized how much he liked her voice. It was breathy and high, very different from Tamara's sultry voice back at the clinic. It was no less provocative, even when she was telling him about the old guy's last meal and BM.

Once they reached the hospital, his imagination reluctantly relinquished him to the present moment. Mike was grateful to send the geezer and his granddaughter off to the nurses along with his notes. Tiffany tried to return the blanket, but Mike's eyes flickered to her blouse and he clumsily handed it back to her.

"Give it to the front desk once your gramps is out of here." He didn't see her again that night, which was for the best.

All-in-all, it was a successful night. No fatalities, low-stress, and only the tender memories of Tiffany to distract him. Not a single craving for smoke or drink in the last few hours either. Mike clocked out feeling comfortably tired, but undeniably aroused. He sped home through the pink morning light, hoping to catch Angie for a quickie. When he reached the apartment, he dashed up to their floor and there she was in the hallway. She was just locking up.

"Hey pretty lady," Mike called to her.

"Oh Mike. Hi, honey." She let him kiss her cheek as she unlocked the door for him. "Glad I got to see you before I go. I have an early meeting today."

"Isn't that the pits," murmured Mike, holding around her waist from behind. "I was hoping we could have our own little meeting."

Angie giggled. "I'd love to, but this is a new client. They've flown in from Calgary just to see me." Mike slipped his hand down Angie's skirt and pressed her firmly against the door.

"They can wait twenty minutes, can't they? I've driven all across the city just to see you." Angie squirmed beneath him, but for a moment Mike didn't want to let her go. He wanted to just have her anyway. Fuck the new client.

"Sorry, honey."

He removed his hand and yielded.

Angie gave him another kiss. "I'll be back late tonight too. Peach wants to catch a movie tonight with a couple of girlfriends. We're going to see Taken 2."

Mike grasped at his chest dramatically. "That's two strikes for your old man."

Angie only smiled and rolled her eyes. He had to watch her go. He was not angry. It wasn't like he was going to let that kind of thing get to him. After all, he still had the shower and he had the memory of that pretty little thing in his ambulance. He decided to make a morning of it.

Turning on the hot water, Mike let the steam build up. He unbuttoned his uniform, unzipped his pants, and let everything drop to the floor. His stomach looked firmer. He couldn't be sure, but he thought it must just be the night shifts. It was hard to eat enough these weeks.

He opened his mouth. His gums were not as red as they usually were. His tongue looked less yellow. His eyes did not. They weren't jaundiced necessarily, but they were about the colour of a before photo for a toothpaste ad. At least he didn't look as bad as his father had in his last few weeks. Mike still had phlegm building up in the back of his throat, so he horked it up and spat. Satisfied with the subtle, yet perceptible changes, he stepped into the shower.

Under the warm flow, he let his mind wander. He thought of Tiffany, but found that she really couldn't make him hard. The woman who surfaced in the ambulance of his mind was Peach. What he wouldn't give to get her shirt off. Just rip her skirt right off of her too. He'd like to pull her ponytail 'til her back arched. Lift up her breasts. Expose her throat. Watch her wriggle, watch her try to get out from underneath him. He'd like that.

He didn't want to hurt her. He just wanted to watch her squirm. Once he was inside her, she would be okay. She'd take it nicely. She'd like it more than she'd want to admit and that was okay too. He'd ease her into it and she'd relax. Then he could really give it to her, right there between the oxygen tanks and the ECG monitor.

Mike rinsed off with his head hanging under the nozzle. Instantly ashamed again, he let the water run over his eyes, nose, and mouth. He cranked the heat, as if he could scour away his depravity. He only got out once his skin was hot and flushed and raw. Then he towelled himself dry in front of the foggy mirror; glad he didn't have to look into his eyes now. A minute later, he was passed out on the couch. It was nine in the morning.

Felix woke him less than an hour later. Apparently, Angie had neglected to feed him before her big meeting. *Fucking cat.* Mike wiped his mouth. There was a string of saliva connecting him to the couch cushion. He crossed to the kitchen, found the little container of kibble and poured some out. Felix accepted the offering and sat down to eat, his tail flicking happily behind him. Mike suppressed the desire to yank it. Back in the living room, he turned on some inconsequential news story and fell back to sleep.

At 6:25 p.m., Mike bolted back upright, certain in that split second that he was going to be late for work. Groggily he remembered that he wouldn't be late. He would be early by about four days. Transition days often induced this sort of panic attack. Once Mike had oriented himself, he called out to Angie. No answer. He searched the whole apartment for her, idly closing the front door as he passed by, but she was nowhere to be found. He checked his phone; she hadn't messaged him. The clock on the screen read 8:56 p.m. Mike texted Angie, where are u Babe?, but he didn't wait for a reply.

Instead, he fumbled around in the kitchen looking for something to eat. He thought it might have been about sixteen hours since his last meal. There wasn't much on the menu. It was the end of a long and twisted week. A few sad-looking vegetables rolled around when he opened the crisper and a couple of cans of beans shuddered in the cupboard. Mike could have heated up a meal from the freezer, but he had a decidedly different sort of appetite. He wanted something meaty...and greasy. He thought about asking Angie if she'd like to join him for some bar food, but then he remembered she was out with the girls. Since his wife was MIA, he figured he'd slip out for a steak. Maybe he'd get lucky and catch the UFC fight too.

He was lucky. Bigfoot Silva was promising to fight Travis Browne on seven of the eight TVs in the pub. On the other screen was a mediocre-looking college basketball game. The pub was full of men: some single, some in groups, all enthralled with the opening fighters in the octagon. The only women in sight were two matching blonde waitresses and a red-headed bartender.

The blondes were all smiles but tired-eyed. You couldn't call them pretty, cute though, and patient. Mike watched the way they expertly weaved around the bad jokes and pick-up lines. The pair could have been in their late thirties, about Mike's age, still working the scene like he was, in a way. The red-headed bartender was not pretty either. She was drop-dead gorgeous. She had a rack that could give you a heart attack.

Mike ordered a Heineken and a medium-rare steak from said red-head. He noticed that the drink was a reasonable $7.25 and not $9 as it had been at the blues can. Thinking back to that night made Mike remember the text he'd sent Angie. He checked his phone for her reply. Only the home screen photo of their honeymoon was visible, with no little blinking notifications. So, he typed a little "haha I remember now" sort of text.

His steak showed up with a pile of mashed potatoes and gravy. Everything was grey and gelatinous. The food was subpar, but it was the novelty he liked. Angie never nagged him about eating meat, but living with a vegetarian did come with unspoken expectations. Mike was happy to be his own company tonight. *Let my wife have her freedom; let me have mine.* Plus, that bartender looked amiable.

Her hair was not only red, but also curly. Curlier than Peach's; it was straight from the moors of Scotland, he was sure. She had brown eyes, though, not green. She must have been in her twenties, but Mike thought late

Habit

twenties. Her arms were lean and tanned, and freckled of course. Those freckles dropped like shooting stars down the top of her shirt.

"What's your name?" he asked casually, once she had a free moment from the bar.

She replied with a noncommittal smile, "I'm Clare. Can I get you anythin' else?" Her accent was Irish, not Scottish.

"Clare. Nice. I'm Mike." She smiled but didn't say anything else. She had taken away his plate and was waiting for him to order, so he said, "Another, please," and pointed down to his Heineken.

Her eyes tracked his finger and he saw her take one imperceptible scan of him. Just an assessment. He thought she might have liked what she saw, but she wasn't going to show it. He watched her turn and reach for the bottle in the little mini-fridge reserved for imports. She was wearing a tight pair of dark jeans. They fit her perfectly. Mike had a moment of self-hatred for wanting to hurdle over the counter after her, but he stifled both the urge and the loathing.

She cracked the cap off the beer and handed it to Mike. Their fingertips grazed.

"Thanks," he said, and then, "so..." just to stall her retreat one more moment. Their eyes met and he asked, "Do you have a bet in this match?"

"What, the fight?" Clare glanced behind her. "No, I'm opposed to violence, actually."

She looked at him a little triumphantly, he thought. But Mike smiled.

"No, no. Not the fight." He gestured above her with his chin. "I'm talking about the basketball."

She looked up, looked back at him, and smirked. Lazy and final. Mike left it at that. He finished his beer and watched Silva pummel Browne into the ground. When he paid his bill, he left a generous tip. That caught Clare's eye. She thanked him with a genuine and lovely smile. *There you are, you little...*

Angie was home before him, but only just. Mike met her in the hallway again. She didn't notice him at first. His approach was sneaky on the carpeted floors. Leaning to the left, so he'd be out of her line of sight, Mike crept right up behind her.

"Deja vu," he whispered, catching her around the middle. Angie stiffened, then relaxed.

"So, we meet again," she sighed, resting her head back onto Mike's forehead. Mike released Angie and turned her chin to face him. With his other hand he opened the door. He kissed her fully. Her lips parted willingly, though Angie was surprised by Mike's ferocity. She tried to say, "At least wait 'til the door's closed," but Mike wasn't listening.

Right there in their darkened apartment, with the little stripe of light from the hallway, he was already stripping off her shirt and then his own. He unbuckled his pants and helped Angie out of her skirt. He fiddled for thirty seconds with her bra until Angie herself unhooked it for him. Her breasts tumbled out like two puppies out the front porch.

Then Mike pushed her, a little too hard, into the wall. After her cry of protest and his murmured apology, they found a rhythm. With Angie's leg wrapped around him, and her moans surrounding him, Mike felt a surge of power. He wanted to stay like this. He wanted nothing else but to keep giving her that medicine.

He closed his eyes, but Greta Freeman's battered face broke in, threatening to diminish his excitement. Mike pushed the image away with a low growl. Instead, he recalled Peach in the back of his bus again. He had one of Angie's legs up on his forearm now. Being shorter than your wife had its perks: no awkward hunching over. He just drove straight and true and watched her head rise up and down the wall, bumping along at times when she lolled backwards. Mike decided he liked the little thump, thump, her head was tapping against the drywall.

Moaning, Angie dug her nails into Mike's back. That was something that drove him mad. It was her signal. She tore into him when she was about ten seconds away. Mike gave her what she was begging for and her moans rose an octave in three crisp steps before she gasped and held tight and shuddered in his arms.

Normally after sex, Mike would want to smoke three cigarettes at once, but just thinking about smoking made his mom reappear in his mind. Mike was at once repulsed and at the same time intrigued by the image. It was too much like that Clockwork Orange scene where the kid is strapped in with his eyelids stretched wide while the violent tableaux plays across the screen. So, this was rehab. A steady barrage of unpleasantness, an aftershock of

Habit

revulsion, and then voila, recovery. Angie relieved Mike of his reverie by turning on the hallway light.

She'd found her clothes and was hurrying to the bathroom, calling over her shoulder, "So, what did you get up to while I was gone?"

"Oh, you know," said Mike, pulling on his boxers, "just snorting cocaine and picking up hookers." Angie gave a single bark of laughter. Just one *ha*, and she closed the bathroom door. The shower came on. Mike closed the front door and locked it. He tossed the rest of his clothes into the bedroom and then plopped down on the couch in just his shorts. He popped on the highlight reels from that night's fight.

Mike snoozed on the couch while Angie microwaved some popcorn. All the while Felix swaggered around her ankles, hungry again. She filled his little dish and changed the water. With the bowl of popcorn in hand, she sat down next to Mike, who was sound asleep with his feet on the ground and his head thrown back. She tucked her feet up beneath her and Mike didn't stir. He only woke when Felix jumped up onto his lap. One stray claw penetrated his shorts. It gouged Mike's scrotum.

"Fuck!" Mike stood and flung the cat off. Felix hit the coffee table right on the corner.

Angie winced. For the first time in her life, she heard her cat hiss. She didn't blame Mike for overreacting. She saw what happened. She was sure it hurt, but she thought it was out of character. She'd once seen her husband slice his thumb almost in half while cutting a potato. He'd been cool as a cucumber even while receiving twelve stitches.

"Fuck," Mike said again, pawing at himself.

"You okay?" ventured Angie.

"Yeah. I'm good, Angela... Just trying to make sure my balls are still attached."

Mike breathed out and shook his shoulders. Then he slipped one arm around Angie to anchor himself more comfortably. He grasped one of her boobs in his hand. With the other, he stuffed popcorn into his mouth. It was as if all was forgotten. Angie glanced over and saw that Felix still looked perturbed. He was watching them through half-closed eyes. His tail struck out at the air like he was swatting wasps.

Part of Angie wanted to check on the little guy, but she took a deep breath and stayed very still. Past experience with sudden bursts of violence taught her never to draw attention to whatever it was that had brought on the attack. She didn't like the part of herself that was still afraid, but there it was. She told herself that she would not let fear interfere with her daily life. The cat was fine. Her husband was fine. She was fine. Rain ricocheted off their window. Mike turned on some Netflix special and promptly fell asleep, his hand still rising and falling with Angie's breath.

Habit

It was the dream that woke Mike so suddenly. Yet as he sat there blinking in the darkness, he could not recall the scene. He only felt like his hands were sticky. They were. Not with the blood he had dreamt, but with sweat. Mike peeled his wet body off of the couch. He was cold and it took a moment for his feet to stop tingling. Angie was gone. She must have tried to drag him back to bed with her hours ago, but he had been dead to the world. Now he was alone and confused.

Rain rapped its knuckles on the windowpane. Mike listened in wait, letting the blood return to his legs, realizing his bladder was about to blow. On his way to the bathroom, he caught sight of the open front door.

The hairs on the back of his neck stood at attention. Listening for any minute sound over the knocking rain, Mike crept along the wall towards the kitchen. It was empty. He moved back to the hall and closed the front door silently. He latched it and dragged the chain quietly into place. The hallway floor creaked once beneath him and he froze for a whole minute. He could hear nothing, sense nothing. He stalked back to the bedroom to check on Angie. The room was still.

Light from the street crept in between the blinds and laid its yellow hands on Angie's body. Mike was intimately aware of every shadow, every sound. All he heard was Angie's soft breathing. All he saw was her figure lying still under the covers. Once he'd made his way around the perimeter of the room, he was satisfied that they were alone. He must've just left the door wide open when he'd taken Angie in the hallway. The thought of last night made him hard again, but he stifled the feeling. He still had to pee.

The little timer in the bathroom blinked 3:50. Its blue lines bleached Mike's vision. He washed his hands in the darkness and his face too, and then he had a sinking feeling. He had not, in fact, checked the tub. The shower curtain was drawn shut but it didn't matter in the dark anyway. Mike could see nothing. With one hand, he aimed for the light switch. With the other, he reached for the edge of the curtain. He had no weapon, but he hoped speed would catch the intruder off guard. After counting to three in his head, Mike made his move.

The lights burst on and the curtains drew back; the last two hooks ripped out of their sockets. There was no one in the bath. *I would have heard them get in*, thought Mike dumbly. Cursing himself, he attempted to poke the shower curtain rings into two fresh holes. Then he flicked off the lights and felt his way back to bed. The remainder of the night was a mix of nightmares and eroticism. He dreamt about Angie in the back of the ambulance with him.

At first they were having a fine time. But then her face was swollen and bruised and missing teeth, and his hands were bloody again. Mike awoke three more times. His jaw ached from clenching. His throat felt like sandpaper. By the time the alarm started bleating, he was ready to call in sick. He was even dialing the hospital when he remembered that he didn't have to. He didn't work, of course.

Still it was 6 a.m., and phlegm compelled Mike to get up and face the day, so he threw on pants, spat out his morning's communion to the sink, and put on some coffee. After a quick and dirty shower just to get the night's slime off, Mike took his coffee out onto the balcony and watched the world wake up. Sun rays started to lick at the buildings and the trees outside. The day looked to be a break from the rain, which meant there would be more accidents. There usually were. On cue, Mike became aware of an ambulance's distress call in the distance.

On a day like this in October, Mike would have hated to be working. How could anyone enjoy a twelve hour horror show when all around the city, they had to watch other people spread out happily into the sunshine. He considered the fact that rain was worse. It complicated treatment, it slowed down processing, he should hate it. He wondered idly about the warm comfort of working in-hospital. A doctor could at least stay dry and warm.

Sipping his drink, Mike thought about taking advantage of the fair weather. He could go for a run. He hadn't gone for a run since he'd met Angie. He wondered how long it'd take for him to be as strong as he was in his hockey days. He thought that might be a good goal now that he wasn't smoking. It was the first time in a long time he actually considered making a goal for the next few years of his life. After his dad died, there had been a lull in his motivation to live, let alone exercise. Life had been dripping past. Maybe now he could slow the leak.

The traffic sounds below grew more hostile. Mike had to rush to finish his coffee and prepare for another shift. No. No. He didn't work today. He had to keep reminding himself. When was his next hypnosis session? He was about ready to ring Tehrani's neck if this lapse in memory was due to the treatments.

"Felix?" called Angie from the hallway. Mike looked over his shoulder into the kitchen. She appeared wearing one of his oversized t-shirts, but of

Habit

course, she was too tall for it. Her panties peeked out at Mike when she bent to search all the nooks and crannies in the kitchen. She caught sight of him staring. "Is he out there with you?" Mike looked behind the barren planter and checked under the patio table.

"No. Not here, Mama."

"Weird..." Angie shook the little treat bag, but the cat did not come running. "You don't think he got out, do you?" Mike flashed back to the open door last night. He hadn't thought about the cat, but he supposed it was possible that Felix had run out to explore the hall.

"If he did, he won't have gotten far," said Mike. "Everybody knows him. They'll turn him loose once they've had their visit with the charming little bugger." Still, Mike crossed to the front door and opened it to the shared hallway. He checked left and right, there was no fat little grey tabby cat pacing the corridor. Angie filled herself a cup of coffee and sat at the table with it.

As Mike returned, she said, "He's always hungry in the morning. It's not like him to miss a meal." Mike hesitated before trying a reassuring hand on her shoulder.

"Don't worry, Hon. I'm sure he'll turn up tonight."

Felix did not turn up that night. Angie became increasingly anxious, re-checking every corner of the house. Under the bed, she thought she saw him, but it was just a pair of slippers. She came up from under the couch with only a few dust bunnies. Mike calmed her as best as he could and promised that they'd search for the cat first thing in the morning.

It was dark out, and even though the rain was absent, it was getting colder at night. Angie said as much, hoping to begin the search that very evening, but Mike said it wasn't a good idea. It was too dark to see anything. He was right, Angie knew. Felix preferred to hide at night and sleep anyway. His favourite spots were the small, enclosed spaces of the house, like behind computer monitors or up in the linen closet. "The linen closet!" Angie exclaimed then dashed to the hallway and opened the door a little too quickly. Luckily, Felix wasn't there or he might've died from fright.

Angie closed the door sadly. She wasn't going to find him then and there, so she had to content herself with typing up a missing cat sign. The pictures she found for the posters were what finally caused her tears to break. She fell asleep in Mike's arms on the couch. Mike watched the breaking news that a suspect had been found in the disappearance of the college student last week. Some cruel-mouthed convict was in custody. *Good,* was Mike's last conscious thought.

At the crack of dawn, Angie was scanning neighbourhood Facebook pages and the SPCA for any word. Nothing. She couldn't really imagine Felix escaping. He'd never even made an attempt in the past. He was the perfect little homebody. Calling out his name and brandishing his treat bag like an offering, Angie retraced her steps around the apartment until she was satisfied that she'd surveyed every inch. Something must have enticed him outside; a bird, maybe, because he was always after the birds. Angie glanced out at the balcony and felt her stomach sink.

Meanwhile, Mike walked door to door on their floor, canvasing the neighbours. There were shaken heads and well wishes, but no cat. Angie had printed a dozen posters with Felix's funny face on them for Mike to tape to walls around the building and phone poles outside. He couldn't imagine the cat getting outside; it would have been a mission impossible sequence of opened doors, steep staircases, confused neighbours, and one charging cat. Felix wasn't in that kind of shape. He wasn't that smart either. Once Mike made his rounds outside, he stopped underneath the building near their balcony. The sun had risen somewhere, shrouded in rain clouds. Mike stared into the grey alley.

There was one more way that stupid cat could have disappeared. The image was not pleasant, but Mike knew that he should be the one to find the cat, not Angie. It would break her heart to learn that her best friend had chased some pigeon off of their eighth floor balcony and was out here somewhere. Maybe he was okay. Maybe he was dead...or nursing four broken legs.

Angie walked out onto the balcony with the same supposition. She peeked over the edge, unwilling to witness Felix's little body down there. She saw a few mounds of garbage that were vaguely cat-shaped. Deeper in the alley, there was a murder of crows huddling around something. Her thoughts turned grim. *Why do they have to call it a murder anyway? It's so dark.* Other than the birds, she couldn't see anything except Mike coming around the corner. She watched him, gratefully. He was checking so that she wouldn't have to. Still, she watched him. She might not want to see what he found, but she wanted to see his reaction. A single raindrop marked the back of her hand.

Habit

Mike scanned the crumbling asphalt. He saw a pile of dirty clothes, grungy and decomposing. He saw some shredded black garbage bags spilling their guts into the gutter. He saw a gang of crows plotting together farther in. The birds were excited about something, so if Felix were down here, at least Mike wouldn't need to put the cat out of its misery. The rain broke.

Mike approached the black birds, blinking in the sudden flack of rain. He caught sight of grey fur. Large flecks slapped at Mike's skin. The birds parted way reluctantly. One old scraggly crow cawed at him, refusing to go. Mike kicked a stone at it. The bird dodged and kept yelling. Mike ignored the indignant beast; if this really was his cat, he was going to have to take it back with him. He'd have to wrap it up and bury it. That's what Angie would want. Where they'd bury him, he didn't know. They weren't out in the country with miles of rolling hillsides. They were in the middle of a city of 2.2 million.

Stepping right up to the body, Mike stared down at the little pointed ears, the striped tail, the potbelly—pulled open by the crows. But it wasn't the crows' mess that made Mike's heart rate skyrocket. It wasn't rain, but fear that trickled down his neck. Wedged in the animal's chest like a stake was the yellow handle of a screwdriver. Adrenaline licked up and down Mike's spine. He bent down, partly to recover his blood pressure, partly for a closer look. The tool was like so many others Mike had seen, like one he probably had at home. He was suddenly aware of eyes on him, as if somebody were watching and judging. As if they might think he was connected to this crime.

Looking up, he stared straight into Angie's face on the balcony. Even through the rain, he saw she was disquieted. He'd just been standing there for a whole minute, looking over this thing on the ground. He didn't know if she could see the body, but he figured she wouldn't be able to make out the weapon. Mike waved weakly and Angie raised a hand in response. He made to return to the apartment and watched her turn and re-enter the kitchen. Once she was out of sight, he toed the animal all the way behind the huge green dumpster.

Angie was standing in the corridor when he'd made it back inside. Her eyes were pleading. "What was it?" she asked hoarsely.

"Raccoon."

She tried to read his face. Her green eyes scanned his own. He couldn't help scanning her at the same time. Her round face was solemn, the bags under her eyes prominent and stained with yesterday's mascara. This whole ordeal had diluted her beauty. Mike looked up at her pale face, fine-lined and framed by that blue-black hair. Some of her roots were showing grey. The fluorescent lights did nothing to hide the fact.

"Come on," breathed Mike, shaking off his wet coat and criticism. "Let's go eat. I'm starving."

Angie couldn't eat. She was worried about Felix. She thought she should be relieved that the creature in the alley wasn't him, but that just left uncertainty. Knowing was better than not. She had to spend the rest of the day dwelling in that uncertainty. After more calls to every nearby shelter and vet, she still could not put her mind at ease.

Mike didn't seem upset at all. Angie thought about the last few months, ever since Alan's death, how sad he'd been. She wasn't trying to compare a missing cat to the loss of a father, but still. He was all of the sudden concerned about cleaning the house. He said he didn't want her to have to worry about chores on a day like this. He vacuumed and mopped. He cleaned the bathroom. All the while, he looked loose and at ease. In fact, in Angie's eyes, he seemed upbeat. It was unnerving.

Through all this, Mike was experiencing his first day without a death cough and without the acid burn in his throat. He wanted to do something nice for his wife since she was probably having the worst day of her life right now. He cleaned every room in the house and told Angie to just put her feet up and relax. It was the least he could do. She wouldn't relax though. She drifted through the apartment like a ghost. She touched each of Felix's toys as if they were idols. She willed him to appear. Mike was certain he wouldn't.

Outside, the afternoon sun pulled off its veil in one smooth motion. The rain stopped just as quickly as it had begun. Rays of light spilled into the apartment, lighting up Angie as she paced about. She looked horrible. She needed some sunshine the same as Mike did. He was feeling limber, so he decided to go for that jog he'd thought about yesterday, just to test out his lungs. He asked Angie if she wanted to join him, but she declined with a look of disbelief.

"I'm sorry, but I can't stay cooped up on a day like this."

Once he was out in the sun, Mike breathed in fully. The stuffy house and Angie's haunting presence had done a number on him. He ran a block and

Habit

felt pretty alright, so he ran two more blocks and then he felt fine. He ran to Coal Harbour, dodging between pedestrians and cars, breathing hard. He took in the mouldering smell of autumn, breathed the sweet gasoline off the cars, and coughed with the righteous air of working lungs. Halfway back, he did have to stop just to hack up some horrible sludge, but once that was out of his throat, he felt great.

Crossing the alley on his way home, he stole a glance over to where the body lay. The crows couldn't reach it, but Mike wondered if it wouldn't be better to trash the damn thing. He didn't want to touch it. He knew Angie wouldn't go near it. She hated the sight of death. It made her panic. Mike hadn't reacted too well himself. He saw death often and it normally made him numb, but this was too close to home. His heart was racing and it wasn't because of the run. Once his breathing slowed again he felt okay, or at least he felt he was going to be okay.

In fact, he felt almost back to normal, except that when he returned, Angie kept throwing worried glances at him like she thought he was going to bite. Mike ignored her for a minute and took a shower, whistling to the tune of *She'll be Coming 'Round the Mountain*. Once he was clean and shaven, he made a spaghetti dinner and they sat at the table together. Mike poured himself a whiskey on the rocks and offered Angie a glass of wine. She took it solemnly. He could read her distress for her lost pet, but he couldn't shake the feeling she was upset with him too. It was during their meal that Mike caught one of Angie's frantic glances. He stopped mid-bite and placed his fully-loaded fork back on the plate.

"Okay, Angie, what's up?"

Angie put down her own fork and looked at him briefly. "What do you mean?"

Sensing her rising anxiety, Mike spoke in a soft voice. "I mean...why do you keep looking at me like that?"

"Like what?" Her eyes darted away from him.

Mike sighed. "Like you're looking at a predator instead of your husband."

"What?"

"Like you're scared of me!" His voice rose before he could control himself. Angie flinched away. Mike knew better than to frighten her, but he wasn't hallucinating; she had been dodging his gaze, and when she wasn't, she sat staring at him like he were a wild animal.

He waited for her reply. He breathed in and tried to lower his heart rate. He tried to relive his day to find any cause to her unrest. How could she be upset when he spent the morning looking for her damned cat? How could she be angry when he was trying to make the house nice for her? She hadn't seen what he had in the alley. He knew that much. She had been spared. She was acting like he'd killed the animal right in front of her.

"I guess..." Angie started, then stopped. She was so delicate.

"You guess..." Mike prompted.

Angie's brows stitched. That was rude, he knew. She took her time, but now at least she was showing some constitution.

"I guess I think it's strange how you can be smiling all day and then go gallivanting around while our cat is missing."

"Huh?"

It came out with a bit of aggravated spittle. Angie watched the speck of saliva hit the table between them. Mike waited for her to elaborate. She didn't. Her own heart was making an escape attempt. It chiselled painfully against her sternum.

"What do you want me to say, Angie? I was cleaning the house *for you*. I was searching for *your* cat all morning. And give me a break. This is the first time in a long time that I've felt anything other than complete garbage. I went for a run today, Angie—a run. When was the last time I asked you to go for a run with me?"

"Never," she said too quickly, as if that very fact was an admission of guilt.

"Exactly. Look, I'm so, so sorry that the cat is missing. I didn't mean for him to go missing. I don't even know how he got out of this apartment. I think we both have an idea." He pointed to the balcony. "And if that is what happened, then we can't really do anything about it. You want to keep torturing yourself?" He asked it rhetorically, but Angie shook her head emphatically. A few tears loosened themselves and she wiped her eyes.

Mike didn't want to keep arguing. He didn't want to see Angie cry. It made her eyes a fierce green, but of course that was only because they were ringed with red. It washed out her skin until she looked like a wax figurine rather than a live woman. Her scar flushed pink. Mike sighed.

"I *am* sorry, Angie." He said it very softly. She looked up uncertainly at first, but then she managed to compose herself. She shook her head slowly again. Mike pulled his chair right next to hers and wrapped her in his arms. Engulfed in the clean smell of him, Angie tried to relax and rest her head on Mike's shoulder. She knew in her gut that Felix couldn't have gotten out in the nighttime. He must have slipped out while Mike was having his coffee outside.

She told herself it was no one's fault. All she knew is that it felt good to be held. That's all she had wanted today. It was selfish of her, she knew. Mike had cleaned the whole house and she was only upset because he hadn't done the one thing she really needed, curled up with her in his arms.

Mike felt Angie start to tremble. He kissed her hair and sighed again, giving up the lofty dream of taking her to bed. Sometimes it was hard for him to remember how fragile she was.

On Thanksgiving morning Mike rolled out of some relentless dream about the god-damned cat. First, Felix had been chattering at something on the balcony, then he was chasing it over the edge. The next thing Mike knew, the cat was yowling far below and he had to run down the stairs to find him. The stairs were endless, of course. Mike just went around and around with the cat's wails resounding in his ears.

In the waking world, Mike blinked and tore the sheets off. Angie was up already. He heard her in the shower and the thought of a warm, wet body turned him on. Like a vampire rising, Mike floated over to the bathroom and let himself in silently. He could see Angie's shadow on the curtain. Her curves were exaggerated nicely. He watched her shampoo her hair and waited for her to start singing. She always sang when her hair was underwater. That was the perfect time for an ambush.

With a smile on his face, Mike stripped off his boxers. He padded quietly over to the tub. With one swift tug, he pulled back the shower curtain, rebreaking the first two holes. Angie gasped and whipped Mike in the face with her hair as she turned to face him. Oblivious to the sting, Mike was upon her. He slid his fingers between her legs and made her squeal a luscious harmony of indignation and delight.

When they were finished, Mike turned the water even hotter. Angie, breathless, rinsed the rest of the shampoo out of her hair. That was the second time Mike had spooked her. This time, he hadn't even said a word; he'd just gone after her. She scrubbed her body all over again, but found herself smiling. It hadn't been entirely unpleasant. She escaped the tub, but not after Mike had given her one final wet smack on the ass.

"Mother..." Angie gave him a harder one right back, and then left to find her towel. While she dried her hair, she listened to Mike whistling. It was the same tune she'd heard the day before, something about riding six white horses she was sure.

She moved to the kitchen in her bathrobe and bent to replace the little dish of water for Felix before she remembered. A sad sigh left her lips, but she decided she was not going to let it get to her, not today. Today was for festivity. Tomorrow she could worry again. She didn't think one day would make a difference anyway. Felix was gone and if he had run off the balcony. Well, even a cat could be injured from a fall that high. She checked her phone for any word from the shelters. Then her mom called from Ottawa to wish them a happy Thanksgiving and show her all the snow she was missing.

Habit

Angie didn't have the heart to tell her parents about Felix. They weren't animal lovers. They asked after Mike and she was happy enough to report he'd quit smoking.

"That's great," replied her mom, "now you can focus on making us some grandbabies."

Staring down at her phone after the call, Angie felt Mike behind her. She sighed again, and sensing her dismay, Mike clasped his hands on her shoulders and turned her to face him. He smiled reassuringly up at her.

"Don't worry, Hon." He held her in a kiss before moving away to the fridge.

After a quiet breakfast of toast and eggs, Mike asked, "What time are we due at Peach's place tonight?"

"Five," replied Angie.

"Good," said Mike, piling his dishes in the sink. "I have my appointment at three again."

"Oh." Angie had almost forgotten about the hypnotherapy. "He's open on Thanksgiving?"

"I guess so," said Mike.

"Seems strange..."

"Well," Mike shrugged. "Maybe I'm the last patient. He'll still have time to make it home for turkey."

At 2:30, Mike put on a clean, button-up shirt and found a pair of dress pants. He styled his hair and brushed his teeth. Then he set out to find his cologne. It was in the recesses of the medicine cabinet, dusty from disuse. He spritzed himself before kissing Angie goodbye. Angie looked him up and down.

"My, my, Mr. Perry. Don't you look nice."

Mike chuckled. "Only the best for my wife and her friends."

"You smell good too."

Mike kissed her again and winked. "Only the very best."

Mike's mind wandered away from Angie as he drove. Guiltily, he tore his thoughts from Peach too. But as one beautiful woman slipped his mind, another popped in, until he was thinking about Tamara. He wondered if she would be working today. He wondered what she'd be wearing. *Damn it.* He tried to think about Tehrani instead. He thought he'd had some questions for the shrink about after Tom's confession, but he was drawing a blank.

He found parking right in front of the clinic and strolled up to the front door. Pulling it open, Mike was hit with the warm smell of pumpkin pie. He stood there wafting it in, his hand still on the handle. Tamara was watering a plant between a poster of a man on a mountain and one of a woman in the sea. The receptionist stood up on tip-toe to reach the plant and Mike liked the way her legs were tensed. She glanced behind her and gave him a smile fresh out of the oven.

"I'll be with you in a moment."

Mike let the door close behind him as he took her in.

She was wearing a festive little outfit of a coral blouse with frilly sleeves that rested at her elbows since her arms were above her head. The blouse was tucked into a tight brown pencil skirt. The skirt was riding up as she reached up. It came to rest just above her knees. Her brown heels must have been four inches at least, but still she was reaching. Mike watched the muscles in her calves relax as she lowered herself. He imagined taking a bite out of one of those calves.

Tamara's hair swirled around when she turned. She smiled shyly. She'd been stared at by a lot of the men who came into her office. She didn't mind so much if they turned away quickly or blushed. That was normal. That's how Mike had been the last time she'd seen him. This time he just kept staring. He watched her cross the room to her desk. It was unsettling, but she was a professional. With the counter firmly between them, she scanned her scheduler.

"Okay, Mr. Perry. You're our last appointment of the day. The doctor is with another client, though, so you'll have to wait out here a moment."

"That's fine," said Mike amiably. He sat in the chair closest to the counter and set about pretending to read the most recent Psychology Today magazine. As he flipped meaninglessly through the glossy pages, he stole glances up at Tamara. Her blouse was not cut as low as the last shirt he'd seen her in, but the sheer fabric hugged her nicely. Mike couldn't see any bra straps. He hadn't seen any panty lines under her skirt either. He wondered about that.

Habit

When he turned to an article called *Eternal Curves*, he skimmed through the author's theory that men were unintentionally tuned into women's waists. They probably were all subconsciously looking for those procreative qualities. He realized with revulsion he sized up every woman he came across. He didn't think it had anything to do with child-bearing as the study suggested, but wasn't that just the internal struggle? Mike could think of very few women he'd like to raise a child with, but they were the most beautiful, curvy women he knew. The thought made him sad. He had a memory of red rose petals upon the bed. He didn't think Tamara would have done that for a man.

Tamara was increasingly aware of being watched as she sat alone with this stranger two metres away. The fact that he didn't seem to be breathing made her even more self-conscious. Most men she'd sat in silence with made breath sounds: coughs, or grumbles, or sighs. Every once in a while, she looked up, fully expecting Perry's eyes to be on her, but he was only reading one of the periodicals. She wanted to shiver. She could not shake the silent feeling of his eyes on her body.

After an eternity, the door to Dr. Tehrani's office opened and a squirrelly little guy stepped out. Mike thought he recognized him from somewhere. He could have been one of the meth addicts he'd treated. The guy was so skinny and jumpy that he looked like he was about to hold the place up for drug money. Behind the squirrel appeared the doctor. He was dressed in another set of tailored grey slacks and a matching vest, this one a shade or two darker than the last. Underneath, he wore a rust-coloured silk shirt.

Tehrani clapped the little man on the shoulder and said, "Until next week, Mr. Hawk," before ushering Mike to follow him back into the room. Mike passed his eyes over the squirrel named Hawk, who smiled weakly at him. Mike nodded but turned to Tamara. He tipped two fingers to her like a salute and then strode to the office nonchalantly.

Tamara watched him go, feeling suddenly uncertain about how she'd judged him. It wasn't like he'd really been staring. It must have been her imagination. Maybe he was just admiring her, like everyone else did—like the mouse in front of her was doing now. She gave a quick smile.

"Let me make your next appointment, Mr. Hawk."

Mike closed the door softly behind him and let his eyes adjust to the dim room once again. The doctor was already settling into his velvet chair, notepad in hand, pen between his teeth.

"One moment, please," said Tehrani, gesturing towards the sofa with his pen.

Mike took his place and looked around at the rich decorum. On the floor lay an intricately patterned Persian rug with threads of gold and green and red. It matched the landscape in the painting above Mike's couch. The high bookshelf was engraved with grape vines. He hadn't noticed that before, but he remembered how crammed it was; many of the books teetered on the edge, like precariously placed butts on an ashtray.

The polished rosewood desk was piled high with files. Mike couldn't recall if it had been that way last time. He saw the domed clock with its red wooden case facing out from the corner of the desk. The gold pendulum swished back and forth like a cat's tail. It was the same clock from his childhood, how could he forget?

Mike was still mesmerized when Dr. Tehrani lowered the pen to his lap and cleared his throat. Mike turned.

"Thank you for waiting, Mr. Perry."

"No problem."

"So," continued the doctor, steepling his brown hands together and smiling over them towards Mike, "how was your first week?"

In the days leading up to this moment, Mike had thought about all the things he wanted to say to the doctor, all the troubles and memories and lapses he'd been faced with. Now he felt impotent to put it all into words.

"It's been good." That was only a half-lie.

"That's good to hear. What sorts of things have been good about it?"

Mike considered. He hadn't seen much of the cat lately. That was good. Angie and he had had some magnificent sex, but no, that was the week before…

"I've been on time to work all week. Early…sometimes."

"That is good. It's a good sign. You like your work?"

"Yeah, you know, good team, good people. Management is good."

"Glad to hear that. You've been there about four years?"

Mike nodded.

Habit

"It's nice to have a stable career. Are you feeling any stress at work?"

Hellhole. Mike barely kept from flinching. He hid it with a shrug.

"Nothing more than usual."

"That doesn't mean it's easy." The quick remark made Mike regard the doctor.

"No," he replied, a little guarded, "it isn't easy."

Tehrani took the hint and dropped the subject, but he checked a note before continuing. "You say you've really got a good team though. That helps."

Mike nodded and rubbed his palms on his jeans. He hoped this wouldn't take long. He realized with surprise that he wanted to be put under again. He remembered things when he went under, things he never wanted to think about. Maybe he could forget things too.

"How were the cravings?" asked the doctor behind his half-glasses, getting better? About the same? Worse?"

Mike shrugged. "Same, I guess." He recalled the terrible flashes of carnage that accompanied those cravings. "Nothing I couldn't handle though."

"Any relapses?" asked the doctor, lowering his steepled fingers. Mike remembered the coughing spasm that had flung the cigarette out of his hand when he was with Rita.

"Just one...but...I couldn't manage to finish it. The cigarette I mean." The doctor watched him for a moment, then made a note. Mike felt sweat under his arms. He didn't like to be looked over like that. It was too much like the shrink who'd questioned him after his mother's death.

"And what led up to that relapse? Did something happen last week?" The doctor was looking right into his eyes, not intensely, but it felt overwhelming to mike. Heat rose up in his face.

"It was a call at work—"

"You're a paramedic, right?" interrupted Tehrani.

"Right. There was a call that started off as one thing and then turned into something completely different. I don't want to get into specifics—"

"I think you should." He said it so suddenly, that Mike wasn't sure how to respond. He just sat there with his mouth half open. Dr. Tehrani leaned over in his chair with his hands palm up, like he was offering something to Mike.

"Mr. Perry, this could be important for your ability to handle future relapses. We should open this thing up."

Mike glanced at the clock. "I think I'd rather just get on with this thing. Just this time. You know. It was a bad call. A terrible call. I just—" his hands were sweating again. "I can't really talk about it. It just makes it worse, you know."

Tehrani paused for a moment, wanting to press his client, but unwilling to do so. Their rapport was still translucent.

He said, "I get it. It's hard to break the seal once you've tucked some memory away. Why don't we start there though, in the session? Would that be okay? You can start to think about moments just before a craving hits you.

It was already 3:47 p.m. "Ok." Mike agreed, lying back for a moment, then trying to find a comfortable position.

"Now take a deep breath and start at the beginning," Tehrani said once Mike was settled.

Mike breathed in and tried to close his eyes. "It was Monday."

"This happened just after you left my office?"

"Well...hours later, actually." Mike recounted the domestic violence call, glossing over some of the more gruesome details. He spoke openly about wanting a smoke so badly after that, only to have the coughing fit ruin it for him. He left out the part about seeing his mother's face in Rita's. He didn't mention his mother at all, in fact. He didn't feel it pertinent to mention his growing sexual deviance either. He only answered the questions and tried to distance himself from the week's memories. Once the story was out, Mike waited for Tehrani to respond. The doctor only looked at him over his glasses. Those green eyes were sober and patient.

He said, "There's something you're leaving out, Mr. Perry."

Mike stayed quiet, certain that Tehrani could read some underlying condition in his very bone structure.

"What do you mean?"

Habit

"Well, for starters, I haven't heard anything about how this horrible experience made you feel." Mike coughed over a laugh.

"Made me feel?"

Tehrani nodded.

"It didn't make me feel anything..."

Tehrani said nothing for a long time. Mike glared at him and kept his mouth clamped tight. His eyes shifted to the clock and then back to the doctor. Tehrani blinked impassively.

Mike sighed, then said, "Except incapable." Tehrani waited for him to continue. Mike's lip curled. "I should be able to do my job no matter what it entails. I shouldn't be shaken up by every ugly thing I see." Mike's body slumped back down. Tehrani lifted his own shoulders with a breath and settled them again. Mike eyed him, but unconsciously took a breath as well.

"Thank you for sharing that with me, Mr. Perry." Mike met his gaze. "The desire to do our work well is strong for all healthcare workers. The pressure...well, the pressure can be crushing. You stand between your patients and the grim reaper." Mike blinked, but his tension slackened a little. "Mr. Perry, I think you can move through that feeling of being incapable. I think that would be very healthy for you. From what you told me of your father's death, you may need to let go of a kind of hero complex. You can't save everyone. Some people don't want to be saved."

Mike nodded. He was thinking about his mother.

"You, however, were meant to save lives, and right now you have to save your own. I want you to think about the kinds of things you can do for yourself to help you get healthier and stronger."

Mike caught on. "And happier?" They shared a familiar smile for what felt like the first time.

"That's right. Are you ready to begin?"

Mike scanned the room from where he lay and his eyes rested on the clock. Time was contained in a single oscillation behind the glass. His childhood clock. He had the vague notion to smash it. Tehrani took in an audible breath and Mike pulled himself away from the destructive thought. He matched the doctor's soft inhale.

When Mike looked into his eyes again, he said, "I'm ready," and settled down even more, arms loose, eyes up to the ceiling. *Just like mom.*

The doctor sensed his stress and took advantage of it. "I want you to start by contracting every muscle in your body." Mike peered over at the man. Tehrani nodded. "Contract every muscle until your entire body is tense and shaking."

Mike followed the order. He squeezed his legs, his arms, his fists, his feet. He pinched his eyes shut. He shook with the pent up energy until he thought he would explode.

Tehrani said, "Hold."

Mike held. He held until he could feel the sweat between his shoulder blades and under his arms.

Calmly, Tehrani said, "Harder." Mike's body trembled with exertion. His jaw clicked under the pressure. His left buttock spasmed and he got a cramp in the bottom of his foot.

"Hold it."

He thought that at any moment his body would give, but still Mike held.

Finally, Tehrani whispered, "Release."

When Mike let go of his grip, a surge ripped through his tired body. He felt the effects of yesterday's run like a blade dragged over his legs. He shuddered and his breathing came out in rasps.

Tehrani said, "Easy now. Breathe normally. Feel the tension leave your body until you're left only with the remnants. Even that pressure is only a memory. Your body is at ease. Totally at ease. So is your mind. Your mind is freed of all tension and distraction."

Mike tried to relax. It sounded great. He listened for the doctor's next instruction, but for a long time, Tehrani said nothing. So, Mike let his mind float down, attracted to the sudden nothingness. His breathing normalized.

In a voice from above, Tehrani said, "Imagine you are walking down a long staircase. With each step, you drop deeper into relaxation. With each step your muscles loosen..." Mike's body melded into the cushions again. "Your eyes settle." Mike stared through his eyelids into the pink void. "Your jaw relaxes..." Mike's lips parted.

Habit

"Your body moves gently down...down...down, until you are so perfectly at ease that you realize the staircase has brought you to your favourite place in your home." Mike imagined his bed, blankets askew, Angie's imprint still on her side, her smell still in the room.

"In this place, you find a comfortable spot to rest."

Mike laid himself down and covered up with the sheets.

"Now think about the details you leave out when you think about your week."

They were numerous. Whole scenes washed out in swatches of watercolor.

"Look beside you. Find a photo album, or a book with all the causes of distress hidden in its pages..." Mike saw his week in a sort of montage. One image after the next projected in his mind's eye: the night shifts, the flashbacks, the cat. It all came out frame by frame, distorted and fuzzy, but disturbing nonetheless. Mike tried to distance himself.

"Everything you see here is only a memory, Mike. Memories want to be real. They try to make us feel real emotions, real worries. But memories are not real. They are like the negatives of a photograph; they can only show an imprint of what really happened. I want you to open the album." Mike hesitated. He couldn't bring himself to commit to the onslaught that he was sure would drown him. The furrow of his brow exposed his stress.

"You can let go. You can and you will. Open the album, but don't read into it. This album is going to be burned, so you can let the memories come up. You don't have to try to blur them out. When you smoke, you get a break, Don't you? You can catch a break in many different ways. Think about the room you chose, you can always reset in there. Think about a place outdoors. You can be in nature and get a longer lasting break."

Mike heard the words and slowly let his resolve flicker out. He didn't want to let go, but he didn't want to get burned either. Fear was stitched into his forehead.

Tehrani said, soothingly, "Everyone deserves a fresh start. You have to give yourself permission to reset without shame and self-defeat. Cigarettes cannot give you the release you're looking for. Only you can give yourself that freedom." Mike couldn't feel the tear, but Tehrani watched it roll down.

"That's right. You deserve to live without shame. Now, take a lighter out and touch it to the corner of one of those memories. Watch the emotions attached to it take flame. Feel the heat from the fire."

Mike tried to imagine the scenes from his life without the feelings that always accompanied them. He saw his father's corpse, but could no longer blame himself for not saving him. He saw Peach, but could no longer shame himself for wanting her. He saw... He saw his mother, stretched out in death, and felt nothing, the way he always did.

The doctor acknowledged a fluttering release in Mike's lips. When he'd finally relaxed, Dr. Tehrani repeated, "Memories cannot hurt you. You have to let yourself recover."

Tehrani waited to continue, "Okay. Take your time leaving this space. Picture yourself stepping back up the stairs." Mike tried to envision himself walking up to his apartment, but it was sort of like floating up through the dark. "Take a step up and feel your chest rise and fall with your breath. Take another step and feel the warmth of your body return. Another step and you feel your eyes, your mouth, your fingers, your toes... I'm going to snap my fingers and you'll be fully awake, fully present. You'll remember that regardless of your memories, your emotions, your dreams, you are enough."

The snap rang out and something like a medicine ball rolled off Mike's chest. He released a sputtering gasp. He shivered and opened his eyes. Tehrani was making a note. He waited until Mike had cleared the tears from his eyes before observing him again.

"Well, how do you feel?"

"I feel...better."

"I'm glad to hear it."

Mike stood unsteadily. The doctor rose and extended his hand. Mike shook that hand very slowly.

"You've taken great strides today, Mr. Perry. Don't be alarmed if this calm wears off. Things might get worse before they get better, but we'll pick up again next week." Mike nodded gravely.

When he strode out of the office, he anticipated Tamara to be seated at her station like a vision. Perhaps she'd see him as a changed man. The waiting room was empty though. The front door was locked. Mike would not let his disappointment show, though. Tehrani was the one to jot down his next appointment for the following Monday.

"It will have to be at six p.m."

"That's fine. I'm not working Monday."

Tehrani locked the door behind him and Mike hustled back to his vehicle. The Ford's clock read 4:42. Mike hadn't realized how long he'd been inside. It felt like a blip in time. He checked his mirrors and skirted out onto the main drive. The journey to Peach's was relatively uneventful until he caught a text from Angie asking him to pick up the pumpkin pie she'd forgotten at the apartment. *Fuck*. Mike pulled around the next block and headed back towards home.

He parked in the alley behind the building and ran to the back door. Still running, he took the stairs two at a time, then unlocked their unit with one smooth motion. In his head he was on a countdown. He found the pie and balanced it on his fingertips as he locked back up. Then he thought twice and went back inside to collect the whipping cream he was certain Angie would have in the fridge. There it was in a little pink carton. He imagined the surprise on her face as she realized she'd forgotten to ask, but then her delight when he showed up with it anyway.

He was still imagining Angie's smile, and then Peach's, as he stepped back out to the alley. Movement caught his eye and he turned towards it. The pie plummeted from his hand, and with it, the last sane thought in Mike's mind.

Staring up at him from two lazy yellow eyes was a fat grey tabby cat. It looked very much like his fat tabby cat, except this one had a screwdriver driven into its chest. Because of this abnormality, its gait was disjointed. As it approached, the front legs wobbled around the obstruction, making it zig zag as it walked. The cat's fur was sticky brown with blood. Entrails snaked out of a gaping wound in its belly and dragged along on the rocks behind it. Once the cat's back paw landed on the offal. It stopped.

It meowed at him. The sound was garbled, but it echoed off the buildings and struck Mike like a blow. Mike's mouth opened in a silent scream. He backed up into his truck and turned to duck inside. He locked the door beside him. When he finally dared to look out, he saw the cat was right there, ready to leap up onto the hood. Mike scrambled for the keys and almost busted them against the ignition in his haste to get away.

Heart in his throat, Mike peeled out and without realizing it, he crushed the pie under his wheels. The whipping cream spewed out its white guts as the tire rolled over it. The cat eyed his retreating vehicle and then sat on its haunches and licked at the white blood. Mike saw it there in the rear-view mirror. He sped all the way to Peach's house, oblivious to everything, including the red light he blew through. All he could think of were those eyes, glittering with malice. He didn't kill that cat. He had not killed that cat. He hadn't killed that fucking cat.

Mike was exhausted on arrival. He saw Angie's car already parked in front of the little townhouse, plus Val's vehicle, and a red Mazda he didn't recognize parked in the driveway. Mike put the truck in park and leaned his head back. His blood pressure was through the roof, so he closed his eyes and breathed in as deeply as he could. He couldn't go in there like this. He replayed the way the cat's tail had swayed as it walked. He forced the image out with a breath and found it transformed into the swinging pendulum of Tehrani's clock. He was back in that office, listening to the clock's subtle knocking.

Something was very wrong. Where had the doctor's encouragement gone? Whatever happened to *memories can't touch you*? That was the thing, though; whatever the hell he'd just witnessed...it wasn't real. Mike was only being haunted because he hadn't told Angie the truth of what he'd seen being pecked by the birds. Sure, he should have levelled with her, but what the fuck was he supposed to tell her? *Sorry honey, somebody took a screwdriver to your tubby little tabby cat. No, I have no recollection of killing him myself. Of course, I'd tell you if I had!*

Mike opened his eyes again. He had not killed the cat. The truck's digital clock taunted him with the numbers 5:38. Mike turned off the vehicle and stepped into the waning light and the waxing rain. Subconsciously, he felt the droplets soaking through his jacket and his pants, but Mike moved through a fog. He tried to remind himself that memories couldn't hurt him. He squared his shoulders and walked up to the house.

It would be good to see Peach. She was so certain in life. It would be good to watch her smile and laugh and entertain. He knocked on the door and stepped back. Mike needed to hear her sarcasm, needed to bask in her sweet cynical peace of mind. But it was not the beautiful little curly-blonde who let him in. It was a tall, handsome man with a self-deprecating smile and eyes that sparkled glacier blue. He was fair-haired and dressed in an ugly holiday sweater and brown slacks.

Habit

"Welcome," said the man, as if he were letting Mike into his own home. Mike was taken aback. He'd been here many times. This was the correct door.

"Is—is Peach here?"

"Of course. Sorry. I'm Collin." Collin stuck out his hand for Mike to shake. Mike stared at it. So, here stood the new boyfriend, officially debuting with the friends and family on this fine Thanksgiving eve. Mike didn't want to shake that hand. Deep down in some nasty part of himself, he knew that if he did, he'd be letting go of the woman he'd been in love with for four years. The woman in question appeared, just before that hand could hang alone in the air too long. Collin stepped aside and placed that same hand on the small of her back instead.

"Hello Michael," said Peach warmly. She turned her radiant face to Collin then quickly back to Mike. "I'm glad you two could finally meet."

Collin nodded, but his smiling eyes were passing over Mike now. He pressed them upon Peach. Peach didn't look at Collin again and Mike wondered why she kept her eyes on him instead of her supposed lover. The pair of them stepped back to let Mike enter.

Mike recovered himself and said, "Hi, Peach."

"Did you bring the pie?"

"Oh uh..." *Fuck.* "I didn't realize I was supposed to." He lied and reached for his phone as if to check for a text.

"Shit," said Peach, turning to Collin. "I don't suppose you could run out and grab one, Sweetheart?"

Collin amiably agreed and grabbed up his coat just as Mike was taking off his own. Mike glimpsed himself in the hallway mirror and was surprised to find a wet, dishevelled rat with sunken eyes looking back. *So much for the very best*. He swiped pointlessly at the rain on his shoulders and ran his hands through his hair to try to rework the wax in there. Meanwhile, Peach kissed Collin on the cheek and he left.

Then Peach was hugging Mike. Her soft scent wrapped him in its arms. He inhaled. Quick as she'd come, Peach was leading him into the dining room where Angie, Val, and Peach's parents were seated around an ornate table. The tablecloth was a lattice of lace. There were red, yellow, and orange maple leaves in amongst the wine glasses and hors d'oeuvres. A threesome of drooping sunflowers sat in a clay vase surrounded by miniature pumpkins. Mr. Müller held the seat at one end of the table and his wife was to his left. Val sat to his right and there was an empty space between him and Angie.

Angie stood to kiss Mike. She asked, "Where's the pie?"

"I..." started Mike.

"Don't worry. Collin popped out to grab one. Mike didn't get your text in time." Peach moved her fingers out in front of her, like a magician casting a spell. "He just got back from hypnotherapy." She said it the way you might say Abracadabra, or Frankenstein.

Val and Peach's father both chuckled. Mike coughed uncomfortably.

"Oh. Well. It's my fault, really," Angie was saying as she settled back down. Mike pulled up the chair between his wife and Val. "I had the pie and the whipping cream ready to go. I guess they'll just be sitting in the fridge waiting for us."

Mike felt like he had straw caught in his throat. He coughed again. Peach's mom poured him a glass of water. He thanked her and nodded over at Mr. Müller in greeting. Mr. Müller raised his glass to Mike. Peach was moving to the kitchen, asking Mike if he'd like any wine. He said he would, but it was Angie who poured him a glass of red.

Val clapped him on the back. "What's this about hypnotherapy?" he asked.

"It's... I'm quitting smoking," Mike mumbled.

"Oh, I've heard of that," exclaimed Mrs. Müller. "There's all sorts of tapes you can buy and listen to before bed."

Mike nodded and gratefully took a swig of the wine that Angie handed him.

"And it works?" asked Mr. Müller incredulously.

"Well..." began Mike, but Angie continued for him.

"He only started last Monday, but he hasn't had a smoke all week."

"Fascinating." Mr. Müller steepled his fingers thoughtfully. Mike was reminded of Tehrani.

Habit

Mrs. Müller leaned in conspiratorially and asked, "What's it like?"

Mike thought back to the dim room and the doctor's intoning voice. He remembered the photographs, the feelings that he'd burned to a crisp. His disgrace drifted off in the ashes. That all seemed a very long time ago after what he'd just experienced in the alley. They were all watching him, so Mike cleared his throat.

"It's a bit like a dream, I guess. Like having someone guide you—through the dream. They tell you things you sort of already know, but when you hear them...they have more power." There was a subtle shifting around the table. Mike's gaze rested on the sunflower centrepiece. "It's like everything you really want is right there waiting for you to take it and so you do."

A solemn moment went by while the others nodded wistfully.

"It sounds wonderful, Michael," said Peach, entering from the kitchen with a steaming plate of dinner rolls. Mike smiled up at her, detecting the subtle sprinkling of sarcasm. Peach. He hadn't noticed how lovely she was tonight. He'd been too busy staring daggers at her new playboy.

Half of Peach's curly hair was up, held by a black barrette in the shape of a flower. She wore a silvery silk shirt that accentuated the absence of any bra. Her long black skirt was decorated with white flowers. In it, her plump hips moved beautifully under the warm central light. She had a half smile all the while that she laid down the buns and took a seat at the other end of the table. Val was the first to reach out for a bun and he dropped it on his plate with a little grimace.

"Careful," said Peach, "they're still warm."

Angie giggled beside him, and feeling penitent all over again, Mike turned to take her in as well. She wore her hair down. It looked shiny and clean. It covered the one thing Mike had to thank Jackson Fucking Forcier for. If he hadn't cut Angie, then she never would have left him and Mike never would have met her. He never would have married her. Her lips were their signature red. Her heavy mascara fanned her lashes out demurely. Mike could only see traces of tiredness around her mouth and eyes, as if she'd still been crying. She was wearing a green, voluminous sweater that did nothing to hide her large breasts but did hug her waist nicely. Angie caught him staring. She smiled at him with coy eyes that asked, *What are you looking at?* But Mike's eyes were drawn back to Peach as she leaned over to refill his wine.

"So, Mike," Mr. Müller was saying as he reached for his own bun. "Val tells us you had a rather nasty call the other week. I think I saw something about it in the news."

Mike winced. How could any film crew put that hellhole on the air?

"Shame about the little girl."

Mike's heart stopped. "Little girl?" As if on a slide show, each of the victims that night made an appearance in his mind. The cat, the dog, the bird, the wife. Wasn't there a nursery rhyme about that? No. There had been no little girl.

"Yes...the one struck by the truck?" Eyes were on him now. Mike took a drink of wine and then finally understood which call they were talking about.

"Let's not bring up work, Dad." Peach gave her father a sad look across the table. "It's not really something we want to relive on Thanksgiving. You understand." Mr. Müller would understand. He'd been an emergency surgeon for nearly twenty years. He worked for the same shop of horrors as Mike, Peach, and Val.

His wife chimed in, "I, for one, am just so grateful for all of our front line workers here tonight." She raised her glass in a toast and it was quickly taken up by the others. Mike sipped from his long-stemmed glass, happy for the break in conversation.

It wasn't long after that that the front door opened and Collin returned. Peach stood and went to him in the front hall. Mike could hear them kiss in the foyer and Collin made some dumb joke about fighting off an old lady for the last pie. Mike idly tore away the corner of his napkin.

Angie watched him fidget as the couple reappeared hand in hand.

Peach held the prized pie along with a tub of Cool Whip in her free hand. She brought them to the kitchen and Angie followed her. The two of them laughed about something and returned to the table, arms full of dishes of roasted vegetables and baked yams. After two more trips, they had the table laden with mashed potatoes, gravy, Brussels sprouts, cranberry sauce, stuffing, and a shiny brown turkey.

Peach settled beside Collin, who had taken her seat at the head of the table, *like he had the right*. He solemnly took up a carving knife in one hand and a large fork in the other, *like it was his honour*. The turkey sat at the mercy of his hands. Mike ruefully remembered the handshake. It felt like a

Habit

win. He hadn't had to make peace yet. He was torn from his steely thoughts when Angie dropped a fork beside him.

With a smile for everyone around the table, Collin said, "Let's dig in."

The food was delicious. The conversation was warm and informal. Only Mike seemed to be at a loss for words. Everyone else chatted about Angie's newest client who was an exciting new Calgary tech company, and about Collin's stupid sweater. Mike found himself zoning in and out of the talk, focusing on his wine more than anything else. The only thing he managed to say was, "The food was delicious, Peach."

Peach smiled at him and nodded for Collin to continue with whatever origin story he'd been on. Angie noticed when Mike emptied his third glass in an hour and she put her hand on his thigh as he went to fill it again. Mike looked at his wife with a mix of surprise and agitation. *She's really going to govern my drinking?* He thought back to the night at the blues club and relented—sort of. He only took a half glass.

Somewhere into the meal, Val asked, "So, Collin. How did you meet our Peach?"

Collin looked lovingly to the youngest Müller before replying, "Well, it's a funny story." His hand was on Peach's thigh. Mike couldn't see it, but he knew it was there from the angle of his arm. He wasn't listening to the story; it was something to do with his runaway dog that just so happened to choose Peach as its potential new owner. He thought about that hand on Peach's thigh and wondered how many times Collin had fucked her.

Val was saying something then; some joke because there were laughs around the table. Then Collin's voice again. He'd moved his hand off Peach's thigh and Mike's eyes lifted up with it. Mike heard his own name spoken, not by Collin but by Angie.

"Right, Hon?" They were all looking at him. He racked his brain for what she'd just told them. He read the faces, all with downturned lips and furrowed brows. Something sad then.

"Right," said Mike soberly. The correct response he supposed because they nodded sadly and patiently.

Mrs. Müller asked, "And you have no idea how he got out?" Mike clued in that they were talking about the cat. He grimaced and closed his eyes. The fucking cat walked towards him in the alley again and he had to open them again.

"No," replied Angie. "We searched all day on Sunday and I've called all the shelters and the vets. Mike put up signs around the block and everything." She was worried about Mike now. He looked unwell. When she put her hand on his, he didn't seem to notice.

"I'm sorry, Cricket," Peach's voice was almost a whisper. She and Angie shared a comforting look. A moment of silence passed, then the superhero, Collin, started to clear the plates as if that would bring the cat back. Val stood up to help him. Angie nudged Mike with her foot and he stood too. The three younger men cleared the table swiftly and set to work in the kitchen washing and drying the dishes.

"Shame about the cat, Mike," said Val once the water was running. "But I suppose Angie was more cut up about it than you were."

"Why would you say that?" Mike asked defensively.

"Hey, don't take it personally. I just remember you complaining about the damn thing; all the fur, all the toys, all the shit?" Mike clamped up. He glanced over his shoulder towards the dining room, but the others were laughing about something in there.

"I don't blame you," cordial Collin was saying. "I don't much care for cats myself. I'm a dog man." He said it like it was a career, like it was something to be proud of. Maybe Mike would buy the guy a name tag. *Hi, I'm Collin. I'm a Dog Man.*

They finished with the dishes, and Collin divvied out the pie with a dollop of Cool Whip on each piece. Mike and Val acted as delivery boys. They were met with gleeful oohs and ahhs, as if they were handing out Strawberries Arnaud instead of store-bought pumpkin pie.

When they'd finished the dessert and another bottle of wine, the conversation grew sleepy. Val was the first to depart, stating that he didn't want to be late to work tomorrow. He clapped Mike's back one more time. Angie nudged Mike with her toe again and he agreed that they'd better be off too. Peach hugged the three of them at the door. Mike thought she lingered with him a moment longer than with the other two. He could smell her fragrant perfume again.

Habit

Then fucking Collin did the thing that Mike should have anticipated. In front of everyone, he held out his hand and said, "Pleasure to meet you, Mikey."

Mike watched the shit-eating grin spread across his face. With what he hoped was only a moment's hesitation, Mike took the man's hand and looked him square in the eye.

"And you," *can go for a long walk off a short dock.* He let go again almost reluctantly. Val took Collin's hand next. Mike moved on to shake with Mr. Müller and to hug Peach's mother. Out on the porch, Angie said goodbye and Mike kissed her cheek before the two of them retreated to their separate vehicles.

Angie drove home bewildered. Something was up with her husband. It looked like he was treating Peach's new partner like a rival, which was stupid. She kept telling herself, *It's just my own insecurity.* But she didn't feel insecure, she felt disconcerted.

The pair of them arrived home within a minute of each other. Angie walked up from the parkade in time to see Mike dumping something in the trash behind the building. When he turned, he must have seen the question in her eyes.

"Junk from my truck."

Angie nodded, but the question was still there. Mike tried a smile. He was moving his hands around in his pockets. He looked like he was searching for his pack of smokes. Angie shivered. She realized the wine had been what was keeping her warm. She turned to go inside.

Mike wanted desperately to peek behind the dumpster to prove to himself that animal was still there. He decided against it and followed his wife instead. He got ahead of her and unlocked the door. He held it open and tried another smile. Angie relented.

"Thank you," she whispered. Mike smiled a little brighter. He watched her go up the stairs, her ass moving side to side as she climbed. He liked the way she moved. He thought her dark jeans fit that round ass very nicely. Just watching her gave him the idea that he'd never been with a woman in a staircase. It could be fun to bend her over the corner right here, right now—hold onto her with one hand and have the other on the banister to steady himself.

Around the next corner, Mike thought he smelled Peach's perfume. He reached for his wife's hand. She paused and met his eyes. He was looking at her the way he had for that fleeting moment at dinner. He stepped in close and kissed her ear. He made a necklace of kisses across Angie's skin as he maneuvered himself around her to a higher step.

Heat rose up to Angie's cheeks the same as it always did with Mike. There was no mistake. Those kisses were meant just for her. Mike had not been staring at Collin with Peach. He had just been zoned out from all the wine. Angie could smell it on him now and she swore she'd never let him drive home in that state again. Mike nibbled on her neck. He was unzipping her coat right there on the stairs. Before she knew it his hand was under her sweater, but Angie pulled away.

"Come on, you fiend. Let's not get arrested for public indecency."

"No one's going to see us," Mike whispered in her ear.

"Everyone and their mother is going to hear us." Mike couldn't argue with that. They lived in the corner unit on the back end of the hallway and they still sometimes heard people moving up and down the stairwell.

In the living room of their apartment, Mike threw off his coat and relieved Angie of her sweater and her pants and then her panties. He let her figure out the damn contraption around her tits. Fully naked, Angie crossed her arms and simpered devilishly.

"Your turn."

Mike undid his belt with pleasure. He bent it in half and for a moment considered spanking her with it, but Angie raised an eyebrow at him. By the time his pants were off, he was already aching to have her. He pulled off his shirt and practically tackled Angie over the couch. She giggled and tried to wriggle away. It didn't feel like a game to Mike though. He was throbbing. Just as he bent Angie over, he was imagining taking Peach in her own home. Wouldn't that be the thing. Strip her down just like this. Mike really would take the strap to Peach though. Sometimes he thought she needed a good hiding, especially after this nonsense with Collin. God, but it would be good to hear her howl. Mike wasn't even inside Angie yet. She had only put her hand on him to guide him. He exploded with a single feral thrust.

Angie felt the warmth on her hand and her thigh just as she felt him groan. She let go of Mike, confused at first. This hadn't happened to her since high school. She was about to say as much but thought it cruel.

She laughed a little and said instead, "I guess the wine won this battle." Mike did not laugh. She didn't catch his expression at all. As she turned, he was already walking away from her. She figured he was embarrassed. The bathroom door smacked closed. Fair enough.

Unwilling to pester him on his performance, she let him take that trip alone. She crossed to the kitchen and washed herself off. Standing there on her own, Angela Perry thought she deserved another glass of white wine. She pulled open the fridge. The mix of condiments in the door jingled cheerfully, but Angie's arm stopped dead, mid-swing.

"Mike?"

Mike opened the bathroom door a crack. "Yes?"

Angie heard the defeat in his voice. He probably thought she was going to say something about the sex. She turned back to the fridge. She found the white wine in the door and closed it again.

"No—it's nothing."

"You're sure?" asked Mike.

"I'm sure."

Angie thought she was the first to wake up. It was still pitch black outside, but she couldn't sleep any longer. She rolled over and felt for Mike, but there wasn't even a pool of drool on his pillow. He had been on the couch when she went to bed. He said he couldn't sleep, but he looked dead on his feet. She figured he just needed to come to terms with what had happened. It wasn't that big of a deal, but she wasn't going to patronize him. She slipped out of bed and padded through the darkness to the kitchen.

She almost dropped dead. There was Mike blocking the doorway with his back to her—just standing there in the dark.

"Mike?"

No response.

"Mike?!"

He turned slowly as if through molasses.

"Sorry. I was somewhere else." He brushed her shoulder on his way back to the bedroom. Angie watched him go. He was like a zombie. She shook off a chill and put on the coffee. Then she used the bathroom. There, her thoughts turned instantly to Felix. He used to love to rub against her while she sat on the toilet. They had a little ritual in there. He liked to be brushed with her old comb while she sat. He'd waddle back and forth, meowing like she'd made him the happiest cat in the world.

A teardrop hit the linoleum and splashed Angie's toes. When she was finished, she collected the litter box from beside the toilet. Holding it out in front of her like a body, Angie brought the box down the stairs and out to the alley. The dawn was still a while away and Angie moved through the darkness and the frost. She opened the lid of the great green dumpster and poured out the gravel. Then she sighed heavily and dumped the box in too. The lid closed with a metal bang. It felt a lot like giving up, but a little like letting go.

Angie climbed the stairs again. She wiped her eyes before entering the apartment. The smell of coffee was comforting. Mike was in the kitchen, fully present and accounted for this time. He'd noticed the missing litter box. Meeting her eyes, he handed her a hot mug of coffee. She accepted his peace offering with both hands and the steam from the coffee mingled with fresh tears on her face.

Habit

Mike and Angie left for work together. Mike kissed his wife goodbye and felt another pang of disgrace. He'd remembered how the mere thought of Peach had sent him into a frenzy the night before. When he should have been getting off to his wife right in front of him, he was busy coming to another woman. Tehrani's instructions cut through the shame and he tried to imagine closing the album.

On his way out to his truck, Mike remembered something else from last night. He sidetracked to the back alley. Some sinking feeling told him he would not find that skewered creature there, not after it had come back like something out of Pet Sematary. When he circled the dumpster, there it was like a message—like a provocation. He lifted it by the tail and swung open the dumpster. *Good riddance*, he thought, tossing it into the back corner of the bin. The screwdriver dislodged itself during the overhand throw and it clanged against the wall of the dumpster. Mike froze while the reverberation ran through him. It was loud enough to wake the dead. He waited for silence to return and then slowly turned his back on it.

Mike was getting used to being early to work. He caught sight of Peach's raised eyebrows and wandered over to chat. He found himself acutely aware of her perfume, the same brand from last night. He'd thought about that smell while he was kissing Angie in the stairs and that had been his first mistake. Now here Peach was, leading him on with her sweet fragrance.

Peach felt a prickle of concern when she saw Mike's face. He looked clean shaven and his hair was styled, but he had bags under his eyes he could have carried his car keys in.

"You're awake," said Peach dubiously.

"Yeah, I feel fine."

"Not hungover?"

"Not even a little bit."

"Not smoking?"

"Not even a puff." He winked at her.

Peach's eyebrows climbed even higher up her forehead. She looked Mike up and down and nodded. "Good work. Keep it up 'til Christmas and I might not have to fire you."

Old Val looked fresh out of the dryer. His grey hair was clean and crisp, so was his uniform. He gave Mike a high five and the two of them had just enough time to do their inspection before the first call. Then they were headed to an accident on Georgia Street.

The sun crept over the horizon waving a white flag. The air was cold, the sky was clear, and everything was covered in a frosty film. There were no pedestrians out yet, only the sentries curled up in their sleeping bags and cardboard boxes.

The first call was routine. Two injured drivers; one woman with whiplash, probably, and one man with a seized back, possible slipped disk. They looked after the woman and another bus came for the man. The woman was in her mid-fifties and had big bouncy breasts that kept getting in the way. Mike accidentally brushed one when he was taking her blood pressure. He apologized and she shook her head, unfazed. He had his hand right between them when he was listening to her breathing through the stethoscope and she wasn't bothered by that either. Right afterwards, Mike was disturbed to find he was nursing a halfy. He suppressed it. The day passed merrily by.

All around, people had a palpable goodwill towards others. It might have been because they were all still full from Thanksgiving dinner, though Mike figured it was because they didn't have to fight each other for space under the awnings, the way they did when it rained. That entire Tuesday shift, there wasn't a single death. Mike felt like a hero on a sunny day like this. It made him happy to be a paramedic and not a doctor. There was a sense of freedom and mobility that beat being cooped up in a hospital under fluorescent lights all day. Plus, he rarely had to see the same patients twice. Though he wouldn't really mind seeing that stroke victim again—so long as his granddaughter could join.

Mike bathed in the mundane dance of sunshine, stoplights, and sirens, and when he got home that evening he felt warm and clean. Normally he wanted to rush to the shower and scour the day off, but he felt genuinely good. Angie was on the couch, curled around a heating pad, watching CBC. She turned when he came in and gave a wan smile. She was probably still upset about the cat, but Mike chose not to ask. He kissed the top of her head and caught wind of the story on TV. The body of the missing college student had been found in the marsh south of Pitt Lake. The suspect had been released on bail.

"Bullshit," said Mike under his breath. Angie blinked at him.

Habit

Unbuttoning his uniform, Mike continued, "Somebody killed that woman and dumped her in the lake. I hope they find *his* body in a fucking lake." Angie watched her husband undress. She found it difficult not to notice his hard body, his hard face. Her eyes stalled across the rows of round burns on his chest. They made him look even more like the hero under the uniform, denouncing violence against women. She wasn't aroused, just proud, she thought. Then she remembered the missing pie. She turned back to the screen.

Mike noticed her looking at him but decided against coming on to her. He wasn't ready to face what had come over him last night. He made his way to the bathroom, still pulling off his clothes along the way. The shower tap screeched and the water ran hot until the room was muggy.

Under the steam, he fantasized about saving lives. He imagined making it to the house before Freeman had gone mental. He imagined how it would be to take down a man that size. He imagined that if Collin ever tried to hurt Peach, she'd call Mike for help. He'd be there so fucking fast. He'd destroy that preppy little shit.

Peach. He'd rescue her. Maybe he'd even drive the ambulance to her place; he'd have to if he were on call. He'd settle her into the back to check for any damage. He'd want to do a full examination to make sure she wasn't harmed. He'd pull that curly hair back and taste her health. If she freaked out, he'd give her something to calm her. She'd like that. She'd like the way he could keep her calm yet on the edge of her seat.

Mike finished and stood under the steady scalding stream for a long time. His mind was comfortably blank. Then he dried off and checked the fridge for dinner; there was nothing. He looked at Angie, still lounging on the couch, but decided not to make a big deal out of it. *She works too*, he reminded himself. He found some frozen veggie burgers and asked if she wanted one.

Angie was fighting off some monstrous cramps and had the heating pad pressed to her stomach like a shield. She said, "No. Thanks though."

Mike ate at the table and then sat beside his wife on the couch. The news was finished and there was some cheesy cop show on TV. With his arm around his wife, Mike forgot his resolve not to come on to her. He started kissing her neck. Angie tucked her ear to her shoulder.

"Not now, Mike. I've got my period."

"Oh," said Mike. "That makes sense."

Angie turned to regard him flatly.

Mike met her gaze. "No, come on. I was just wondering what was wrong."

Angie blinked, slow as a cat, and looked back towards the screen. If he didn't know what was wrong then he was living under a fucking rock. Her cat was gone and her husband was acting weird. Now he wanted to fuck. What could possibly be wrong with that? She hadn't realized she was sitting bolted into place until Mike tried to ease his arm around her.

Angie stiffened and Mike asked, "Is this about the cat or the baby?"

Shocked, Angie glared at him. "How can you even ask that?"

"Tell me the truth. I remember how excited you were. I was excited too."

"This is not about having a baby." Angie almost laughed.

"So, it's about the cat then."

Angie did not answer.

"Angie?"

Nothing.

"Look, Sweetheart, I'm sorry that he's dead, but—"

Angie leapt to her feet. Her hands were over her mouth and tears burst out of her eyes.

"You said it was a raccoon!" The word raccoon came out cracked. "You lied to me. You lied to me and then you acted as if everything was okay. As if you didn't give a fuck that he was dead. No, it's worse." She pointed her finger at him. "It's like you were happy he was dead." The words crackled as she choked through her tears. Her face was in her hands. Everything fell away to muffled sobs until she looked down at Mike accusingly.

What Angie saw in her husband's eyes she could not explain. There was a blank space where his brow should have creased. Where his lips should have been set tight, they were unperturbed. In place of his eyes, were two dark pools. She stepped back subconsciously. Mike was absolutely silent. Absolutely still. He stared at her as if staring at empty space. Then, with visible strain, he softened his gaze and really looked at her again.

Habit

"Angie, I'm sorry. I didn't want you to have any idea what I saw out there. I didn't want you to know what had happened. I thought it would be better if you didn't find out, and anyway, you know I loved that cat. I loved that cat, Angie." Angie lowered her hands away from her mouth and challenged her husband's gaze.

"What did you do with the body, Mike?" *Why can't you even say Felix's name?*

Mike thought back. He hadn't been satisfied with the animal on the ground anymore, not after it had reanimated and come after him. But he knew that wasn't the story he should tell her.

"I think it was taken away."

"You think it was taken... By what?"

"A coyote, probably. It isn't in the alley anymore."

"Is that...is that what you were throwing out last night?"

"No!" It was the truth, but Mike wasn't ready to admit the other half of that truth. "Angie, you have to believe me. I loved that cat. It was horrible to see what happened."

"What *did* happen?"

Mike waited a beat but decided against the grisly truth. "You know what happened. His body was right there on the ground. The fucking crows..."

Angie put up a hand. Her stomach was threatening to turn. She stood there watching her husband for a moment, but she'd had enough.

"I'm going to bed." She walked around the couch and yanked out the cord of her heating pad.

Mike asked over his shoulder, "Are you sure you're going to be okay?"

"I'm going to be fine." She was already in the hallway. Her heart was loud in her ears. She skipped the zolpidem and went straight for a Xanax, washing it down with water from the tap. Angie took a long look at herself in the mirror. If he had lied about this, what else had he lied about? She thought of the pie, but that didn't make any sense. *None of this makes any fucking sense.*

Mike's own thoughts milled about in his head as he heard his wife slam the bedroom door. He wanted to make things right. There must be something he could say to make her forget the fucking cat. He wanted to forget the cat. He couldn't. That cat had come for him. Why had he come for him? The mere memory made him stand up. He looked around the hallway corner and listened for Angie. There were only muffled noises from the bedroom. Crossing to the hallway closet, Mike held his breath. He opened the accordion door slowly so it wouldn't squeak.

The toolbox was there on the floor. The screwdrivers were a clutter of sizes and colours: blue handled, yellow handled, red. Mike stared blankly down at them. He had no way of knowing if he was missing one. He squatted down and rifled through them quietly. He willed the truth to the surface. Nothing came. Mike pushed the box back into the closet and closed the door. It let out a banshee's cry, but Mike ignored it and went back to the couch.

The more he thought about the cat, the more he wondered what it meant if he didn't remember killing it, but he couldn't prove that he hadn't. Was he still guilty if it turned out he had? He'd never purposefully killed an animal before, except when he was a kid. Back then, he'd shot at crows with BB guns, he caught rabbits in snares, he'd even had to mercy kill a couple farm dogs. Country boys did that, though. They learned about life by dealing with death. Even when he'd had to put down that little kitten, he'd learned that sometimes it's more humane than watching them suffer.

Eventually, Mike's thoughts carried him into a dream state. He saw his mother again. He was spying on her through the window like he did as a kid. She wasn't having a party, though, but she was sitting with his kitten. She was speaking softly to it. Mike climbed in through the window and then she was speaking softly to him. He couldn't hear what she was saying; it was only the gibberish of dreams.

After a chilly night, Mike and Angie awoke to another frosty dawn. Angie saw Mike rising from the couch and had no words for him. She didn't want to accuse him of anything and she didn't want to talk about it. She'd had a disturbing dream. It was probably just the Xanax, but she'd woken up out of sorts. In her dream, Mike had been looking up at her from the alley again. Only this time, he was in uniform. He was pushing a gurney. There was nobody on it, but Mike stopped under the balcony and lit up a cigarette.

"You okay, Babe?" asked the real Mike.

Angie was leaning against the balcony window. She needed air.

Habit

"I'm fine. I just have an early meeting." A few minutes later, she left the apartment without so much as a coffee for the road. It wasn't even a quarter to six yet, but Mike let her go. She needed some space and so did he. He was guilty of nothing he could recall, and certainly nothing Angie could find out about now. He'd lied about the cat to spare her feelings. That's all.

Mike decided that he needed to get out of the house too. He threw on some running clothes and took off down the street. The neighbourhood was quiet. Mist hugged the buildings and kept his footsteps soft. After a while, he picked up his pace. He let his mind go blank, allowing his thoughts to turn from conception to perception, until he was only a man running down the street. Just an ordinary face you might find in the crowd, like a background character in a movie. The sensation was emptiness. The sounds of the city entered that space in Mike's mind, and he was only vaguely aware of anything other than the people on the street, the cars on the road, the jingle of keys and bells and electronics.

Once the clock in his head told him he'd run about twenty minutes, he headed home. He set the coffee on and took a shower and cleared the buildup out of his lungs. Once she was clean and caffeinated, he was off to work. He arrived early enough to the hospital to spend a few precious minutes with Peach again.

She had just gotten in and she was still wearing her coat at her desk. She had a coffee in one hand and a pen in the other. She looked relaxed. She looked good, too. Her makeup was subtle, except for a pair of maroon lips the colour of ripe cherries. Her strawberry-blonde hair was up in a bun and a few curly strands dangled in front of her ears. Mike imagined coiling one of those strands around his finger.

"How are you, Michael?" asked Peach without looking up.

Mike stepped into the office.

"Could be better," he said honestly.

Peach finished her note and set down the pen. She folded her hands and leaned back in her chair, gesturing with her head towards the seat in front of her desk.

When he was settled, Peach asked, "What's up?"

"Ah, well. Angie and I had a little tiff about the cat. I didn't have the heart to tell her that I found him dead, but she found out anyway."

Peach whistled and sat upright. She looked at Mike intently and said, "Well, what the fuck were you thinking?"

Mike smiled. He liked her frankness. It matched those dark lips, turned down though they were. He stopped smiling and shook his head apologetically.

"I just...choked. I mean, I didn't want her to be hurt and instead I wound up hurting her myself."

Peach kept her eyes on him. She sat perfectly still, relaxed, but watchful.

She asked, "Have you apologized?"

"Of course."

"Apologize again. And buy flowers. Take her out to the ocean and throw a rose into the water for the little guy."

God, he loved her.

He followed her every word with a bowed head. He was watching those cherry lips. She was giving him instructions that could save his marriage, but he was imagining a kiss from those lips, the colour of Merlot staining his own.

"You got all that, Michael?"

He chewed his lip and nodded. "You're a lifesaver, Peach. Thank you."

"Just don't mess it up. Angie is under enough stress with her new client. She needs you to start picking up the slack."

With a humble smile, Mike thanked her again and then almost as an afterthought, he asked about Collin.

Peach beamed. "Collin's great. He wants to have you and Angie over for drinks some time."

"That'd be swell," replied Mike. *Since when the fuck do I say swell?* "Guess I'd better get to it." Peach watched him go. She couldn't tell what was up with him, but something more than just the cat, she figured.

Val came in, but stopped short when he saw Mike there before him. For a while, they shot the shit with Tom and Sara and another pair from the night shift. Tom had apparently decided to speak to the crisis line since his dreams were getting worse.

Habit

"Now it's like I'm Freeman. I see my wife underneath me and I've pummelled her." There were grave nods and heavy shuffling feet.

Trying to lighten the mood, Mike said, "Well it's a good thing you're into guys then, isn't it?" Tom squinted at him. "You know...you won't have a wife to...to beat up."

Val gave a sympathetic smile. Tom grimaced, but the female paramedics present just shook their heads and turned away. Mike had never really gotten to know any of them. Sara was only here on nights with Tom. Brenda and Pat had been hired as a unit. They all stuck to night shifts, like true vampires. Mike chanced a glance at Sara to gauge her reaction. Her rosebud mouth was crinkled in an uncomfortable frown. Her glossy brown hair was in a bun, but her uniform was undone. The white undershirt was visible behind her folded arms. She was shaped flat and boyish; cute rather than pretty. Next to the older women though, she was a cherry blossom.

Val slapped Mike's back and said, "Time to clock in. We'd better let these kids get some sleep." They parted ways and Mike and Val had some free time to begin with. Nearly a whole hour passed by before they had to set out. After that, they had four successful emergencies. One after the next, Mike and Val transported four living, breathing individuals to the hospital, all of which appeared to be on their way to recovery.

The whole day they were comrades, reading what the other needed, coordinating perfectly to make their patients calm, safe, and stable. Many high fives and a well-deserved doughnut break later, Mike felt like the king of the world. He wasn't in the slightest worried about his ability to perform. Last week's mayhem was gone. The violence and amnesia, far away. Around 4 p.m., they were still riding the heroic high towards a new scene on East Hastings. Then Mike killed the dog.

It was a little terrier thing, with scruffy fur and beady eyes. Mike had been bitten by a dog like it a thousand years ago. The light turned yellow in front of his ambulance, so Mike slowed and checked for traffic. The creature was on the other side of the intersection, crossing the road to sniff at something. Once it had marked its territory, the mongrel looked up at Mike's bus, and then to the other side of the road. It began to cross again, so Mike waited before entering the crossway. The sirens swore angrily, but the mutt didn't notice them. It stopped to gnaw on a flattened pigeon still in Mike's lane. Cars in the intersection stayed where they were to allow the ambulance pass, so Mike eased forward. The dog didn't move.

Mike had an inexpressible desire to floor the gas. He thought he wanted to see how fast the dog could run. Obviously, he instead drove slowly, firmly, onwards. All the while the sirens howled. The dog didn't run off. Instead, it tore at the bird, which was sticking to the pavement. The ambulance was almost on top of it now. Mike checked his mirrors. He didn't see it run off, but it had to be out of the way of his tires. He released the brake.

The garbled sound of bone beneath rubber was barely audible above the dog's yelp. The high-pitched cry cut through the siren. Val's eyes widened. He'd been watching the whole thing. He thought Mike had seen the dog move out of the way before driving through. Mike swore under his breath and kicked his foot down on the brake again once he was sure the tire had rolled off the terrier. Val flipped off the siren but kept the lights flashing. Anxious silence settled between the two men. Mike did not need to look to know Val's eyes were on him. He pulled the emergency brake and got out without meeting those eyes.

Kneeling down behind the driver's side tire, he saw the animal. It was crushed against the pavement. Blood trickled out of its nose. The weight of the vehicle must have crushed its spine because it was already dead. Mike grabbed its front legs and heaved it out with a little too much force. Its limp head lolled back. Blood sloshed out of its open mouth onto the pavement. A driver trying to get around the bus gasped behind her hand when she saw him there.

Mike grimaced and held the dog far out in front of him. He was waiting for the blood to stop dripping when two paradoxical thoughts came to him. At once he regretted killing the little cur, but at the same time he wished he were wearing gloves.

With the dog outstretched in his bare hands, Mike suddenly lost sight of what the best option would be. He didn't want to hold it anymore. More blood was splattering onto the sidewalk and staining his shoes. He wasn't going to waste a body bag and he certainly wasn't going to put the thing in the back of the bus like this either. The only viable option seemed to be the least compassionate. Mike b-lined to the bus stop and opened up the garbage bin. He thanked the gods it wasn't overflowing and he scooped the body inside. Then he tied up the bag so no unsuspecting person would see it there.

Re-entering the ambulance, Mike was again aware of Val's eyes. He met them this time and thought he saw a wall of shock and disapproval. The man who had been like his brother-in-arms was now judging his morality. *Fuck him.*

Val shrugged, but to Mike it seemed more of an ironic gesture than an offer of indifference.

Mike tried to explain himself, "I figured it would move...but it didn't."

"And here we are." Val shrugged again. "Come on, we need to book it. Now." He turned the sirens back on. They arrived at the call too late. Probably it wouldn't have mattered if the episode with the dog hadn't happened, but it was never a good feeling to lose a patient. Police were on scene. The accident had involved a biker and a Volvo. The hockey mom was comatose, oblivious to the two screaming children beside her and the cop trying to take down her information. Mike chose to head to the body of the biker rather than deal with the family.

The biker was dead. Mike knew it before he reached him. He knew it before the cop beside the body told him. The biker's neck was broken. He had on his helmet and Mike couldn't see his face, but under the mirrored surface, the kid's eyes were pointed right over his shoulder from where he lay belly-down on the pavement. Mike felt his cervical spine with a gloved hand and found two broken vertebrae, one seemingly dislodged. No pulse.

Val managed to wind the driver back into her body. One officer took down her details and the other one fended off traffic while Mike and Val put the biker in a bag.

When they were heading back into the cab, Val said, "I'll drive."

Mike saw that he had his glasses on already, so he handed over the keys. With silence falling over them on the way back to base, Mike decided he should be the one to let Peach know what happened with the dog before she heard about it from some disgruntled pedestrian. He wished he had a cigarette. The thought alone made his stomach weak. He took out his phone and called Peach.

"Hello, Michael." There was an unspoken question behind her greeting: What *did you do to merit a phone call when you should be at the scene?*

"Hey, Peach," said Mike cautiously. "I wanted you to hear it from me. I killed a dog today."

"A dog?"

"Yeah."

"Like somebody's pet?"

"No, it was definitely a stray. No collar, no meat on the thing. It walked right in front of the bus and wouldn't move."

"Why didn't you honk?"

"I-I did." *Did I?*

"Why didn't you try to shoo it away?"

"To be honest, I thought the sight of a five tonne ambulance would be enough to shoo it away." Mike felt a smile creep across his lips. He switched his phone to his left hand to hide his face from Val. He hoped Peach wouldn't hear it in his voice. She was quiet for a while, probably writing this down. The silence was hard to swallow. Mike had been prepared to defend himself. He was not prepared to await judgment.

"Peach?"

"I'm still here. Still trying to wrap my head around this. What did you do with the dog?"

"What did I do with it? I mean, I couldn't just leave it there…"

"So?"

"So, I…disposed of the body."

"You were sure it was dead?"

"Yes." *Wasn't it?*

"Well, I'm sure we'll get some pretty angry phone calls about it…but shit happens I guess. Jesus, Mike, a dog? And you're sure it was a stray?"

"I'm sure. Hey, Peach?"

"Yea?"

"Can we not tell Angie about this one? It would break her heart."

There was a long pause. Then Peach said, "I agree."

Once they'd hung up, Mike contemplated the event once more in his mind. He couldn't gauge his feelings. It was too surreal, too far from his ordinary experience. He hadn't meant to kill the dog. He couldn't deny wanting to watch it dance. only remembered running over one other animal in his life; a deer he'd smoked on the highway towards a party in Terrace. He was seventeen. His mom had been three years dead and the old farmhouse was sold off. He and his dad were happily moved into their new place in the city. That event with the deer had been a true accident. The fucking thing just jumped in front of him and destroyed its own legs trying to clear the hood.

This wasn't like that at all. Mike couldn't even lie to himself about his desire to see the dog dance. He just wanted to put a little fright into the thing. Get it to move the fuck out of the way. Well, it hadn't budged. Maybe it figured he would go around it. Maybe he should have.

Val kept an eye on his partner for the rest of the drive, trying to see any changes in his behaviour. He had been zoned out ever since Thanksgiving supper. Not that it was any of Val's business, but it seemed Tom was right. Mike was getting a bit sterile in his old age. He was still a bang-up paramedic; apart from the last call, they'd been on a roll. Val turned the corner to the hospital.

With this sequence of thoughts taking centre stage for the rest of their shift, Mike forgot all about the apology he still owed his wife. He forgot about the flowers and the ocean funeral. He was craving Chinese food, so he brought home some takeout and they ate quietly together in front of the TV.

Even though he didn't want to talk about the day, he did want to have sex. Guilt kept him from trying anything, though. He knew Angie was still on the rag and he finally remembered what Peach had told him to do. *Fuck*. Mike looked over at his wife. Angie looked tired. Her hair was unwashed and she was tucked into an oversized grey BCIT sweater with matching grey sweatpants. She noticed him looking and turned to blink at him.

"Hey, Ange," began Mike, "I was thinking we could have a little memorial for Felix."

Angie arched her eyebrow.

"You know, tomorrow night. We could go down to the boardwalk and lay a flower in the water for him or something. Would you like that?"

Angie's eyes brimmed with tears and she wiped at them.

"Yeah," she said in a choked voice. "Yes. I think that would be good."

Mike tucked his arm around her and they finished their meal. *Thank you, Peach.*

Habit

There was still a full twelve-hour shift between Mike and his reconciliation. With a tired smile, he realized he was just as excited about getting some make up sex as he was about making things right with Angie. He didn't consider her period to be an obstacle. He just prayed he could get her into the mood and everything would take care of itself. From the moment he got to work he was bombarded by cravings, not for cigarettes, but for intimacy.

A glance at Peach bending for something in her purse set him off and so did another glimpse at Sara's white undershirt. He couldn't stop thinking of what they'd feel like. Peach would be warm and soft and yielding. Sara would be bony, but scrumptiously squirmy. These fantasies were better than the nightmares from last week, but still, he wasn't sure if this was the second stage of treatment with Tehrani or if it was all an outpouring of his own depravity and repression. Mike was pretty sure he'd never been a pervert before. As far back as he could remember he'd kept his mind out of the gutter. Today he wanted to wallow in it.

While he was tending to a skinny, scabby teenager who'd overdosed on some kind of opiate, he got the feeling he was being watched. Mike looked up and saw a plain-faced hooker, who smiled grimly at him. She wore fishnets and an oversized leather jacket. She took a puff off of a cigarette just as Mike was injecting the kid with naloxone.

Mike was reminded of some of the women his mom used to have over; the ones who rode on the backs of motorcycles with no helmets on. Mike had a rather uncomfortable memory from when he'd peeked in at them all in the living room. It was the leather jacket that did it to him. He'd seen his mom wearing one just like it, and nothing else.

Once he'd stabilized the kid, they had to rush him into the ambulance. Mike didn't look back at the prostitute. He was afraid of how he might react. Before they'd reached the emergency room, Mike had given the kid fifteen minutes of CPR and another shot of naloxone. It was a lost cause after all.

Mike's brain dipped back into the gutter over the course of the shift, despite his best efforts to ignore the way every female EMT and emerge nurse seemed to be flirting with him. One laid her hand on his when she took away the stretcher with the dead kid on it. Another touched the small of his back and smiled when she ducked around him. Back at headquarters, Peach paused to visit them in the break room. Mike could smell her intoxicating perfume when she drew close. That was the last straw.

It was the first time he'd ever done anything like this at work, but it had to be done. He told himself it was nothing untoward. He just needed five minutes alone in the washroom, and he'd be clear-headed again. It was Peach who helped him make it quick. Just the thought of her strapped down to the stretcher was enough. He imagined how even with restraints, Peach would do everything she could to get close to him, to get that sweet little body pushed right up into him as he ground down into her. When he was done, Mike washed his hands twice. He could still feel the guilt running down the back of his neck though, so he dabbed at it with paper towel.

In a way, he was right. The rest of the shift was wholly manageable once his mind was at ease. He made the appropriate small talk and was able to drive straight and provide triage. He even managed to save the next overdose, even though he was pretty sure he'd already saved this one two weeks ago. His level headedness lasted right up until the end of his shift.

On his way to buy the roses for the little ceremony he'd promised Angie, Mike saw the most gorgeous blonde he'd ever seen. Her body was round but tight, her legs and arms thick enough to squeeze, her face angled as if it were photoshopped. Her breasts bounced perkily in the chilly evening air. She wore only sneakers, biking shorts, and a white cotton shirt. She was just casually jogging down the street as if she weren't heaven-sent. Mike kept one eye on her until he almost rear-ended the car in front. This at least shook him back into his own plane of existence. He was instantly imagining taking her right there in the parking lot, and he had to let the feeling pass before he could exit the vehicle.

In the grocery store's floral section, Mike chose white roses. He paid, and a chubby teenage boy came over to wrap the flowers in plastic and then paper. Mike was impressed to see that the kid was a professional; the package was crisp and even, and Mike asked him to leave the top open so Angie could see the flowers. The kid nodded and tied two plastic ribbons into bows around the base. He used a pair of scissors to curl the edges.

Mike texted Angie and by the time he'd parked his truck, she met him outside. He presented her with the flowers and she thanked him with a smile that was both sad and silly-looking. When was the last time he'd bought her flowers? She took them and together, they walked arm-in-arm towards New Brighton Park. Mike could hear Angie sniffling and he wished he had a handkerchief like he might have in a silent movie. She just used her sleeve discreetly and they wandered closer to the water's edge.

Habit

Along the way, they were met with an unmistakable street-people stench. Mike recognized the campers even though he'd never seen them here before. The man recognized Mike as well. One of his dogs, a shaky chihuahua, started barking.

"Shut up," hissed the woman. Her partner held out a grimy hand to Mike hopefully. Mike started to rifle through his pocket for the change from the flowers, but the thought that *It's just going to prolong the inevitable,* made him shake his head and turn to leave. The dogs caught his attention. There were three in total. Two mangy pitbulls and the aforementioned chihuahua.

For as long as Mike had known these people, they'd had four dogs. Mike only counted three, no matter how he searched their nest of sleeping bags. The dawning of that realization left him clammy. The chihuahua barked again. Mike tried to recall what kind of a dog the fourth had been. The pitbulls started growling. Angie tugged him away.

Once they arrived at the water's edge, they found a bench and sat together in silence for a long time. It wasn't uncomfortable, only necessary. Angie needed space to cry and Mike needed time to think. Would it have mattered if it were their dog he killed? He would be doing them a service really. One less mouth to feed. One less way to contract fleas or norovirus.

Mike breathed in the sweaty sea air and tried to focus on his surroundings. It was nice to just be, quietly watching the black waters under the black sky, nothing at all to worry about in the universe at large. The stars were far away and far between. It must have been a new moon behind the clouds because "out there" was only a concept above the park lights.

The ocean lapped at the rocks below them. It lulled them both into an exhausted calm. Mike began fantasizing, this time about taking Angie in the park. It was dark enough in the trees behind them. There weren't any late night walkers around either. But Angie was still crying. She was in no condition for a public rendezvous. Mike squeezed her shoulder, taking her mind off of her grief and his own mind off of corruption.

"Should we lay a flower in the water for him?"

Angie's lips trembled, but she nodded. She carefully plucked two white roses from the bouquet and handed one to Mike. They braved the slippery rocks and made it to the water. Mike asked Angie if she wanted to say anything, but she only cried harder, so he recited something he'd read in a card at the grocery store.

"The friendship of a pet is one of the greatest gifts we can receive. Felix was a great friend. We will always remember him."

Mike tossed his flower into the black water and, after a moment, so did Angie. The long-stemmed roses floated there on the surface, awash with the twinkling debris of the ocean: plastic bags, Styrofoam, and some kind of beach ball, deflated and dead looking in the pale light. Mike thought about the dog he'd run over yesterday. It was probably floating on an isle of garbage too. Or rather, it was growing hot and putrid in its black bag, buried under the weight of a thousand other black bags. By now, so was their precious cat.

The roses were pressed right up against the chunks of Styrofoam now. In the dark it was hard to tell them apart. Mike grimaced and hoped Angie wasn't taking all of this in. She was looking far out in the distance, seeing the other side of the channel, or perhaps not seeing anything at all.

In the end, it was her idea to leave. She held the remaining ten roses in the crook of one arm, and with the other she clung to Mike. On cue, the rain began, trickling and ponderous. The wind picked up once they were back on their block and they escaped to the apartment building before the real storm began.

Inside the apartment, Mike asked Angie if she'd like to shower with him. He tried to keep his face neutral, even though he felt a pressure building under his belt. Angie shook her head after a moment of feigned consideration, so he went alone. In the kitchen, Angie cut the stems of her roses and placed them in a vase on the table. She admired them. It was a sweet gesture, but it made her sad to remember the rose petals she'd laid out on Mike's birthday.

She sighed and got started on a curry for dinner. The smell of it enticed Mike even though walking through it with wet hair made him smell like he'd showered in spice.

They sat at the table together and Mike asked, "How is your newest gig going?"

Angie's surprise showed when she opened her mouth. It had been a long time since Mike had asked her about work. She didn't hold it against him. He was dealing with a lot right now, although Angie supposed he must be through the thick of it. She hadn't smelled smoke on him once this week, or last. He was smiling again too.

Habit

Angie swallowed a mouthful of food. "It's been really good." Mike chewed quietly and watched her attentively, so she continued, "He agreed to our initial proposal, including the price, and now my graphics team is working on the logo and my writing team is brainstorming some slogans. We'll start with billboards and online ads. They've got a really great product and it looks like they want us along for the ride."

"That's a good feeling," said Mike, smiling around a mouthful.

"Yeah," agreed Angie. She returned his smile. "Yeah it is." She looked down and stopped pushing food around with her fork before meeting her husband's eyes again. "Man, it feels like we haven't had a good talk for ages. How is work treating you?"

Mike tilted his head in a comme-ci comme-ça motion. "Well, it hasn't killed me yet. Val and I were on fire yesterday and today—for the most part. You should've seen us. Peach is looking good too. She wants to have us over sometime for drinks with her and Dog Man," It slipped out just like that.

Angie's fork stopped midway to her mouth. She laughed. "Dog Man? Care to explain that one?"

Mike admonished himself. "Shit. It was something he said over dinner the other day. Val was razzing me about the cat and *Collin* said he was on my side. He called himself a Dog Man." Mike puffed out his chest when he said it. He laughed and shovelled more food in his mouth. But Angie had stopped laughing.

When he turned to her, he saw her face was blank.

"Angie?"

"Why would Val razz you about the cat? Did you usually talk about how much you hated Felix?"

"Oh. Honey. No. No, it's not like that. No, I just, you know. I'd complain about the fur and the litter box and stupid stuff like that. Val was trying to cheer me up because he figured I was feeling guilty."

Angie set down her fork. "What would you have to feel guilty about? Was it you who left the balcony door open?"

Too easy, said a voice in Mike's head. He took Angie's hand in his own and said, "Angie, I woke up on the couch that night and the door was open—just a crack, but still. I didn't think to look for the cat, and... I'm sorry."

Angie's gaze did not soften. She took her hand out of Mike's and said flatly, "I'm sorry too. I guess it could have happened any time." Except it couldn't. Angie knew this. She knew this because she specifically remembered checking that both doors were closed and latched. Mike could not have woken up to either ajar.

The rest of the meal was silent. Mike cleared up after dinner and Angie sat at the table for a moment longer before moving cautiously to the couch. She felt hollow and confused. Her stomach felt weak. She didn't understand what Mike could possibly be trying to hide. She didn't think he'd kill a cat. She'd never seen that side of him. He was the kind of guy who caught spiders in a cup and brought them outside. Hell, his job was to save lives, not take them. But it wasn't just that Felix was gone, it was the whole weird episode with Thanksgiving.

Mike startled her out of this thought when he flopped down beside her on the couch. She didn't quite gasp, but she flinched back. She couldn't figure out why he was suddenly so stealthy. It was like he enjoyed sneaking up on her.

Mike thought it was strange that his wife was just staring at a black screen, so he plopped himself beside her and grabbed the remote. He wasn't really interested in anything the TV had to say, but he thought Angie might like some background noise to whatever disaster she was thinking herself into. Her thoughts were making her flighty. She looked lovely though. Her eyes shone green inside those rims, red from crying. Just being this close to her made Mike want to try to make things up to her again.

He placed a hand softly on the back of her neck and gave it a gentle massage. Angie relaxed a quarter of an inch, so Mike moved over to her shoulder. He waited until she softened a little more before he leaned in close and brushed her neck with his lips.

After a few more minutes of kneading, Angie let out a breath. Mike slid closer. He tried kissing her up and down her neck the way she liked, but she was unresponsive. She only smiled meekly and tried to watch TV around him. Her heart was a knot.

Mike turned off the TV, but that was worse because Angie said, "I'm not in the mood tonight, Hon. I'm sorry." Mike pulled away slowly. He watched his wife for a moment. Angie didn't meet his gaze.

Mike clicked the TV back on. He turned towards the screen and tried to pay attention to it. His leg started to shake. What the fuck had he done to this woman? Okay. He lied about the cat. So what? Every Rom Com in the history of the world taught us that when a man lies to protect a woman's feelings, he gets three scenes of discomfort and then incredible make-up sex. Mike no longer wanted to watch TV. He stood up very slowly, so Angie wouldn't think he was upset, and he went to the bedroom.

He had an erection that he needed to deal with. It was not going away on its own. His wife was on the verge of a panic attack. She'd cower on the couch, filled with dread, until she was sure he was asleep. Then she'd creep in next to him. In the morning, she'd probably let him have her just so he wouldn't think she was mad at him. Until then, Mike needed to deal with his current predicament. He flipped open the old laptop they kept in the bedroom. It took a solid minute to wake up. Mike thought about the porn sites he'd been to in the past. It had been a while since he'd needed one.

He chose Pornhub. It would be in good enough taste, nothing too rapey. A couple of brunettes promised to please him and so he turned off the sound and clicked on their thumbnail. The problem with porn was that Mike could always tell he was watching actors. It was so obvious these two were not lesbians that he couldn't even get into the scene. He scrolled for a long time until one picture caught his eye. It was a curly blonde with her leg up in the air. She was being held against a tree. The caption read, "Cot her alone in the woods." Mike clicked.

The blonde had a button nose and full, pouty lips. She was fully clothed, but the sun was out, so that only meant that she had shorts on and a tight t-shirt. No bra. Her thong showed when she bent to pick some flowers. Behind her, a man slowly peeked around a tree. He watched her just as Mike watched her. Mike watched him watching her. The peeping Tom's expression was scripted. No guesswork. No flirting required. The man knew he'd have no real fight. He knew he didn't have to look over his shoulder, but he did it anyway, for the camera.

Mike undid his pants.

When the video ended, he exited the site and cleared his browser history with his left hand. He breathed out through pursed lips and stood carefully. He listened at the door. No movement, so he pulled it open and crept to the bathroom to clean up.

Mike slithered back onto the bed. The curly blonde's cute face came to mind along with an admonishment, *how the fuck did that make me come?* The actress had looked surprised the way people did when they already knew about the birthday party long before the lights flipped on. Mike thought back to his ambush on Angie in the shower. Now, that had been a real surprise. He remembered the way she'd melted for him, under the stream of water. That was pleasure. That was real. *Was it?*

At one point, Angie turned off the TV and went to the bedroom, ready to crash. Then she caught the soft grunting of her husband. She froze with her hand on the doorknob. She was not ready to walk in on that. Not after the night she was having. She crept back to the living room and waited him out. Only once he'd been in and out of the bathroom did she tip-toe to bed. She lay beside her sleeping husband and wanted to cry all over again.

Habit

On Saturday night, Mike drove Angie in her car to Peach's house. The car had no heat. The week hung in the frosty air between them. Angie had spent the days trying to focus on the demands of her job, while simultaneously worrying about Mike at work, Mike at home, Mike in that zoned out space between the waking world and the next, Mike sleeping on the couch. Mike in her dreams.

Meanwhile, Mike had managed to resuscitate two patients, transport a dozen more with various injuries, and hand off more than a few overdoses with heartbeats to emerge. He'd lost four more people. At some point, they'd solidified plans for drinks and now here they were, in the car together. It was late. He was late. Again. Mike glanced from the wheel over at Angie. She was beautiful in the warm streetlights. He really fucked up his chance to make amends. Now he had to just give her space until he could be sure what would make her happy again.

Maybe a night out with friends was exactly what the doctor ordered. He was sure that if he just played his cards right tonight and didn't do anything stupid, he'd be back in Angie's good books, and Peach's for that matter. *No.* Mike was not going there. He was going to be a gentleman to Peach and that was all. He was going to be civil to Collin. He was not going to lose his mind just because Peach had a new boyfriend.

Angie glanced nervously at her husband as he drove. He was gripping the steering wheel too tightly. His eyes were narrowed. It was raining, but it was always raining. He was thinking about something and whatever it was, it was upsetting him.

Mike caught her looking at him and he smiled. It was brief, but warm. He put his hand on her thigh. It was cold, but comforting. He squeezed a little too hard, but Angie put her hand over his anyway. She looked out the window.

They arrived at Peach's townhouse and Mike parked behind the red Mazda. He breathed out and recalibrated himself for the evening. He put on a smile for his wife that he hoped was reassuring. Angie took him in. His hair was styled nicely, slicked back, but not greasy. He was clean shaven and his brown eyes were bright. He wore his old leather jacket—the black one his dad gave him a few years back. Under that was a simple blue patterned shirt. He looked good. His smile was genuine. Angie returned it. Mike stepped out and she watched him for a moment longer before she exited the vehicle herself.

He really was trying. Maybe tonight could be a milestone for them. They'd survived the loss of a parent and now a pet. Every marriage had these moments. Now was the time to move on. Angie joined her husband on the porch and Mike knocked jovially. As expected, Collin was the one to answer. He gave them a conspiratorial smile and made two guns with his hands.

Shooting at his guests, he said, "Ayyy, yous guys!"

Angie giggled.

Mike's face was stone for an instant, but then crumbled into a smile. "You've been watching mobster movies."

"Guilty as charged," said Collin, putting his hands up and stepping back so they could enter. Peach joined them in the foyer. She had on a simple, strappy, navy-blue top with sequins along the bottom. The top was layered loosely and it swooped low over the curve of her breasts. She was carrying a plate full of nachos that smelled inviting.

Peach said, "Hi guys, come on in. Don't worry Angie, there's no hamburger in these." Mike smiled and watched Peach turn on her heel to head to the living room with the platter. In her dark, embroidered jeans, her round ass looked like a piece of jewelled fruit.

Angie smiled too, though for a different reason. She felt warmer already. It was good to be with Peach. All her anxieties seemed to fade when she didn't have to focus solely on Mike. She remembered that she had a friend who knew her better than anyone. Seeing what Peach wore made her glad she'd dressed up, though her outfit was significantly less revealing than Peach's. Angie had chosen a green, long-sleeved dress with an embroidered flower that began at the cinched waist and blossomed up her back. The neckline was only a lowercase v. Angie thought Peach might fall out of her shirt if she ever had to bend over.

Collin took Angie's coat and smiled at the flower on her back. "Nice dress," he said. Angie met his smiling eyes. He really was stunning. She could see why Peach had chosen him. He was sweet even if he was a little dorky. Between the blonde hair, the lips, and the blue eyes, he could have been a movie star.

"Thank you," she said, hoping her voice wasn't as breathy as it sounded in her ears. Mike hung his own coat, nearly knocking over the vase that stood on a pillar beside the closet. He grimaced, but Collin caught the urn

Habit

before it could fall. Mike gave Angie a smile and then Collin. Collin reciprocated, but Angie was smiling down at her shoes. When she looked up, she sighed inwardly. The two men seemed to be on better terms already. Mike was just wondering how on earth his own wife could be enamoured with this guy.

They entered the living room simply by moving past the open staircase and the wide hall. Peach had painted this room in darker colours than the dining room and entrance. Here, three walls were cobalt blue, the fourth was a striking forest green. There was only one painting on the wall; it was a splatter of reds, blues, greens, and yellows. It could have contained any image, but it seemed to Mike that someone had merely snorted the paint and sneezed it onto the canvas. Once, he told Peach this and Angie had punched him in the arm pretty hard. Apparently Peach's mother had painted the thing, but she had laughed like a maniac at his joke.

Mike touched his arm reflexively, but smiled at that moment they'd shared. He found his place on the love seat. Angie sat gracefully down beside him. She looked lovely tonight. Half of her hair was pulled up, the rest hung in loose curls. Mike liked when she curled her hair. Peach's own curly hair was up in a bun like it had been the other day. The coils hung coyly out of place.

When they were all seated on the sofas, Peach with red wine, Angie with white, and the men with rum & cokes, Mike asked, "So Collin, I pretty much know how work went for Peach this week, but what about you? I'm not sure I even caught what you do for a living."

"Oh," Collin smiled and looked to Peach for confirmation before saying, "I'm actually retired."

"Retired?" Angie exclaimed. "Peach told me you were a real-estate consultant."

"Well, semi-retired. I still do some consulting on the side. I went to law school in the states and worked my butt off for a land and property firm in my twenties. I was lucky enough to invest in several lucrative ventures and so now I spend most of my time hiking, biking, or sailing with Luna."

"Who's Luna?" asked Mike. He looked Collin over; he hadn't thought of the guy as a rich man, but Mike supposed he must have money. The emblem on his fleece sweater read Patagonia. He wore a class ring of some sort on his right hand, along with a high-tech watch, most likely a Garmin.

Otherwise, there was no outward sign of wealth, but wasn't that the point of being wealthy? His good looks helped to complete the image, Mike couldn't deny that.

"Luna is my dog. She's a Bernedoodle."

Angie almost spat out her wine. "A what?"

"A Bernese Mountain Dog crossed with a Poodle," he said with an acme British accent and a wide smile that showed his white teeth.

Angie laughed again and said, "How fancy. It's funny, I never really knew the breeds of any of my family dogs."

Mike looked up at the ceiling and thought about the feral dogs around the farm. "Not sure I even knew the names of any of the dogs we had."

No one had a response to that, so Angie said, "Luna sounds like a nice animal."

Collin beamed. "Oh, you'd love her. She's quiet as a mouse, and never barks or drools or anything. Actually," he looked at Peach again, "we might need a dogsitter when we go away next month."

"If we go away next month," corrected Peach. "I haven't received the okay from work yet."

"Where are you going?" asked Mike. He wondered what made Peach so hesitant to agree to the vacation.

Collin replied, "We're heading to Belize where I've spent the last four winters. This year I plan on a shorter visit because of Luna. But I want Peach to join me for the sun, the beach, and the adventure."

"That sounds incredible," said Angie, smiling encouragement at her friend. Mike was looking between Collin and Peach. He had a smile plastered on his face, but he was watching the subtle exchange between them. Collin was holding Peach's hand. She wasn't holding his. Collin was smiling a genuine smile. Peach's looked a little forced.

Peach took a long drink of her wine and through a sour face she said, "Like I said, I need to clear it with work first." She turned to Mike pleadingly. "You know how it is."

Habit

Mike nodded. "Yes, I do." He remembered trying to take two weeks off for his honeymoon with Angie. That had required support from three other paramedics just to make the times line up.

Collin nodded gravely between Mike and Peach. "Well, where there's a will, there's a way." He clapped his hands. "How about a game of Pictionary?" They agreed, but Peach insisted on getting more drinks first.

"If I'm going to lose a game, I intend to have a damn good reason for it." Mike wondered if she didn't need to drink for some other reason. He thought she looked a little stiff, though when he saw her walking away towards the kitchen, she moved like a salsa dancer. The sparkles on her jeans gave the impression of twinkling special effects from the Eighties.

She brought Mike another glass of rum with fresh ice and a splash of coke. When she leaned down to place it on the side table next to him, the folds of her top fell away and revealed two soft pale breasts. Her nipples were the only mystery left to him, but that was almost more provocative. Mike looked away. The image remained. *She wants me to see her.*

Angie caught the sight too and thought to herself, *I knew that would happen.* She was proud that Mike hadn't gawked. That would have been embarrassing. Collin didn't seem aware and neither did Peach, truth be told. She was already circling around to Angie. Angie thanked her as she handed her another glass of wine. Then Peach retrieved two more drinks and took a seat next to Collin on the larger couch.

Mike shifted on the sofa beside her, and Angie's eyes happened to glance down at his lap. What she noticed there, she hoped no one else would. She looked quickly away. She couldn't remember that ever happening to Mike in public. Angie willed it away. While Collin brought out the game pieces, she peeked again and it was still there, pressing against the zipper of Mike's jeans. It thrilled some primal part of Angie's brain, but brought panic to her frontal cortex. She drew a breath and sipped her wine and prayed he wouldn't have to stand up at any point. Was he even aware of this thing? He had to be.

Mike was well aware of his body's betrayal and he was painfully aware of his wife's attention to it. The bulge was aching against his thin denim pants. He crossed his right ankle over his left knee and tried to angle everything to block the view from the two sitting across from him.

Collin was busy setting up, while going over the rules of the game as if this were anyone's first time. Mike didn't mind. He was following Collin's instructions with his eyes, willing himself to calm down. His blood pressure had spiked. Along with the spiteful thing in his pants, came a salty anxiety throughout his entire body.

Peach noticed the shift in him as Mike started to tap his foot in the air. She looked to Angie but Angie was smiling benignly at Collin. Mike wiped his hands on his thighs and looked like he was trying to hold his breath, or else he was trying to hold back a laugh. She hoped he wasn't going to be sick.

She interrupted Collin's riveting explanation and asked, "Michael, are you doing okay?" The sound of her ER voice made Mike fidget. He had thought he would be able to get things under control, but now she'd set him back. He raised his eyebrows, though, and tried to look confused.

"I'm doing swell, Peach. Thanks." He took up the new rum and coke beside him and drank deeply. Peach shrugged. Angie, still smiling, unconsciously pulled at the dress around her middle.

Collin said, "Okay...well, I suppose we've all got it. Let's get started. Shall we have couples or guys versus gals?"

At the same time that Peach was saying, "Guys versus gals," Mike and Angie simultaneously blurted, "Couples!" louder than either had meant to.

Collin looked up at them from the box he'd been studying, then he looked to Peach. "I guess it's settled then." He handed a pad of paper to both Angie and Peach. "Ladies first."

Mike concentrated on lowering his heart rate. He thought about being back in Tehrani's office with his eyes closed and his mind settled. He thought about the gentle ticking of the clock, and in response his excitement diminished. It took a minute until he was able to look at Peach again without an influx. Only then did he know he was back. He still wanted to take her right then and there in front of her own boyfriend and his own wife, but he submerged that thought way down in the murky swamp of his mind.

Angie tried not to stare at his crotch, but she thought she could feel him relax, so she breathed out again. Peach studied a card and then handed it to Angie. Mike uncrossed his legs and settled into a more comfortable position. When the timer was flipped, the women began madly swirling their pencils about.

Habit

Collin shouted, "Cloud!" but Peach shook her head.

Mike called out, "Cauliflower." Angie shook her head. Then Peach squiggled a little tail on her creation and Mike peeked over.

"Brain," said Mike and Collin in unison. They caught each other's eyes and Collin lit up. Both women dropped their pencils.

"Nice," said Angie. "What do we do when there's a tie?"

Collin extended his hand to Mike and asked, "Rock, paper, scissors?" Mike flashed back to the day he'd met this man and the handshake that felt like it would end him. He didn't feel competitive today. Mike put out his hand. In three shakes, the tie was broken when Mike chose rock and Collin chose paper. Being the preppy jock that he was, Collin had to physically cover Mike's fist with his hand to prove that he'd won. It felt like subtle retribution for the moment they'd met on the threshold. Collin laughed and removed his hand.

Mike lowered his hand and the thought, *May he be struck by a truck*, flitted through his mind, but he smiled and said, "You got me."

Collin rolled and drew something that could have been any number of four-legged animals with antlers, and Peach tried guessing a dozen. To each, Collin shook his head until he added bigger antlers and Peach squealed, "Caribou! Caribou," and pointed down at the picture like she was casting a spell on it. The last grain of sand dropped down.

"No, it was a moose," said Collin with a wry smile.

"Fuck," said Peach. "I'm a bad Canadian." She took a swig of wine.

Mike thought her squeal had been delectable. Her profanity tasted even better. She wasn't his sagacious boss tonight; she was just a woman enjoying herself. She smiled at him and he returned the grin. His body behaved itself this time. He was in control now. It was his turn next, so Mike took up the pencil and flipped the page of paper. He rolled and landed on a *difficult* square. He pulled a card out that read, *Curiosity Killed The Cat*. Mike sucked his teeth and grimaced.

He showed the card to Collin, who said, "Ooh...yeah, no," and tucked the card blindly into the stack. Collin waved away the question on both women's lips. This time he read the card before handing it to Mike. He smiled and gave a little wink.

Ignoring him, Mike read the card, and put his pencil to paper when Peach flipped the timer and gave him the go ahead. First Mike drew an oval, then two closed eyes with a v for the eyebrows and a frowning mouth.

Angie said doubtfully, "Angry?" Mike shook his head.

He drew a light bulb that to Angie must have looked like an insect.

"Stung by a bee?"

Mike shook his head.

He tried to draw the stick figure's hands in front of his eyes.

"Swatting a bee? Or a wasp?"

Mike shook his head vigorously.

He tried to draw the light rays shining into the guy's face.

Angie was drawing a blank and Mike was about to try drawing a better light bulb, but the timer ran out.

"*Blinded by the light*," he sang in his best Chris Thompson voice.

Angie clapped his thigh, saying, "I thought that thing was a bug." Mike looked down and shook his head in mock despair.

"Don't worry," chimed in Peach with a nod towards her mom's painting, "there's still hope for you as an abstract artist, Mike."

There were chuckles all around, though Collin didn't fully understand the reference. Mike smiled his most winning smile at her. *She remembers*.

Peach flushed and hid her smile behind her glass, but Mike saw it. He saw it in the way she took too large a sip and wound up splashing her lips and her throat with wine. *I'd like to lick her clean*. Mike wasn't even fazed by the thought. He was determined.

Peach excused herself and dashed to the kitchen. Collin watched her go as he took a drink, feeling like the luckiest man in the world. Mike crossed his legs again. It was Angie's turn to flush. Mike's hard-on was back with a vengeance and she thought she might be sick. *What the actual fuck?* Angie pulled at the material of her dress again.

"So," Mike asked Collin, just to clear the silence, "how long have you and Peach been seeing each other?"

Habit

"Oh." He smiled over at Mike. "It's been about a month now. I guess."

Mike snickered to himself, but said in a mostly steady voice, "That's pretty recent. And you two are already planning a vacation alone together?"

Collin turned to see Mike's expression. He wasn't jeering—not quite—but his eyes were a little too questioning, his brows a little too incredulous. Still Collin shrugged and grinned guiltily.

"Come on, Mikey. It'll have been two months by the time we leave."

Mike smiled, but it didn't touch his eyes. "I guess that's long enough to be able to trust one another."

"Well, I mean..." Collin felt uncomfortable. He thought that Mike was over whatever bone he had been picking last time, but apparently not. Then he gave his rebuttal with a short laugh, "I suppose you two could come along and chaperone if you wanted."

Angie gave a nervous giggle. She'd been looking from Collin's eyes to her husband's.

Mike wasn't really sure why he said what he said next, but there it was, coming out of his mouth just as Peach re-entered the room.

"Sure. We'd love to." Even though he smiled, it came out flat. It didn't sound at all like a joke even though he'd willed it to.

It made Peach ask, "Love to what?" Collin maintained Mike's eye contact. He couldn't read the man's intentions, but he didn't like the look he was giving him.

Angie's nerves went off like firecrackers under her skin. She stood up and put a hand to her stomach.

"Peach," she said, moving to her friend, "I'm not feeling too hot." She mouthed the word, *period*.

Collin broke eye contact first. He looked up at Angie and then stood. Mike stood as well; his eyes slowly moved from Collin to his wife. That was when Collin glanced down and saw it.

"Awe, Cricket," said Peach. "Do you need anything?" She put an arm around Angie.

"No, I just think it'd be best to call off the games night a little early. Mike can drive us home and we'll all hang out another time. We should catch a movie or something." Angie and Peach walked arm in arm to the front door and Mike followed after. Collin held back. When he did start moving, his heart sounded very loud in his ears.

"I hope you feel better soon, Hon." Peach hugged Angie and Collin gave them both a weak smile.

Mike said, "Don't worry, Collin. I'm sure the two of you will have a blast in Belize. I was only yanking your chain."

Peach looked between the two men, uncertain of what exactly was transpiring, certain it had little to do with Angie. Mike was grinning unevenly. Collin looked disgruntled. Peach embraced Mike in a hug.

The proximity made bile rise up in Collin's throat. Mike saw his discomfort and inwardly enjoyed it. Once Peach closed the door behind them, she turned back to her partner.

"You alright, Hon? You look like you've seen a ghost."

Collin blinked back into his body. He had to decide whether or not to regale her with what he'd witnessed. Some guys had problems.

Peach could tell Collin still needed time to mull over whatever was bugging him. She thought he could spell it out for her *after* they'd tended to other worldly matters. Peach crossed to her partner and pressed her lips against his. Collin smiled from the corner of his mouth. Some of the colour was coming back to his face. When Peach turned away and climbed the stairs, he followed. The matter could wait.

In Angie's Toyota, the two sat quietly for most of the drive. Mike was at the helm and Angie was trying to keep herself together. She was flashing back to the day she was seventeen, when she'd walked in on her parents having sex. This felt a lot like that except without the humorous apologies. Mike was silently twirling his fingers against his thigh. He was smiling to himself, like he was in on some joke Angie wouldn't know anything about. Something tickled the nape of her neck and Angie shuddered.

"You alright, Babe?" Mike glanced away from the road to look at her. His gaze was empty, devoid of anything, let alone guilt or embarrassment. Angie thought for a moment that maybe she'd blown things out of proportion. Maybe he was just a male mammal reacting to stimuli. That had happened

Habit

the other night. It was happening again. She held his gaze a moment, searching for her husband in that blank visage. She found nothing.

"Babe," he said again, this time without inflection. Angie had been programmed in her last relationship never to let a question go stale.

"I—I have to talk to you," she said carefully, gathering herself.

"Yes?" Mike could sense Angie's agitation in her darting eyes. He knew she was about to bring up the thing he couldn't seem to bring down. He wanted her to say it though. Something inside Mike wanted his wife to have to say it.

"I—" Angie started again but stopped. Her heart was trying to flee. She could feel its wings beating in her chest. Before she could lose her nerve, she said, "I think you've been acting inappropriately around our friends."

"Oh," said Mike, surprised she was able to get that out. "And how would you like me to act?"

His answer wasn't an admission. Angie looked at him. Now his face had a little shit-eating grin on it that only made her angry. She guessed she could thank him for that; it gave her resolve.

"I want you to be able to keep your temper with Collin and I want you to keep it in your pants around Peach. What the hell was going on back there, Mike?"

Mike could have laughed, but he felt his blood go cold. They were alone on the road. He slowed to a stop at the next light. It wasn't red. He looked directly into Angie's eyes, his face expressionless. There were no words.

The light turned red. They were mere blocks from their apartment. Angie felt like he held her eyes in a vice. His mouth did not move even though her own fell open. He did not blink. He did not seem to breathe. Angie felt her own rapid inhales threaten to wind her.

A thousand miles away, the light changed back to green. Angie could not look away. Mike's eyes narrowed and it was like he'd tightened his grip on her. She tried to speak but her throat was blocked. It was not terror. Angie was not going to be afraid of this man. *Please*. Not when he'd treated her better than anyone she'd ever been with.

Angie was still collecting her thoughts when Mike's lips flittered. He blinked and then his lips curled lazily. He smiled a casual smile, the one he reserved for her in restaurants when they were laughing about someone in the room. It made her blood pressure drop. He looked toward the road again, that smile still on his face, and drove on through the light.

Mike liked the pheromones in the air. There was a twist of anxious uncertainty mingled with his own arousal. He knew Angie wouldn't be "in the mood" tonight, but Mike wasn't in any mood at all. He took a deep breath in and then a feather of guilt did land on his shoulder. Mike changed his expression. He glanced at Angie, remembering to have a little crease in his eyebrows.

Mike said, "You know, Babe. I'm really not feeling like myself tonight. I haven't treated you kindly and I apologize. How about I drop you off and take myself for a drive? You know," he scanned the space between them, "clear my head."

Angie searched his eyes. The electrical storm around him had dissipated, but before she could answer, Mike glanced away and pulled up to the front door. He punched the car into park and looked at her.

"Would that be alright?"

"Yeah. Of course."

Mike put his hand on her thigh and kissed her deeply before she had time to register his movements. The kiss lasted a long time, and no time at all. He released her and she sat motionless for a moment before finding her seatbelt and then the door handle. Mike watched her all the while, his expression bittersweet. He waited for her to go inside the building before peeling off into the night.

Angie peeked through the slat window as he retreated. *I was too hard on him.* She realized how tightly she was gripping her phone. The screen came on and there was their wedding photo, with Mike in his tux, feeding her the first morsel of cake. *Something is seriously wrong and I shamed him.* Angie's field of vision closed in like the snapping of a photo. *He needs me right now and I can't stop blaming him for things he can't control.* Her throat cinched shut. She groped for something to grip onto and landed awkwardly on the first stair. Mike had lost control of himself tonight, but he wasn't going to hurt her. He just needed space.

Angie needed air, she needed to breathe, but she couldn't. She had to calm down enough to make it up the fucking stairs to take her medicine. Also,

Habit

Mike had the keys to the apartment. Just the thought of needing to contact him just to get into her house sent Angie's heart rate skyrocketing.

Breathe out. Only out. Just breathe out. Only out. Only out. Breathe out. Breathe. Breathe. Out. Slowly the mantra took effect. Instead of a straw, Angie was breathing through a tube. Her vision cleared. Her phone was in her hand. She waited until she could see the screen, then she dialed Mike's number. Glancing up the staircase behind her, Angie flashed back to Thanksgiving. The last time Mike had lost control, they'd been in the heat of passion and she had what? Laughed in his face.

Mike rolled down the windows and let the cool, damp air into the car. His phone rang and he pictured Angie's stricken face in his head again, but in that moment he wasn't concerned about apologies or make up sex, so he let it go to voicemail. His thoughts were taken up by the image of Peach leaning those pearls right over his nose, like she'd wanted him to admire them. She had wanted him. He knew this now. She was having second thoughts now that Collin was getting too pushy. She knew that Mike's own relationship was on the rocks, so she was giving him a signal. They had to be subtle. It was up to Mike to read between the lines.

He drove steadily on through the drizzling rain. Tracers of light tried to night-blind him but he was used to this lack of visibility. He wasn't used to the chill. Angie's heater gave a wheeze when he turned the knob, but that was all. His hands were going numb, so he snapped open the glove box and found Angie's mitts. It was handy to bed a big woman; her gloves fit perfectly.

His phone rang again and Mike turned it off. Angie should know better than anyone that distracted driving can kill. How many people had her husband scraped off the pavement? Mike tried to distract himself with the view outside. It wasn't exactly a beautiful night for a drive. The chill was bone deep. It took a moment to take in the grid he'd subconsciously followed. He hadn't fooled anyone. All along, he knew where he was headed.

The house looked warm. The upstairs lights were on, even though the porch light had been turned off. Mike could see movement upstairs through the Venetian blinds. At first he was confused to see a man's silhouette. Of course, Collin's Mazda was still in the driveway. Mike stopped short of the property and parked across the street. He killed the engine and with it the lights. For a long time, he just sat in the darkness, his eyes on what he assumed was the upstairs bedroom. Mike thought he saw Peach's figure as she slipped out of that scant little top. He could almost hear the fabric slide over her smooth skin.

Mike checked his mirrors. He listened hard for a moment, both for anyone walking by and for any sounds coming from the houses. He thought he heard a squeal. Mike closed his eyes and listened for it again. He wondered if Peach was ticklish. He thought she might be. She might be being tickled at that moment. With one index finger underneath his shirt, Mike trailed a path across his own skin. It was Peach's finger and he *was* ticklish. A tantalizing

Habit

shiver leapt up. Mike exhaled and laid his head back against the seat. He thought he heard someone behind the car, but it was only a cat.

A fucking cat. Mike twisted hard in his seat to stare after it. It must have been long gone. Mike's stomach itched. He realized he'd been stroking himself with wool mitts on. Irritated, he shoved the gloves in his pocket. One last look all around him set his mind at ease. Another barely audible giggle drew him back to Peach.

Peach. Hadn't she been wearing the same perfume tonight that she had on Thanksgiving? He imagined it was still on his collar where her cheek had rested in that brief goodbye. Mike could feel her head on his shoulder now. It felt good to be this close to a woman like Peach. She was upstairs and enjoying herself. Probably the dog man was going down on her. Probably, it wasn't enough. Mike thought she sounded like she needed him to step in and give her what no other man could.

Mike kept his eye on the window, spying every flicker of light and sensing that Peach was in the throes now. He could almost hear her staccato breath, her tremulous moan. Even though her so-called boyfriend was with her, she was begging for more. She couldn't leave for Belize. She wouldn't be happy there. She needed Mike. Who else could fulfill her? Fill her when the job had bled her dry. Who else understood her?

She needed Mike like he needed her. Yet here they were—so close Mike could feel her trembling in his arms, still, separated by a wife who couldn't even meet his eyes and a pretty boy who could never feed her flame. Mike imagined the heat of her. He imagined the taste of her, clean and sour. He imagined being deep inside her, coming, hard, coming, coming to a grinding halt. Someone rattled the handle. A gasp escaped Mike and his eyes squeezed open, only to stare into his own mother's eyes. Her rancid breath was fogging up the glass.

Mike's ecstasy was sheared by terror. The sickly apparition glared through the window, her face contorted in disgust. She opened her maw as if to accost him. Even as his hand was being covered in his mess, all the warmth was ripped away in the claws of an ear-splitting yowl. Mike covered his face with his free arm as the phantom outside his door aimed to throw her whole body through the glass. The needling sound came so suddenly and so close, Mike swore there was a fucking cat in the back seat of his car.

When the glass didn't shatter, he jerked his head around and stared at the empty backseat even as the howl still echoed in his ears. It was all in his head. He was sure of that much as he turned hesitantly back to the darkness outside his vehicle. He checked all around. Nothing. He rechecked the locks and scanned the street again. He swore if he saw so much as the flick of a tail, he'd run the fucker down. He was alone on the street.

He had to say out loud, "She's dead." Then he threw his head back and cursed louder than he'd meant to. He glanced across the street. Peach's lights were still on upstairs, but there were no more sounds of satisfaction. Only the horrid pulse of his own heartbeat in his ear. He checked his mirrors again. There was a man walking two tiny dogs across the street behind him. Mike watched for any reaction. None. The stranger hadn't heard. No one had.

Once his heart was finally settled, he became aware of two voices. At first he was sure it would be his mother calling him out of his fort. She had some new game she wanted him to play with her drugged out friends.

He looked through the foggy glass and cursed silently when he witnessed Collin kissing Peach good night on the porch. Mike dropped his head down low, so not to be spotted. The chilly night meant Peach didn't move all the way out of her house. She didn't catch sight of Angie's car. Collin hit a button and his Mazda chirped happily. He got in and started it up. After one final farewell wave from beyond the threshold, Peach closed the door and Collin drove off.

Mike stared across in confusion. If Peach were his, he'd never leave her alone at night. But then, of course, Collin needed to get back to his bitch. Disgusted, Mike put his hands on the steering wheel. The stickiness surprised him and he took his hands away again. His revulsion turned inward. He was suddenly eleven years old with the results of his first wet dream coating his bed sheets. He'd been shoving them into the washer when his mom caught him.

Fucking bastard. She'd slapped him into the wall. A phantom sting made Mike trace a scar on his trap. She needed both hands free to deal with his mess so she'd put out her cigarette right there on his shoulder. Had he screamed that first time? He didn't remember. He flicked on the overhead lights as if to ward off the memory.

Thank God, Angie kept a tube of Clorox wipes in the back of her vehicle. When he was confident he'd wiped down every surface, including his own pants, he turned off the lights again and sat in the dark for a moment longer.

Habit

Looking back up at the house, he thought about how Peach must feel. All alone in that big house. All alone when he was only metres away. She wouldn't be alone for long. He registered how cold the vehicle was. The fog he'd made earlier had turned to frost. Mike started the vehicle.

The engine stuttered into life. He flipped a toggle and watched the wipers glide half-heartedly over the windshield, spreading the washer fluid until he could see clearly. The shame he should have felt earlier caught up to him once he was on the road again. He was back in his old bedroom. His mother loomed over him. He'd lost count of how many times she'd burned him. How many times had she dislocated his arm? The sight of her blurred his vision and he had to wipe his eyes just to face the leering city lights. In that moment, he wondered as he had so many times why his father never asked about those scars.

When Mike was a kid, Alan never saw them because beaches and swimming pools weren't part of his childhood, but his dad knew about the broken collarbone. He'd seen Mike in countless dressing rooms before and after hockey games. Alan Perry never questioned any of the marks of the past. It was too painful for both of them. Angie just thought he'd been playing chicken in college. Peach... Mike hoped he could confide in Peach one day. He tried to imagine how that conversation would go but had to stop himself.

She'd probably just swear and spit on his mom's grave, but that was exactly what he needed right now. He didn't want to wallow in it all. He wanted a woman who could kick him into the present moment and keep him out of his flashbacks.

When he reached his own dark block, Mike eased Angie's car into a spot outside their building. Exhausted, he hauled himself inside, but stopped dead in the foyer.

"Angie?" She looked horrible. Tears had stained her cheeks and made streaks through her makeup. She turned two stricken eyes towards him.

"You turned off your phone."

"It died," he lied.

Angie tried to convince herself that was the truth. He stood to turn. "You had the house key. I've been waiting for you all this time."

Mik waited until she had a head start before he followed her up the stairs. The empty hallway greeted them with a ghostly silence and they made it to the apartment right as the hairs on the nape of Mike's neck stood on end. He whipped around.

"What's wrong?" asked Angie fearfully.

Mike scanned the empty corridor. "Nothing." He turned back and slid his key into the lock. The silence broke.

At first it was a faint and misty sound; just some animal in the night. Mike looked down one side of the corridor and then the next. Still nothing. Angie was agitated now. She couldn't sense what he could. He turned the knob and the door creaked open. Then a screech—the same harrowing howl that had sliced through him in the car now chased them inside. He pushed Angie through first, then banged the door closed behind him and pressed his weight up against it.

"What was that about?" *Just someone's cat.* Mike locked the door. "Mike?" *That's all.* He bolted it. Someone's cat had heard them in the hallway and it was merely alerting its owner to their presence. There was no other sound around him, except a buzz in his ear.

Mike lurched through the darkness and into the bathroom. Blinded momentarily by the overhead lights, he unzipped to relieve himself. Angie was on his tail, but she paused at the bathroom door.

"Mike?"

"Yeah?"

"Are you okay?"

"...Fine. You?"

"...Fine." She could hear the stream start up.

"Listen, Hon," said Mike, "sorry you had to wait on me. I just—" He stopped short. His ears pricked up to a distant mewling.

Angie stepped around the corner to look at him. "You just what?"

Mike registered the alarm in her voice and tried to settle himself and his wife. "I just need to get some sleep."

Habit

Angie's jaw dropped. Her eyes narrowed. She couldn't find any words for the fury roiling in her stomach. She banged open the medicine cabinet and shook out two pills from her more powerful prescription.

Mike watched her swallow the pills without water. He waited for more terrifying sounds, but nothing came. His blood pressure dropped unevenly. He wanted to say something kind to his wife, but he had no words. She gave him one last chance. Then she stalked off to bed.

Mike glanced at the timer on the toilet. 1:38. *Fuck.* He brushed his teeth and listened to the strokes of the toothbrush for a long time. It was soothing to look in the mirror and see nothing but his own eyes. He heard nothing but the shushing rhythm of the toothbrush.

Time passed as Mike lulled himself into that blissful nothingness. When he was aware again, he felt at ease. He glanced at his reflection. There was a new scratch on the side of his face. He picked at it idly. A dribble of blood freed itself from the red wound and Mike wiped it away. He flicked off the lights. The toilet timer gleamed in the darkness, 3:45.

Under the cover of night, he made his way to the bedroom and crawled in beside Angie on the bed. He'd forgotten to sleep on the couch the way they'd seemed to arrange that week. Angie was warm and limp. She didn't acknowledge Mike. He'd hoped that in her drugged stupor, she could forget the discomfort he'd put her through. Angie was well past that point. Her oblivion meant he could even curl his arms around her. He was dreaming that his arms held Peach. Angie was dreaming about the black Hawaiian beach where they'd had their honeymoon.

Angie woke when her dream flipped and Mike was rolling a gurney across the sand. Again, he had a cigarette in hand. This time, he blew his smoke in her face. Angie's eyes flew open. She could smell tar in the air. No. It was eggs.

Angie groggily followed the smell to the kitchen where Mike was making them breakfast. She rubbed her eyes. The clock on the stove said 12:04. She'd slept in. She rubbed her eyes and watched Mike work. He was naked to the waist. It seemed to Angie that he was in better shape than he'd ever been. The muscles of his back rolled as he flipped the omelettes and tossed the hashbrowns and poured the coffee. He wasn't the same gaunt figure she'd seen in her nightmare. The real Mike held out a cup of Joe to his wife without looking behind him. Angie crossed and took it from him.

"Hungry?" asked Mike, smiling at her now.

Angie nodded and flicked away the sleep from her eyes. She sat at the table with both hands around the warm mug and watched her husband. He moved fluidly through the kitchen until he had two plates full of food. He presented one to her. Angie thanked him but didn't eat right away. He was still moving around confidently, a little tune escaping him in a whistle. Angie didn't recognize the song. She didn't recognize Mike either for that matter. Last night he had looked frightened and edgy. She thought she should be happy for him.

He hadn't touched a cigarette in two weeks now and that was what Angie wanted. So why did she feel like that wasn't the only thing that had changed? Last night had been creepy, to put it nicely, and now here he was, setting their food on the table like everything was alright. Mike caught her glance as he was turning back to collect his coffee. He gave a little flourish.

"Bon apple tea."

Angie picked up her fork and looked at it the way one might look at a foreign medical instrument. The voice in her head scolded her. *He's trying to make things right. You have nothing to complain about.* Mike took his seat across the table and doused his food in ketchup. Angie watched him take the first forkful.

Without looking at his wife, he said, "I'm going to pretend you're not giving me the evil eye."

Angie looked down at her hand. The fork was still empty. She set it down.

"Actually," continued Mike, chewing and swallowing, "I want to thank you."

"Thank me?"

"For being so supportive of me at this point in my life. After all," Mike took another bite of food and spoke as he chewed, "it was your idea for me to go to hypnotherapy." He didn't think his wife saw how closely he was gauging her reaction. *She did this to me. She and that fucking doctor have unlocked some psychotic part of me.*

Angie was frozen in place. Her eyes were locked on her plate, like she could avoid the rising anxiety if she could only avert her eyes.

Habit

Mike swallowed a smile. "You've really stood by me through all this and I'm grateful."

This time Angie braved a smile. She looked to him for confirmation. Mike smiled back. She knew she was being selfish. *Always so fucking selfish.* Mike finished off his meal soon after. Angie was still trying to muster the strength to chew her food when he rose to clatter his plate in the sink.

Angie opened her mouth to ask what was his hurry, but Mike was already past her, on his way into the hall. He had decided he'd like to get out of the city and called over his shoulder, "I'm going for a hike today. Care to join me?"

"No," came her response. She was gripping her mug of coffee in two hands.

"Suit yourself." He took no time at all to grab his pack and leave her there, her meal hardly touched.

The highway north of Vancouver wound through the thickening trees, hugging the mountainside. Below the highway, the ocean peeked out of the greenery. Mike found himself daydreaming about being out on the road like his dad. How incredible it could be to just drive for miles with only the trees and the sky for company. From this height, the ocean seemed the most peaceful thing in the world. There were no crashing waves or wild storms on the water. It was a rolling bruise of blue.

Mike drove his truck lazily with the weekend traffic and was reminded of the road between the farmhouse and Prince Rupert. The trees were smaller here, the highway was busier, but the towering cliffs that seemed to cradle his vehicle were just the same. He drove until he saw a blue sign promising a hiking area and ended up on an old forestry road east of Lions Bay.

He parked off of the main road and checked a little bulletin board for a map of the West Lion Trail. Then he set off. The rain was being held back behind a shower curtain of clouds, but Mike didn't mind if it rained now. He hadn't been out of the city for months, he realized, and it felt good just to get some fresh air. The woods were lit with streamers of sunshine. There were patches of snow higher up in the forest, kept cool under the canopy of trees.

A chipmunk chattered at him and a few birds stirred overhead, but otherwise he was alone. No other hikers had braved the cold weather or the slick trail. Mike climbed unhurriedly up the steep terrain, proud that he'd made the sharp decision to get out. Angie didn't know what she was missing. How could she? She hadn't grown up in the woods like he had; she grew up in the city. It was too bad. He thought being out here was better than any kind of fucking therapy.

The air was crisp and damp, but Mike was soon shedding his jacket and stuffing it in the small backpack with his water. He only had on a pair of old Nikes, so he moved slowly and slipped just once on a few of the slick black roots. He whistled tunelessly as he made his way up, feeling peaceful in the quiet autumn.

His mind tried to guilt him again for the way he'd spoken to his wife, but Mike was determined. He would not baby Angela anymore. A little tough love was just what she needed. Hell, all he'd received as a kid was tough love and look at him now. If his mother hadn't kicked him around he'd be just as soft. He was glad for it in a way.

Habit

Back at the apartment, Angie's cellphone stirred her out of the tears that had racked her since Mike left. She retrieved the phone from her nightstand and saw that it was Peach calling.

"Hello," Angie sniffed.

"Angie? Are you sick?"

"Hi Peach, no, just tired." Angie wiped her eyes miserably.

"Still having cramps, Hon?"

"No." Angie flopped down on the bed. "No, I'm alright. It's just—"

"Are things okay between you and Michael?" That was it. Peach always knew her thoughts and as always, Angie was grateful for her frankness.

"I don't know," she said truthfully. "Everything's been weird since..."

"Since Felix died?"

"You knew he was dead?"

"Sure. I mean, Michael told me a couple of days ago. Did you two get the chance to send him off?"

So, it was Peach's idea. "Yeah, we did. But it was strange, Peach. Everything is so messy. And now Mike is out hiking somewhere and he left me here alone."

"Hiking? Since when does Mike hike?"

"That's just it, Peach. He's changing. He's changing so quickly that I can't keep track of it at all." Peach was quiet for a while and a few more tears escaped Angie as she listened to the silence.

"Angie, why don't you come over here and we'll have a girl's night?" Angie looked absently out to the hall, wondering if it was a good idea. For a second, she thought Mike might be angry if he came home to an empty house.

"I don't know, Peach..."

"Come on. Mike probably just needs to cool off."

Angie fidgeted with her hair, letting it roll through her fingers. She reminded herself that it wouldn't matter if Mike were upset. She was allowed to see her friends. Angie said, "Okay. Yeah, okay. I think it would be good for me. I need to take a shower first though."

"Damn right it will be good for you! Come over whenever." They hung up and Angie felt some of the pressure in her chest relax.

The hike was ceaselessly steep. Mike climbed until the trees were dwarfed around him. He climbed higher still until the trees gave way to scraggly brush and crags. He stopped when he found himself on top of a crumbling bluff. He could see the West Lion now, its muzzle lifted to the sky. Mike could see where he'd need to scale its face to the top. The clouds were darkening and the smell of rain hung in the air. Mike stepped carefully onward, his legs stiff and tired from the exertion. Part of him wanted to head back, but he pressed on. He wasn't going to give up now that he was nearly at the top.

Once he was a mere 100 metres from the summit, splotches of rain appeared on the rocks and he pushed himself to climb faster even as his limbs were ready to give. His chest felt like it was filling with fluid and he had to rest just to clear the rising mucus. By the time the coughing fit was over, he wanted to bury his red face in a patch of snow. With his airway free, he huffed and coughed and drove his body onward.

His feet met flat ground at the plateau and Mike steadied himself on the Lion's mane. He sat down and when that didn't slow his breathing enough, he lay with his shirt rolled up to expose his steaming stomach and back. Rain chilled his bare flesh but Mike felt better than he had in weeks. For a long time, he simply lay like that, with his arms over his eyes and his mouth hanging open. Catching rain. Then he stretched and flexed his muscles, revelling in the sensations there. The rain was baptizing him where he lay and he knew that this was the freedom Tehrani had promised. He wished he could share it with someone.

A crunch of rock reached him from somewhere far below and he snapped one eye open, towards the trail. A lone woman was braving the rain and the slippery rocks towards his perch. He watched her figure come into view. At first, his heart leapt because he thought he was watching Peach herself climbing up towards him. He knew that was impossible. Still, the woman had a beautiful body, curvy, but petite. She had wavy blonde hair pulled into a neat ponytail that swished back and forth as she climbed. Mike turned his whole body towards her now. She was looking down and didn't notice him

Habit

watching her. He observed her tight-fitting t-shirt and the effect the rain was having on it. The cotton was clung to her breasts. Her breasts shuddered with every step. Mike watched her careful progression. Her legs worked hard and it took no time for her to reach the final stretch where she was out of view beneath him.

Mike felt a bit like a kid again, spying on something he shouldn't be. He didn't want her to see him lazing around like this with his eyes on her. He decided he didn't really want her to know he was here at all. He checked over his shoulder and found an outcrop that he could squat behind. He went there and waited patiently for her final approach. He could hear her heavy breathing and the sound of the rocks beneath her feet. He liked the little inhales she took and the sigh that escaped her when she reached the last step.

She came into view, and she lay on her back right where he had a moment earlier. The swell of her breasts rose and fell. Her fine lips were parted and she breathed in with a small smile on her face. She covered her eyes with one arm, very much the same way Mike had. Watching her was like watching that porn video all over again. Except this time, Mike was the peeping Tom looking to get his fix. Mike licked his lips.

He looked well beyond where he and the woman had come. There was no movement that he could see from this angle. He listened hard to the sounds of the forest. Besides the steady splatter of water on stone, there wasn't a single sound; no voices, no laughter. This woman had come alone like he had. She was wonderfully alone and unaware that anyone else was even up here.

What the fuck am I thinking? some part of Mike tried to ask. It was wiped out by a sudden gust of wind that tousled his hair and sent a shiver over the woman's body. Mike stiffened. He watched her body tense and then relax. He wondered how long she would stay here, or whether the wind and the rain would rush her back down the mountain. He wondered if he should follow her into the trees where they'd be dry. She might notice him behind her. How would she react if she did?

As he thought about all this, stress rose up and he wondered what exactly he hoped to accomplish here with this stranger on the mountain. He didn't want to hurt her. He only wanted to see what was under that cotton shirt.

Angie pulled off her t-shirt slowly. She stepped into the shower and only then did she make a sound. It was a low hum that soothed her on the inside, while the water soothed her skin. Twirling around and around slowly she took her time, still humming. The sound grew louder. It drowned out the memories, not only from these last two weeks, but from her past as well. She took up the soap and began with her shoulders. The bar stuttered over the toughened skin on her collarbone. It was a scar she shared with Mike. He got his playing hockey, she thought. She winced when she remembered how hard she'd hit the ground when Jackson's fist struck the side of her face. It didn't hurt anymore where she'd broken it, not really. It too was only a memory.

Mike made another scan with his eyes and ears. There was no one. He checked over his shoulder even though he knew he didn't have to.

"Strumming my pain..." The words reverberated through the small space before she was aware that she'd sung them out loud. *Yes he was*.

Mike moved from his hiding spot absolutely silently, as if he were stalking a deer. His slow, methodical steps made no sound at all on the stone and he drew up right next to the woman. When he blocked her light, she opened her eyes and screamed.

"Sorry," said Mike stupidly. She rolled away.

"You scared the shit out of me," she said, still scrambling backwards. Her eyes were wide and her chest was heaving.

"Sorry," he said again. His eyes were on her breasts. He took a step towards her.

She tried to stand too quickly and her foot slipped off a rock. She lost her balance. There was nothing but air to catch her. Her scream raked its nails across Mike's face. He ran to the edge, far too late to save her. He was just in time to see her head hit the rocks below. Her body crumbled after her. Mike didn't need to be a paramedic to know she was dead. Mike opened his mouth in a silent scream.

Habit

It felt good to let the water wash over her lips as Angie sang. She sang a few lines from all her favourite love songs. It felt good to be alone with her body. Once she'd dried off and combed her hair, she started applying her makeup and stopped. She decided against covering the scar. Peach always told her it didn't matter anyway. Then Angie thought about sitting at stop lights, walking up to the house, maybe seeing Collin.

After her foundation was applied she was able to meet her eyes in the mirror. It wasn't an anxiety thing. She just felt more like herself when *his* mark wasn't visible. With a little effort, she smiled.

Angie found a comfortable outfit, locked the apartment, and walked down to the parkade. At first she panicked when she couldn't find her car, but then she remembered how Mike usually left it outside. In the rain. She rolled her eyes and pressed the unlock button until she spotted her Matrix's blinking lights. The driver's seat was too far forward. She set it right. Her mittens weren't in the glove box where she'd left them.

Mike fled back to the city. He swerved in and out of traffic, oblivious to the rain and the hapless honking of other drivers. His heart was driving a nail into his chest, but he just kept his foot to the floor. The image of that woman somersaulting down sent a bolt of lightning through his stomach. *It will be okay*. Everything would be fine. He'd get home and explain to Angie and the cops how she had fallen. He had tried to grab her at the end, but she slipped out of his hands.

No excuses could bring his blood pressure back down though. None of the calming scenery could save him. Mike looked down at the fresh pack of Export A's still wrapped in plastic on the passenger seat. He didn't want to smoke, but he needed to. These were extraneous circumstances. Tehrani would get it. Angie would understand. Except...they wouldn't. No one would. Mike kept one hand on the steering wheel and tore open the packaging with the other. He pulled one little soldier from its ranks and pocketed the pack.

Mike was driving home knowing this was the end. He glanced between the road and the cigarette. There wouldn't be a trial. He was so completely guilty he might as well finish himself off. Mike fumbled to light the dart.

Water had pooled in a dip on the highway. As Mike's front tires hit the divot, they slid out from under him. At the same moment, Mike inhaled steeply and smoke clogged his throat. A cough quaked through him and he unconsciously slapped the brakes, knowing full well it was the wrong move. His truck hydroplaned and spun two full circles before lilting onto one side and depositing him neatly on four wheels into the ditch. His only injury was self-inflicted. He bit his tongue. He was lucky he hadn't flipped. Mike's heart was climbing up the back of his throat. He opened his door and thought he might throw it up.

Only hot foam and spit escaped him as he clung, dry heaving, to the swinging door. Somehow he'd held onto the cigarette through all this and he was tempted to take another drag. A semi-truck raged past him. The truck's airstream whipped at his hair. It tore the dart out of his fingers. Mike was watching the cigarette dance across the blacktop when a black SUV containing three young guys pulled up right behind him.

The driver leaned out of his window and called out, "Are you okay, Dude?"

Mike wiped his mouth but couldn't speak. He waved them away. They didn't move.

The back passenger called out, "Should we call 911?"

"No," Mike almost shouted. He composed himself and said in a more controlled voice, "No, I'm fine. I spun out. That's all." When they still didn't drive off, he said, "Thanks for stopping." Then he willed his body back into the driver's seat. He slammed his door and righted the vehicle. In his haste to speed off, he left rubber remnants on the pavement next to the still-sputtering little soldier.

Peach dipped the little applicator back into the rose-red nail polish. She listened intently as Angie tried to relay the events of the last week.

"I wish I knew what to tell you," Peach said, carefully applying the second coat to Angie's index fingernail. "His behaviour is not okay. You know it and I know it. I just don't get it. He seems normal at work, even cheerier maybe." Angie snorted and Peach gave her friend a sympathetic look. "Sorry. I just thought he was getting a handle on things."

Peach would support Angie whether she stayed with Mike or not. But she didn't want to feed this new-found fear either. Mike's mellow nature was the reason Peach introduced him to her best friend in the first place. She felt responsible for these two. She didn't want to bring up the dog. The way Val told it, it hadn't been Mike's fault, so no point incriminating him.

"That's what's so weird about it, Peach. I don't know what's real anymore. He's been flipping like a switch." Angie didn't want to bring up how she'd heard him masturbating. Their last sexual encounter had been difficult too. No point incriminating him.

Peach asked, "Have you two been talking about a baby again?"

Angie shook her head vigorously. "Not at all. That's the last thing we need right now." The two women sat quietly for a moment, just watching the red lacquer slide over Angie's nails.

"Well," said Peach finally. "You know he's under a lot of stress. You know he's trying to keep things together. Maybe this is the one time in your life when you have to give a guy the benefit of the doubt. I know that usually I'm the first to tell you to dump that asshole, but Mike..."

"Isn't Jackson... I know."

Mike reached the apartment door and put his arms above his head, resting them against the cold metal. He willed himself to act normally. No one knew what he had done. He had to remind himself of this. No one had even the slightest idea about what that hike had turned into. Angie wouldn't know anything unless he spilled his fucking guts. No. He would be cool. He just had to relax. He thought about setting fire to the whole memory.

Picturing what had happened as if it were in a closed book actually did help. But the woman had cried out. She had clawed him. That knowledge made him bristle. He had to unclench his fists against the door. He was not about to go down just because that bitch had tripped. With a deep breath, he gripped the doorknob and tried to turn it. It was locked.

The house was empty. It was a relief not to have to lie to his wife outright. He had a few moments to clean up and wash the stench of sweat and fear off of his skin. He went straight to the bathroom and threw the heat on in the shower. He rubbed his face with both hands and cursed. The skin stung on the left side of his face. In the mirror he saw the set of scratches. Mike wanted to vomit again. What eventually threw him over the side of the toilet was the fact that he already had a simple explanation in mind. He'd lost a fight with a bush. His dad used to say that when he got scuffed up at work or out hunting. Mike flushed down the remains of his granola bar and wiped his mouth on his arm. He stripped off his clothes.

He stepped under the scalding shower and closed his mouth over a scream. It served him right. Retribution for his blunder. When would he learn to control himself? He rubbed soap over his body. The searing water eased his muscles out of their rigor. He bowed his head to the onslaught and allowed his scalp to be cooked. It felt just. It felt cleansing. His heart finally settled back down into place. He had to make a choice; he could live in guilt and fear for the rest of his days, or he could accept that this mistake had to be his last.

Whoever found that hiker would think it was a fall. It *was* a fall. With any luck she'd be out there for a long time, maybe long enough for a grizzly to find her. If he was unlucky, some boyfriend or her mom knew exactly where she was. Search and Rescue would know exactly where to look. One day, a helicopter loops through that park and three days later, a warrant for a DNA sample. Except. He hadn't touched her. She hadn't really been the one to scratch him. He'd crashed into a tree on his way out of that forest. Hadn't he?

Keep it together. Mike switched the tap from hot to cold and allowed the glacial water to snake down his body. His breathing became rapid. His skin was in goosebumps. He revelled in the extreme calm he had to hold onto just to withstand the barrage. If he could only keep from caving. He only had to keep his cool.

When Angie returned, the house was dark. It was 8:30 p.m. and she realized that she hadn't even told Mike where she was going. She didn't think he'd mind; Mike would have called once he was home. But Angie was dealing with the memory of another man who would have beat her for not saying exactly where she was going and exactly how long she would be there. She fingered the disfigured skin on her cheek. *No.* Mike was not Jackson. She took a breath and flipped on the hallway light. For a second she expected Felix to rush to greet her. She hung up her jacket and remembered just as his name left her lips.

Then she listened but did not call Mike. Her heart was hammering, but she told herself it was only from the stairs. She reminded herself that she was safe. It took three counts of ten before she could convince herself. The moment she did, guilt stole into her stomach. Frantic questions flashed through Angie's mind as she checked every room of the house for her husband. *What if he's hurt? What if he's lying in a gully somewhere? Where did he even go?* She took out her cellphone and called him. Her breath was shallow and her head felt so light that she had to stagger to the bathroom to take a pill. Mike answered his phone just as she had the zolpidem in her hand.

"Hello?" His voice was distant, like he was speaking to her through the truck's Bluetooth.

"Mike? Where are you? Are you okay?"

"Oh, Angie. I'm touched that you called. Yeah, I'm fine. Never better."

"Where are you, Hon? How was the hike?"

"It was...," Angie could picture him tilting his head side to side as he said, "exhilarating." A breath of relief steadied her hands and she unscrewed the bottle. Mike could hear the shake of the medication. He said, "I'll have to take you up there sometime, Sweetheart. I think it would be good for you." Angie considered the pill as she listened. She didn't think taking up a new hobby was what their marriage needed right now.

"When will you be home, Mike? Where are you anyway?" Mike glanced over his dashboard. He checked the time on his phone.

"Oh, I won't be much longer I don't think. I was hungry when I got back. I wasn't sure where you'd gone, so I went out." Angie knew he hadn't meant to guilt her, but she felt a residual pang anyway. The pill looked like a good idea.

"Okay, well drive safe, Hon."

"I will."

"See you soon."

"See you."

He had seen her.

He watched her through the living room window when he circled around Peach's row of houses. He counted himself lucky that neither woman looked into the back alley, or they probably would have seen him too. He knew he shouldn't be angry with his wife for being there, but that didn't stop his hands from curling into fists. She was only visiting her best friend. There was nothing wrong with that. There was a perceptible taste of betrayal on his tongue that was bitter and briny. He watched the women laugh and drink in front of a Rom-Com on TV. Then he watched his wife hug Peach goodbye and he tasted battery acid.

Stalking back around the house, he spied Angie on the sidewalk and heard the last little joke the women shared together. He should have smiled to hear them speak so freely, but when he caught his name on his wife's lips and the delectable laughter from Peach, there was only rage bursting in his mouth like a piece of rancid fat.

Mike spat and crept around to the back gate. It wouldn't budge. He cursed and moved into the shadows again. A thought crossed his mind that this was crazy. Whatever he was planning to do, he didn't want any part in it. A sneer crossed his lips, but he relented to this timid little conscience.

Crossing under the streetlamps back to his truck was nerve-racking enough for one night. Mike had to content himself to sit in the cab and watch Peach's place from afar. He thought it might be funny to see if her pet dog would make a late-night appearance. He did not. By the time Angie called, Mike had lost track of time. He was already thinking about retreating home. He hung up and drove slowly. He hadn't noticed the rain, but he was drenched.

He thought about the two women embracing in the low light of the living room. He shouldn't have been jealous. He should have been turned on. What a fantasy, being caught between a raven-haired Amazon and a fair-haired cherub.

He shifted in his seat as a traffic light ahead turned yellow. He slowed, trying to keep his eyes on the road while the rain blotted the city lights into a liquid kaleidoscope. An ambulance sounded in the distance. It tore through his mind like a scream. He was struck by the sudden beat of helicopter blades. SAR was on their way to that mountain. He knew it was impossible for them to find anything in the darkness, but Mike's heart rate jumped and the throbbing pain at his temples diminished whatever fantasy he'd been having. Mike was paying too much attention to the chopper to notice the red inkblots change to green. His delay earned him the blast of a car horn behind him.

Mike eyed the driver through his rear-view mirror and let off of the brake very slowly. When he turned his attention back to the road, that fucking cat was in the middle of his lane. He was just crouching there with his belly open and that screwdriver hanging out of his bloody, matted fur. Mike cursed under his breath but did not brake again. He relished in the fact that this was just a vision. He drove over the animal and carried on, even though he heard the screech and the rumble beneath him and another blast of a horn.

"Ghosts," Mike muttered. It was like driving through Alfred Hitchcock's neighbourhood and having all the demons rising out to scare him. He could have sworn he saw his mother shooting up in an alley, but it was only a street person. Her empty eyes followed him when he drove on. His block was coated in midnight nothingness but pockmarked with spectral yellow porch lights. Mike ignored the gloom all around him. He arrived home and slammed the truck's door behind him.

When he caught the rear end of a grey tabby rounding the corner of the building, Mike ran forward to greet it. The cat was the least of his problems now, and he refused to be afraid of it. He leaned on the cement wall and followed it around. There was nothing there. Mike looked behind him. Only phantoms in the yellow light.

In the stairwell, Mike listened to see if there would be any more meowing. All was quiet. He entered their apartment for the third time that day and felt like he'd gotten away with murder. Angie watched him come in.

She'd been determined not to fall asleep, so opted out of a pill. She chose a full glass of pinot gris instead and had been here alone in the dark, in her black leather armchair, for forty minutes. She wanted to see her husband.

She wanted *his* eyes made of brown earth and not stone. *His* voice—not the cold one he'd acquired this week, but the old one that used to call her Mama. She wanted *his* touch. When she heard Mike come in, she stopped swirling the last splash of white wine in her glass. The only light came from the bathroom, but Angie could tell Mike was drenched. He shook off excess water as he took off his jacket and hung it on the back of the door. Otherwise, he seemed at ease.

Angie thought about questioning him, but anxiety held her tongue. He clicked on the hallway light and stood haloed in the warm glow. His hair was wet and slicked flat against his head. It shone darkly. Angie liked the way one strand opposed him and lay over his left eye. He ran his fingers through his hair and while that rebel hair was pressed flat, another took its place over the right eye. In this light, he could have been Rick O'Connell about to vanquish the Scorpion King.

Maybe Angie was buzzed from the wine, or maybe deciding against the zolpidem had helped her libido because she felt tipsy and relaxed. She was enjoying watching her husband without him knowing she was there. It was her turn to play the voyeur. That's when Angie noticed the scratches. She couldn't keep quiet any longer.

"What happened to your face?"

Mike froze, found her in the dark, and then recovered in one fluid motion.

"I lost a fight with a bush."

He peeled his wet white cotton shirt over his head. Light glinted off of his chest. Angie lost track of her last thought. The joke chased it off. She laughed a little too melodically. Mike glanced over and gave a side smirk. He saw the way she was watching him from her perch on the armchair. She was playing with her hair now. Her eyelashes fluttered down. Mike didn't want to get his hopes up, but that kind of look from Angie was a rare gem.

"What's up, Mama?"

Angie's lips parted. She searched his eyes. No menace, only honest appeal. He wanted her, but would he wait for her to make the first move? Mike unbuckled his soaked pants. His eyes were on her, but he didn't advance. The sound of his zipper and the smell of wine put a memory in Angie's head. She had been bumping along the wall right next to where her husband now stood. The image excited her. Yet apprehension mingled with

Habit

the memory. It was new to be needed so completely that just the sight of her body turned Mike into an animal.

Angie needed one more moment to consider her next move. She noticed that the muscles in his stomach were more pronounced than she could remember. His pecks looked solid, edible. The opening in his jeans wasn't wide enough to tell her how he felt. She bit her lip. He took the cue and stepped out of his pants. Angie peeked, and blushed. Mike hesitated at the threshold.

Angie heard herself saying very quietly, "Come here." Like a soldier, Mike came and stood before her. Angie could get used to this. Her eyes moved up his body just as his eyes moved down hers. They met in the middle again, and Mike smirked.

Without waiting for instruction, he sat on the arm of her chair. *She can't control herself.* Angie lifted her chin and Mike met her in a kiss. His lips were cool and wet. Angie thought she could taste the rain on them. His naked arms encircled her and the chill was enticing.

Mike explored her body with one hand but kept his other on the small of her back, pressing her forward so that she had to lean on him to stay steady. When he found her yielding, he pulled her up to her feet by her lips. Angie let herself move without urgency. Mike was losing himself in his explorations and forgot to be gentle as he imagined tearing off her clothes and bending her over the chair.

When he started to put his plan into action, Angie grabbed his hands off of her shirt. She stepped away from the kiss and removed her blouse by herself. Mike tingled more with every button undone. He hardly waited for the blouse to be off her shoulders before he lowered her bra straps too. The sight of those ivory white breasts nearly put him over the edge, but Angie grabbed his hands again and tried to lead him in another kiss.

Mike bit her lip just to keep himself under control. Angie flinched, but tried to salvage the kiss. She let Mike play with her breasts, rubbing circles around her nipples and squeezing them like ripe grapefruits. *Let him have his moment,* even if it did feel like a breast exam. Only, Mike squeezed harder, forgetting himself perhaps and not noticing when his pressure became worthy of a mammogram. Angie yelped and pulled away.

"What, are you trying to squeeze them into oblivion?" She giggled, but then saw right away that Mike wasn't laughing. He had a little O on his face, like he was surprised or like he'd just... Angie looked down and saw the growing grey splatter on his boxers. Mike threw his hands down to cover himself. Angie didn't know how to react, but she tried to be reassuring. "It's okay, Hon. It happens to everybody."

Mike's eyes darkened. "You would know."

Angie didn't know how to take that. She didn't have time to respond because Mike was turning to head to the bathroom. Alone in the living room, Angie thought she caught his drift. It was so cold that she shrank back down in her chair. She pulled her bra back up over her pink and tender skin. Retrieving her blouse, she sat there clutching it to her chest. She looked over her shoulder to the window. The curtains were drawn, but she couldn't shake the judgment that moved over her like a pair of eyes.

Mike peeled off his drawers and threw them into the bathroom trash. He had royally fucked up. He had been thinking about that little blonde on the mountain and it was enough to ruin everything. God, but her tits had been wonderful. He'd been imagining them while he was caressing Angie. Before he knew what was happening, Angie was laughing and he was ejaculating. It was middle school all over again.

Worse, Angie's laugh made him think of his mother. She was always fucking laughing at him. Even after he was old enough to clean his own bed sheets it didn't stop her from taunting him. It didn't stop her from calling him by that pet name. It was her fault he'd come as soon as her hand was around him. If she had just slowed down, maybe he could control himself.

Mike angrily washed off in the sink. The stabbing pain of reopening his memories almost made him crack the mirror with his fist. Mike flattened his palm in time and just stood there, cradling his cock with one hand and holding his life together with the other.

Shame dripped off the tip of Mike's penis and onto the floor. He hung his head, unable to look at himself in the mirror. He tried to remember that memories couldn't touch him. What had Tehrani said? *They are like the negatives of a photo.*

Mike blew air through his lips. He worried for a moment about what he would need to say to Angie. No doubt there was another crisis unfolding in his living room. No doubt it would require days of slowly making things up to his wife, whom he'd called a slut in the wake of his own poor performance.

Habit

Fuck it, said that voice like the devil in his ear. Mike listened in for any other sage advice, but the thought went cold. He shook his head and dried himself off. Then he stood naked looking into the mirror, leaning both palms on the sink. His eyes were no longer yellow, though the circles underneath them were as purple as ever. He didn't look as sorry as he felt. His forehead was unwrinkled. His mouth was relaxed. He stood up straight. He clasped his right wrist with his left hand in front of himself. The image in the mirror was of a secret service agent or a cage fighter.

Fuck it. Mike's eye twitched, but he held still. He watched rather than felt his jaw clench. With an effort, he forced his chin up. With an effort, he smiled.

That night, Mike slept soundly in bed while Angie feigned sleep on the couch. For a long time she fought with herself about what to do next. Then she remembered that in about six hours she would need to present her entire marketing campaign to CalSol Solutions. She caved and took a Xanax. This was something she hadn't done twice in one month since her first marriage. In that silent time before the capsule released, she lay still on the lumpy cushions and knew she would have to leave Mike. She would stay with Peach. She would file for divorce. The benefit of the doubt was no longer on the table. He had so much to answer for, but Angie was worried she wouldn't be able to hear him out. Hot tears flooded her eyes.

She loved Mike. She couldn't lie to herself. Whatever was happening to him now, it couldn't be his fault. He lost his dad this year. He lost his mom when he was only a kid. That does something to a person. Maybe he needed more than just a hypnotherapist. He needed a psychologist. Yes. Okay. If Mike was willing to get real help, then she'd stand by him.

Angie shifted onto her back and what she saw across the room made her stop breathing. A dark spectre hung in the hallway. It was shaped like a man, but it was swaying as it approached, as if it were held up by strings. It was naked. Its skin was black, made out of the night itself. She screamed and Mike came out of his stupor, confused and upset. He glared out at the darkness until he caught sight of his wife's eyes, wide and white like those of a frightened horse.

"What's wrong, Angie?"

"You...you." She thought she'd swallowed a rock. She tried to calm her voice. "You were sleepwalking?"

Mike observed the space around him. He only remembered dreaming about that cat moving through the house. In his dream, he'd had something in his hand. He looked down but he wasn't holding anything.

"I guess I was."

"Have you done that before?"

"I guess when I was a kid. Scared my mom a couple of times."

Angie's heart settled back in her chest, but she kept her eyes on her husband. He looked distant and not all there. Maybe he was still dreaming. Angie sometimes spoke while she dreamed. Even when she was aware of

Mike responding, she usually stayed asleep too. Mike yawned and turned back down the hallway.

Over his shoulder he said, "Come to bed, Hon."

Not a fucking chance. Angie said, "In a bit." The initial adrenaline swept through her body and left her drained. She couldn't close her eyes though. She kept looking up, expecting to see Mike hovering over her. Eventually the xanax made a second break for her brain, but when she finally drifted off to sleep, a knock at the door slammed her back into her body. Angie rose like a woman under a spell. She thought about waking Mike to answer the door. That was stupid. She'd use the spyhole. She could always call the cops if it was a stranger.

It was the cops. An older man with a tidy moustache and a younger woman with her dark hair slicked back to a bun. In the fish-eyed lens, the man's hand shot out towards the door. The second bout of knocking sent Angie back a pace. The floor squeaked beneath her. The man called, "Police. Please open up."

Angie took a full breath before sliding back the chain and unlocking the dead bolt. When she slowly pulled open the door, she stood halfway behind it. Only, that made her feel like a girl peering around her mother's skirts. She tried to casually move into the light.

"Hello ma'am," said the male cop. "I'm Officer Harly and this is Officer Reid. We're here because there was a scream heard from this floor. Is everything alright in there?"

"No," Angie said too quickly. "No, that—that was me."

The female officer stepped forward. "You were screaming?"

"No, I mean, it was nothing. My husband was...sleepwalking and he came into the living room and woke me up. It scared the crap out of me."

"Did he hurt you?" asked the woman, Reid.

"No. I was just scared."

"Is your husband awake now?" The grey-haired officer, Harly, asked.

"No. No, of course not." Angie felt her cheeks burn. "I don't think he even woke up when I screamed, to tell you the truth."

The cops shared a look and Officer Reid said, "We'd like to check things out."

Angie tensed. She didn't want the police in her apartment. It was only going to cause trouble for her. *No.* She was safe. Mike was not Jackson. Let them have a good look around. Angie opened the door all the way and stood to the side.

They went room to room, turning on the lights in their wake. They came to the bedroom and saw Mike sound asleep, a fishing line of saliva clinging to his pillow. Ben shined his flashlight around the room. For a split second, Amanda Reid thought she recognized the man on the bed.

"Do you...want me to wake him up?" asked Angie.

Ben looked to Amanda. She considered it. Even if this guy was who she thought he was, there was nothing going on here. This was just a weird coincidence. Amanda looked to the wife. She was fine, but she was nervous. Amanda turned the question back to Angie as gently as she could.

"Do you want us to wake him?"

A little flutter creased Angie's brow for a second and then she steadied herself. She tried a smile as she shrugged.

"Not really," she lied, "he works in the morning."

Officer Reid searched her eyes but found only discomfort, nothing life-threatening. She looked to her senior partner and shook her head. On their way back down the hall, though, she pulled out her card.

At the door, Officer Harly said goodnight and stepped back to the corridor, leaving Reid alone with the wife. Reid gently took the woman's hand in hers and placed the card directly on her palm.

Reid said, "Call me if you ever need anything, Mrs..."

"Perry." Angie looked down at the card. "Angela Perry."

"Angela. Perry. Okay. If you need *anything*..."

"Thanks."

Reid smiled grimly and left. Angie closed the door softly, before committing herself to the asylum of the couch.

"What do you think?" Harly asked his partner on her way back down the stairs.

"I didn't hear the TV," replied Officer Reid. Harly reached the front door and held it open. He paused for a moment considering that statement with his whole face.

"So?"

"So, it was weird she was sleeping alone on the couch."

The rest of the night moved over Angie's eyes like a bad dream. She half expected Mike to reappear as a terror in the hallway again. He slept peacefully in bed instead. She half believed he'd show up in her dreams pushing that gurney again, but she only dreamt about driving to work. She was still stuck in traffic when dawn suddenly draped an ugly grey light over the room. Angie got up groggily and started a pot of coffee. She drank it alone on the balcony, wrapped up in a blanket. The warm drink soothed her nerves but Angie couldn't fully relax.

As the city struggled to life beneath her, Angie knew that her decisions today could inform the rest of her life. She could still make this marriage work, but she would not be a sway in the wind. Mike needed to convince her there was something here to save. Her temperature rose just thinking about the potential confrontation, but Angie planned out what she would say the way her therapist had taught her. She considered what she'd accept from him as an answer.

Mike's alarm murdered whatever fantasy had caused him to awake with a fiery erection. He was alone in bed and his thoughts turned instantly to the woman on the mountain. She'd spent the night alone between two boulders where he'd dragged her body. No. That was the dream. She had fallen. He should have been more careful. He should have taken things slowly, not only with her, but with his wife. He listened for Angie's sounds in the house and when he didn't hear her, he tossed aside the blankets and lay naked in the gloom.

His bladder wouldn't let him linger on any particular source of self-loathing, so with a groan, he crossed to the bathroom. Thoughts of how to spend his Monday before the session with Tehrani came and went. He thought about going for a hike—just to clear his mind. He felt his throat close, thinking about losing control like that again. If he so much as spotted a woman out there, he'd run the opposite direction. God, if only things had been different. If only she hadn't tried to get away.

Mike flushed the thought down and tried to shift to something less oppressive. At least he'd get to see Tamara tonight. The thought of her always brightened his day. Through the bedroom window, it looked like there could actually be sun somewhere amid the grey. Mike decided to settle for a run. He dressed in shorts and a sweater and went to find his wife.

Angie was out on the balcony watching the world go by. Bundled in a blanket, she could have been a queen in furs, except she looked small. Mike slid open the door just wide enough to poke his head through. He remembered with a cringe how he had spoken to her last night.

When she turned to him, Mike asked, "How did you sleep?"

"Fine." Angie tried to sound indifferent. "You?"

"Yeah good. What time did you hit the sack?"

"Late."

"Right. You probably want to relax before work. Or would you like to join me for a run?"

Angie gave him a tired look, "Mike, we need to talk." She said it like he should have seen it coming, and he had. He raised his shoulders in a shrug, though, as he stepped out onto the deck. Angie took a deep breath.

She gathered the blanket around her like a shield. "Something's happening to…us." Mike crossed his arms, then consciously uncrossed them. He would listen to what she had to say. "You're going through a lot right now and I want to support you, but I feel like you're not able to accept my support. Maybe it's because I don't have the tools to help." *Maybe it's because you don't respect me.* "But, I think I'd like us to take some couple's therapy sessions, Mike."

Mike stifled a snort behind his hand. "First hypnotherapy, now couple's therapy…"

Angie didn't respond.

"It's a lot to think about." Angie frowned, but Mike asked, "What would you like to accomplish with all this?"

She opened her mouth. Then she closed it.

Habit

"Why don't I give you some time to think about that? I've already got a therapy session scheduled for this evening, and it would be nice to know that you're behind me, instead of quitting and moving on to the next great thing."

Angie looked down. Her face was burning. She thought her ears were bright red, which always happened when she had to deal with conflict. She looked up, but Mike had slipped back into the kitchen, leaving the sliding door ajar. She heard him whistle as he fetched his running shoes. It was like nails on a chalkboard. She went to take a drink of coffee, but her mug had been empty for a long time. She peeked over her shoulder just in time to see her husband leave. Over her other shoulder, she read the clock on the oven. It was ten to seven, she had to face her day.

Mike started jogging towards the harbour. The morning wrapped long grey fingers around the buildings. It cast long shadows over the people in the streets. Mike was still sore from the day before. He thought he might have pulled a muscle in his back and didn't want to remember how that had happened. Near the familiar sleeping bags, Mike quickened his pace. The couple were still buried in their covers trying to black out the dawn. One of their dogs barked and then another and then another. Probably they didn't see many inner city runners. They started to rise. They weren't on any kind of leashes. Mike decided against kicking at them and instead he crossed the street. A wind picked up and played in his hair.

God, it felt good to be alive. With his lungs working and his heart pumping, Mike wondered why he ever worried about anything at all. So, a woman had met with an unfortunate accident yesterday. That had nothing to do with him. She'd tripped. He saw it with his own two eyes. Here in the present, he was not going to be bogged down by guilt or any other feeling his mother had once tried to ram down his throat.

Mike hopped over a pile of what could have been dog shit but looked questionably human. It felt like a metaphor. He wished he could forget all the shit he'd been through, but he supposed he would just have to rise above. He had to rise above every memory of his mother cornering him in his room. He had to remember that his mother was dead and he was not. She had tried to hurt him and had only hurt herself. Karma was a bitch.

By the time he got home and had a shower, he felt more in control. Angie was gone, which was for the best. Mike spent the day lounging on the couch, flipping through the channels until he saw it. A breaking story about a missing woman from Squamish. Mike's throat closed. The image of the smiling woman showing off a huge engagement ring sent him reeling. So that was what her real smile looked like. What he would have given to see it live.

When the fiancé came on, Mike stood up and paced in front of the TV. He thought about wanting a cigarette, but there would be no solace there. The news anchors were asking anyone with information about the woman's whereabouts to come forward. They hadn't mentioned the hike though. Maybe she'd been like Mike. Maybe no one knew where she'd gone. There was no information that linked her to the Lion.

When the clock on his phone read 5:08, Mike put on a nice shirt and wore his favourite dark jeans with a pair of Eddie Bauer shoes. He locked up the little apartment with no inclination that this would be the last time he'd see his home.

The clinic smelled faintly of vanilla when Mike stepped through the door. He inhaled deeply and his eyes were drawn to Tamara, as if she were the source of that sexual aroma. She was busily sorting through paperwork. When he entered, she gave a winning smile before really registering who he was. It was a reflex for her. But she remembered how his eyes left their mark on her skin. She greeted him curtly and ducked her head back down. She was determined to finish up with her files so she could go home.

When Mike didn't take a seat, Tamara spoke to her computer rather than to him. "Dr. Tehrani stepped out, but he'll be back shortly."

Mike said nothing, but he put on a smile. She was avoiding him. He approached the desk and looked down at her. He liked the furtive movements of her eyes and her hands across the keyboard. She looked fetching in her little white blazer that closed with a single clasp. Underneath, the blue fabric of her shirt showed. It stretched smoothly over her breasts. Mike wondered if she was braless again. She had a new haircut and now her blonde hair hung in lively ringlets just past her chin.

Mike reached out to touch one of those curls. He wasn't really aware of the movement until, sensing his presence, Tamara moved her head away.

"Mr. Perry?" she asked, not quite frightened, but vexed.

"Sorry," said Mike hastily pulling back. "Your hair looks great." Tamara started to say something but stopped. She was looking at the scratches on his face. They were superficial, but they didn't look self-inflicted. Mike noticed where her eyes were drawn.

He said, "I had a fight with a bush."

Tamara tried to smile but her jaw felt locked. She rolled her chair discretely out of his reach and looked back down to her papers. She realized she was perspiring and hoped the doctor would return soon.

"Do you have a boyfriend, Tamara?"

She should have seen the question coming, but still it was like a tourniquet. Her heart fought to get enough blood to her brain. She opened her mouth again. Mike smiled at the sight.

The front door jingled open and Tehrani came out of the fading light. He wiped his immaculate shoes on the welcome mat and gave a sunny smile to Mike and Tamara.

"Mr. Perry, you're very early." Tehrani strolled over and shook Mike's hand. He felt the humidity in the room. He looked from Mike to Tamara, but he would not show his concern. "Look at us three," said the doctor. "Ready to take on the world." Mike laughed with him while Tamara tried to swallow her unease.

Tehrani unlocked his office and held the door open for Mike. Mike gave Tamara a wink before stepping through. She tried to go back to her work. *What a fucking tease,* whispered that dark voice in Mike's mind. Tamara looked up with wide eyes, as if she'd read his thoughts, but his back was turned to her. Tehrani met her eyes as he was closing the door. He wanted to ask her what was wrong, but it would have to wait.

Inside the cramped office, Mike was enveloped in the greens, reds, and golds. He slumped down into his regular place on the sofa. Dr. Tehrani took his time to remove his felt coat and hang it over the chair behind his desk.

"My, my, Mr. Perry. I hope you're well. I couldn't help but notice the marks on your face."

Mike exhaled lazily and put his feet up on the sofa. He said, "I had a fight in the bush."

"I see." The doctor took a moment to observe him. He'd meant to say something trivial that Tehrani himself had said after getting scratched up, but that misspeak felt like a Freudian malfunction. And then there was the way Tamara had shrunken away from this man. When Tehrani sat down, he had the forethought to take out his phone and send Tamara home for the night.

"Something wrong?" asked Mike.

"No, no. Just a message from the Mrs.—how is your wife doing, Mr. Perry?"

"She's fine," Mike said sharply.

"Good to hear." Dr. Tehrani didn't look up from his phone. He pretended only to be half-listening. "Did you two get up to anything exciting over the weekend?"

Mike's eyes wandered over the ceiling. He thought about how to dodge the question. "Oh, we had a games night with some friends of ours."

Habit

"That's nice," said the doctor, putting his phone back onto his desk. With feigned indifference he picked up his notes on Mike and asked, "How has your wife been taking your recovery so far?"

Mike frowned. Then he let out a breath and sat up on the sofa. "You know, Doc, I don't think I want to talk about Angela tonight." Dr. Tehrani looked at him over the rim of his glasses. Mike's eyes were icy.

"That's fine. What would you like to talk about?"

"How about my addiction? Since that is what I'm here for. My wife had the bright idea that we need couple's counselling on top of this—"

"Lots of couples choose to talk about their problems with a neutral party. It's very effective."

"It's just a bit much."

"I see," Tehrani put his pen down, "but I have to ask, do you think your addiction is taking a toll on your relationship?"

Mike didn't answer.

"In my experience," continued Tehrani, "addiction can sneak up on a couple. It can drive a wedge between them."

Silence.

"Sometimes we aren't able to be the person our partner has grown accustomed to. Sometimes we change and the person we become isn't who they'd like us to be." The smile appearing on Mike's face looked as though it was pulled up by strings. He laughed then, low and harsh.

"Well, you hit the nail on the head," he said. "You really did. And in your experience, Doc, have any of your patients ever been changed for the worse? I feel better than ever, but my wife won't cut me any slack."

This time Tehrani was silent.

"It seems to me that if a person can't rely on their partner for support, then they should look for someone they can count on."

"Have you found someone else? Someone who supports you?"

Mike shook his head but thought of Peach. He thought of how she'd leaned over him, letting those breasts graze his nose. He had to stop before he lost himself again. He looked around for something to focus on in the room. The clock was there waiting for him.

Tehrani could see him settling back down. He said nothing and simply observed Mike. So, his marriage was suffering. On top of the loss of his father, he was dealing with stress and possibly estrangement at home. That might account for his fascination with Tamara.

Mike shook his head again. "Why aren't you asking me the same questions you did before? Don't you want to know if I had any relapses?"

"Did you?"

"Yeah, as a matter of fact. I bought a pack yesterday. I had one puff and then I threw the rest out the window." Actually, Mike could feel the pack resting against his stomach in the pocket of his coat.

Tehrani nodded, but felt that Mike was keeping something from him. "Well," he said. "I'd call that an improvement. Was this just after your trip to the woods?"

Mike nodded, but when he looked up at the doctor, dread blocked his airway. Standing just over Tehrani's shoulder, was the woman he'd killed. Just standing there, with her hair and clothes dripping from the rain. She watched him with a pair of yellow cat's eyes. That was the only reason he knew she wasn't real. He knew she wasn't real, but still her gleaming eyes melted his resolve and the fear crept out of his pores, staining the back of his shirt.

"Mr. Perry? Is there something wrong?"

She put her hand on the doctor's shoulder.

"No." Mike wanted to faint. Instead, he lay on his back very slowly, with his eyes shut tight, willing away the phantom. His body tensed automatically, but he forced himself to relax. He knew that if he felt even the slightest touch of her cold, dead hands, he'd lose it. He didn't know how else to make this one go away, so he silently willed the doctor to begin. He needed those pleasant words and that soothing voice.

Tehrani sat taking notes for a minute longer. He thought his client had almost fainted and he wasn't about to begin a session now. What this man needed more than anything, was sleep. Beneath his facade were the shadows under his eyes. *So, let him sleep.* The sound of the pen scratch was restful. Mike tried to remember to breathe. He wasn't going to be afraid of ghosts.

Habit

The room remained quiet for a long time. Mike became aware of the clock again. Its subtle tick was like a knock at the door in a far off place. Someone was tapping, not urgently, just in time to the little whisper of the pen. The woman was gone. He knew it without opening his eyes. Her oppressive energy wasted away and underneath the metronome, Mike listened to the doctor's gentle scratching. It was the shuffling of feet. Calloused heels across plain wood boards. Someone moving around the room.

The only other sound was Mike's own breathing. It seemed fast to him. Tehrani had told him once to breathe naturally, but mild panic was making Mike hyperventilate. His skin had cooled below room temperature and there was a chemical smell in the air. Tehrani wouldn't stop pacing the floor. Mike knew that smell. Something between paint thinner and cat piss. Mike's eyes snapped open.

His mother was close enough for her breath to strike him across the face.

She growled, "I'm really fucking sick and tired of you hanging off my tits."

Mike wanted to scream. He was looking at a corpse, but then, that's how she'd really been in life. Her eyes were huge and angry, yellow and shot through with blood. Some of her teeth were brown, or missing. Kerry Perry wore a pair of faded blue Tweety Bird shorts and a black bra that was two sizes too big. Her stomach was wrinkled with loose skin. She'd been actively wasting away as long as Mike could remember. Her breasts should have been shrivelled and thin like the rest of her, but they were pale and full. Blue veins bolted up from her areolae. She opened her mouth to speak again and again her toxic breath made Mike's eyes water.

"I swear to God, if I didn't have my medication, I would fucking kill you." Mike couldn't turn away. He opened his mouth to speak, but only a child's wail escaped him. When she leaned in close to say, "Kill you," he wanted to look away, but his eyes were glued open. She saw him staring at the tits in front of him.

"You're a fucked up kid, Premee, you know that?" She turned her back on her son and went to the kitchen table where her instruments were already laid out. Mike watched his mother tap the syringe and clear the air bubbles expertly up and out, not spilling a drop. "What the fuck is wrong with you, anyway?" She had to dig around in her arm, through one of the open sores where hundreds of needles had gone before. She depressed the plunger and gave a sigh of satisfaction. The needle pulled out of her bruised skin and yellow ooze welled up after it.

Mike was frozen in place. Bile rose in his throat. This was a hallucination too. *No.* Tehrani was nowhere to be found. His desk should have been where his mother now sat.

"I asked you a question." She stood. "Are you stupid?" Mike wanted to stand too. She couldn't hurt him. He wasn't a little boy anymore. Except he was. His mother crossed the room again and towered over him. "You must be fucking stupid. Or else you're a pervert." She grabbed a chunk of his hair. "Are you a pervert?" She aimed to punch him. He closed his eyes for the blow, but it never came.

Tehrani looked up to see the tension in his client's body and said, "It's okay to open your eyes." It took Mike a long time to believe him. He came to and realized the room was as it should be. The ceiling was golden in the low light of the office. He turned his head to see the doctor, alone in his high backed chair. His scratching had stopped. "Would you like to talk about what you just experienced?"

Everything in Mike's body told him to say yes, to just confess and get it over with. How could living with skeletons be better than life behind bars?

"What just happened is that I fell asleep, Doc."

"Did you dream?"

Mike's mouth twitched. "Don't worry. It was just a nightmare." He pushed the image of his mother out and replaced it with the image of Peach in that glittery top. He closed his eyes, and said, "I'm ready," but Dr. Tehrani stayed quiet for a minute longer.

Truthfully, he didn't want to go through with the session. Michael Perry was locking himself up and there was no chance of a breakthrough with someone hellbent on staying sick. He'd texted Tamara to make sure she left early, but she was still in the building. She'd wanted to finish her paperwork before heading out. He could keep Perry in place for a while longer.

He said, "You are going to sleep again, not your mind, only your body. You're exhausted." It was true. "Feel how your breath deepens. Your arms and legs become too heavy to move. Your head feels fuzzy, but your mind is clear."

Mike was daydreaming still. How could his mother feel so real to him, just behind his eyelids, why was he finally remembering her here? The Doctor's voice seemed to drone on and on. "... You don't need to move. You just need to rest. Whatever has been bothering you is gone now. You can't see it anymore. Even if it returns, you only need to focus on your goal."

Mike should have been thinking about the sore throat, the bloody cough, the breathlessness and fatigue. He should have thought about how much he needed to quit smoking and drinking, and how happy he'd be once he did. Instead, he was focusing on Peach behind her desk. Peach serving him a drink. Peach laughing and teasing him. She was everything his mother was not, not that he was seriously comparing the two. Peach was everything Angie had to work so hard to be. Peach was so much more than that. He thought about being with her, *really* being with her. The thought of her alone was not enough. Her presence alone was Mike's sanctuary. Only she could make the memories go away.

"Your goal is close now. Look. Imagine how you'll look, how you'll feel. You already feel like your old self again. Better actually, you feel like a new you. A new you that you've never imagined." Tehrani interpreted Mike's smile as a breakthrough, but Mike was imagining Peach's naked body wrapped around his own. "Yes. That's right. You'll be a stronger, healthier, happier you."

"There is power in this future self. It is a physical power. You can feel electrical currents through your legs...through your arms...through your stomach...through your brain. That electricity is lighting you up. It's telling you to stay on track. Listen to your body." Mike was battling an erection. He felt Peach's writhing body against his own. "Your body wants to be at ease. Your body wants to relax. Be completely at ease." They sat in silence for a while.

Then Tehrani said, "I'm going to snap my fingers and you're going to wake up feeling in control and capable of achieving your goal of beating cigarettes."

Of being with Peach.

The snap was a static shock. Mike's eyes shot open. His body tensed. He thought he might have tachycardia, but the surge passed and he relaxed again. He could still remember the dream he'd had, but he couldn't remember why he'd been so afraid.

"How do you feel?"

"I feel..."

Mike smiled at Tehrani. He was about to say alive, when the clock cracked out the first sharp chime to mark the hour.

Tehrani watched Mike's eyes fall upon the clock. He read something in his patient's face that hadn't appeared last week. He couldn't name it. It was squeezing out of the creases of his forehead, it was hollowed out of his bulging eyes. It wasn't physical pain. More like a psychic trauma.

That clock mimicked the piece that sat in Mike's childhood living room. It was the soundtrack to Saturday morning cartoons he watched on mute while his mother was passed out. Whenever he'd had to sneak back into the house or risk dying in the cold, that clock was the steady tap on his shoulder. The day he'd crept up to his sleeping mother with his revenge in hand, that clock had caught him in the act.

"Mr. Perry? Michael? Are you alright?"

Mike came to, but he couldn't meet the doctor's eyes. "I'm fine. I was just zoned out." It sounded like he was reading a script. Tehrani scanned the very first notes he'd written with Mike in this room. He closed his pen in a fist, angry with himself. He'd missed something. *This was never about the cigarettes.*

"Mr. Perry." Mike made himself look up. "I'd like you to consider having a few counselling sessions with me. I think talking things out is the only thing that can help you right now." Mike blinked.

"Talk?" He wanted to be angry, but he was trapped by that clock. "Talk about what?"

"About everything that's happened with your wife, with your father...with your mother." The subtle twitch at Mike's eye caught Tehrani's attention. He waited a beat, then said, "I never really asked you about your mom. You said she died when you were young." Mike's eyes dilated as he tried to focus on the doctor's face. He heard the question long before he watched it pass through the doctor's lips, "How did it happen?"

In the dim light, everything seemed to blur. The chiming had ended ages ago, but the staccato tick of the clock was growing louder. Mike sat rigidly. He remembered now how the bell had tolled just as he was inserting the needle. That's why he'd pushed it in too far. He was startled by the shrill sound. His mother woke up too, accusation in her eyes.

Mike rubbed his moist hands on his pants, "She—I found her like that...She—I had to call the ambulance."

Tehrani waited for Mike to continue, but when he saw how his patient now gaped and rocked himself back and forth, he said, "I'm sorry. My question upset you."

Mike stood, mummified. He could not answer. He turned towards the door.

Alarmed, Tehrani tried to call him back. "Are you sure you're alright to leave, Mr. Perry?" Mike was already turning the knob and crossing the threshold. Tamara was outside the building, locking the door.

Their eyes met through the glass. Rain was coming down in sheets and Mike couldn't register who she was through the streaks of water. He staggered towards the exit. His vision kept blurring and doubling. This woman was not the beautiful receptionist. She was his mother with her stringy hair pasted to her head. She sneered at him through the window. She'd sold him for the night and now she was locking him out in the cold. He would not let her lock him out, never again.

"Mr. Perry?!" Tamara asked, her voice muffled through the glass. Her hand was frozen on the key in the deadbolt. Mike didn't speak, he only lunged at the locked door. Tamara sprang back, leaving her key and nearly tripping as she turned to run.

Mike didn't realize why he couldn't get through. Then the doctor's firm grip on his shoulders slowly shook him from his stupor.

Tehrani was surprised by how much strength it took to turn Mike around to face him. "Mike, I think you'd better take a moment."

Outside, Tamara disappeared into the safety of the rain. Tehrani waited until she was out of sight before he said, "Why don't I call you a cab?" Mike felt his eyes trying to refocus. He shook his head.

"No. I'm fine. I just thought she'd stolen my phone off the chair. But it's in my pocket. I'm fine. I'll drive." Tehrani wanted to argue, but the other man was relaxing, so he let go of Mike's shoulders.

"Well, I'll call you tomorrow. I want to check in on you and Angela." Mike's vision was still impaired. *She set you up to all this didn't she?* Tehrani continued, "It would be good to meet her." Mike felt the man touch him again, but he was seeing through a telescope. Tehrani's face was too distant, too inconsequential. Mike broke the doctor's grip and careened back towards the door. He managed to unlock it and run blindly into the rain, the same way he'd run into the snow so many years ago.

When he turned to look behind him he could have sworn he saw a ghost. A water-sodden woman with gnarled fingers, straight from clawing out of her rocky grave, was advancing through the downpour. Mike ran. She chased him to his truck. He felt her furious fingers wrap around his throat, but he got the door open and piled inside. He felt like he was breathing down a tube. He looked out his side window, but of course, there was nothing to be afraid of.

He had to get out of this place, but he still couldn't see clearly. His head felt inflamed, like his own mind was threatening a meltdown. He had to confess. He needed someone to know what he'd done. What he'd had to do. It wasn't his fault. It was his mother's. Yes. He'd killed her, but she had been a mad dog that needed to be put down.

Mike keyed the ignition. Now he needed to flee. He threw the truck into gear and sped off. A banshee had his head in its claws and if he didn't get far away, she'd shred him. Her shriek was his mother's piercing voice. *You're pathetic. You're a fucking waste.*

The oncoming car that nearly killed Mike was a splotch of light that seemed too large to avoid. Mike closed his eyes against the onslaught. He lost control of his truck and the other vehicle swerved into a parked car just to avoid him. Their horn's blast cascaded over him until he swerved back into his own lane. He kept on speeding until he reached Cambie bridge.

There he finally slowed. If he could leave his mess on this side of the water, maybe he could lose it on the other side. He felt in his pocket for his pack of cigarettes. It was still there. He wouldn't smoke. He couldn't, but the shape of it soothed him. Driving away from the city core, Mike could finally breathe again. He could finally see again.

All around the vehicle, the skyscrapers collapsed straight into the water. The flat bridge above black waters transported him swiftly out of his mind. On the other side of the bridge commercial buildings crumbled out of the rocky shore. Underlit construction signs promised luxury apartments, but there were only chain-link fences and tatty single-story homes like the ones he'd grown up in after he'd killed his mother. The street lamps here were few and far between. The road offered the kind of dark anonymity that wasn't possible in the blaring downtown backdrop.

Night was dropping in. The sky was abysmal blue. Mike wanted to forget. For a while there, he really had. Now the dam had broken. Black waters stripped away all his childhood memories to their twisted core.

Mike opened his mouth wide, trying to loosen his jaw. The muscles relaxed reluctantly. He rolled his neck to relieve some of the tension that still held him in its talons. The mad panic that had upended him settled into a faint sense of dread.

He could never share the knowledge of his mother's death with Angie. Never. She would never understand what could bring him to do it. She had been abused for years and she never once stood up to her attacker. Mike, on the other hand, had killed a sleeping woman just because he couldn't take it anymore. He didn't even remember what finally broke him. A swirl of assaults fought to break the surface. He forced them back down. He refused to remember the faces of the men she'd sent to his room. But, of course, the penultimate memory came.

She'd stormed his fort—his sanctuary. His dad was not due back for four more days, but Mike thought he was safe the week before his dad returned. He thought because he had his friend, Damien, over for a sleepover that he'd be safe too. He had a witness. He could cry for help. His mother reeked like vodka. He knew by the look in her eye that she'd shot up.

"You were not supposed to have anyone over tonight. Your friend needs to go home now." When he refused to send Damien away, that's when she hit him. The force of that smack sent Mike to his knees. Her threats on Damien's life made the other fourteen-year-old grab his bike and flee into the night.

Mike wanted to kill his mother then, but he was no match for her meth-induced wrath. He tried to punch her, but she caught his wrist and nearly broke his arm twisting it up against his back. She called to whoever had been hiding outside in the trees. Mike saw a man with no face. None at all. Just a blank nightmare where there should have been a man. The bastard held him down while she stripped off his pants. The faceless monster hurled him onto the bed. Before he could turn away, she had licked the fear off of his upper lip.

"There. That's better," cooed his mother. "Now, don't you fucking move until he's done with you. He's going to give you your medicine."

Mike jolted back to the present. Vomit spurted out of his mouth before he even knew he was sick. He rolled down the window and tried to spit it out. Most of it just landed on the glass. He searched his vehicle for napkins and nearly drove his truck into a ditch. He checked his pockets. His pack was there, and so were Angie's mitts. Mike wiped his lips with one of these.

The night he was raped, Mike saw his mother's cigarettes right there like a relic on the coffee table. He swore he would never jab himself with a needle, but he stole the whole pack.

He torched his fort that same night and smoked his very first cigarette while watching the flames threaten to burn down the trees outside his home. Part of him wished they would. His mom and the man who'd paid her in drugs were still asleep inside. Instead, the fort collapsed in a fiery heap and burned itself out.

Mike saved the next cigarette for after he'd killed her. He thought it would be his last, but of course it became the first of many. He'd needed a smoke right after witnessing his mother convulse and finally, choke to death. Nicotine erased the smell of her vomit. He was sick to death after that, but he still wanted another smoke and another. He ran outside with the rest of her pack and chain-smoked right until the police arrived. They took his statement and told him none of this was his fault.

Mike wanted to believe them. But he couldn't shake off what he'd done. He couldn't tell anyone. Smoking, and later, alcohol gave him permission to forget. Mike inhaled fumes and exhaled fury. He let that woman burn to ash on the tip of his cigarette.

Before he knew how long he'd driven, night came down hard on the city. Kamikaze raindrops crashed into his windshield. Every streetlight and traffic light gave off dizzying tracers. Mike touched his pocket for reassurance. They were waiting for him. He turned the truck around before he hit Richmond and drove back through the swirl of inky rain. When he was back on Cambie, his phone buzzed. He knew it was Angie before he hit the Bluetooth button. He answered the call but remained silent.

"Mike?" Mike listened for the subtle inflection in her voice. He wanted to know if Tehrani had gone behind his back and called her.

Habit

"Mike?" He heard no terror, no anger, just the uncertainty that was natural after waiting for the person on the other end.

"I'm here."

"Mike? I just got home from work. Where are you? How was the session?"

"It was fine."

"Oh, good. That's good. Where are you now?" Mike took out the Export A's and slid out a single cigarette.

"I decided to catch a bite to eat."

"Oh...good. Yeah. I'm starving. Where are you?"

Wouldn't you like to know. He twirled the cigarette across his knuckles the way one might walk a coin.

"I'm halfway through the meal, Angela. I'll catch up with you at home." Angie could hear the sound of traffic behind his voice. *More lies.* She felt like she was breathing against a corset.

"When will you be home?"

"Who can say?" The absurdity of that question sent Angie into asthmatic panic.

"W-what's that supposed to mean, Mike? Where are you? What the fuck are you doing?"

"Angela."

Angie's throat closed.

"Calm the fuck down."

Her vision went white.

Mike said, "I'll tell you what I'm not doing. I'm not going to anymore fucking shrinks."

He cut the line and left her gasping like a fish. She clutched her chest. Her lungs seemed to close and she stood to try and find her long-lost inhaler. She wanted to call for help. She wanted to call the cops.

And tell them what?

She picked up the phone.

Queen Elisabeth Park rolled past on Mike's right. Mike turned in on a whim and drove slowly along the parkway. There was no one out in the rain except one poor soul and his shaggy dog. The dog was wearing a yellow reflective raincoat that matched its owner's. Mike did a double take when he saw it had on yellow rubber rain boots too. Even in his angst, this ensemble irritated Mike. Some fucking people. Mike drove to the end of the lane and parked next to the dog run. He sat there in the dark.

At some point he grabbed hold of a lighter and flicked idly at it. He needed Peach. He knew this. He'd always known this. He had needed her since he'd met her and through his own idiocy and procrastination, he'd never told her how he really felt. It was not too late. She had shown him that much when she'd pleaded for his help the other night. He was so wrapped up in his own thoughts, he didn't realize that the dart was lit and pressed to his lips. He coughed once, certain that his body would reject the toxins. But then there was the surge of nicotine coursing through his lungs down to his stomach. He was sick with pleasure.

The stranger and his dog were approaching now. They had come to play fetch in the rain. Mike chuckled. It was ludicrous, but there they were. The man unleashed the hound and tossed a tennis ball for it. Mike blinked in the smoke and had to roll down his window.

The man was tall and sandy-haired. His hair was pasted flat, but the rest of him must've been dry in his heavy-duty raincoat. His back was to Mike. The dog was an unfortunate black and white poodle mix. With its stupid yellow coat, it looked like a shag carpet rolled up in a Pringles tube. When the man turned around to throw in the opposite direction, Mike was in the middle of a luxurious pull on the cigarette. He caught sight of the guy's face and exhaled quickly before he went into another coughing fit.

It was fucking Collin, the dog man. *Well, if that ain't a sign.*

Habit

Collin hadn't noticed Mike or his truck. He was speaking to his bitch. Mike couldn't hear the exact words, but he assumed there was a lot of sex talk. *Good girl, come get it! You like that?* He watched the display in disbelief. Mike was not a religious man, but it felt like God himself was throwing him a bone. He had a problem and here was a solution. Except what was he proposing here? Mike hadn't even come to terms with the accidental death he'd caused just a day ago, now he was plotting murder. But of course, with Superman out of the way, Mike and Peach could finally be together.

For a long moment Mike could only breathe out, long and slow, as he waited for some other option to appear. He was not a killer. He was not going to run down his enemy. He'd taken life before only out of necessity—self-defence. This was the same. Collin wanted to take Peach away and that would kill Mike. It would kill him if one day Angie caught the bouquet at Peach and Collin's wedding. *A slow death is still death*. This was still an act of self-defence. An act of love. Dispose of Collin now, and Peach would be free. Mike would be there to ease her pain. Angie would be easy enough to be rid of. She and Peach could still be friends.

Mike could picture his wife's face while her friend told her the good news. There would be tears, no doubt, but Angie was a reasonable mouse. She had to know there was nothing left for their marriage. Mike inhaled the last dregs and tossed his butt into the rain. His truck was idling evenly. He ran his hands down the steering wheel and smiled. There was enough power under his fingertips to end this without even leaving the comfort of the cab. It didn't make his decision easier, only imperative. Collin would die so that Mike could—so that Peach could—live.

Mike made a full 360° scan of the park. There wasn't a light on in any of the houses across the street. Collin was in the middle of the field, his mutt bouncing around him. They were two rubber ducks in a row. When Mike put the truck into gear, the dog man didn't even look up. He didn't notice Mike carefully pull up onto the curb and cross the sidewalk towards him. Mike had checked for witnesses already, but his eyes scanned the area again, daring someone to interfere. His face twisted maliciously.

Only once Mike's tires bit into the wet grass did Collin turn to see the Ford stalking towards him. Staring into the headlamps, he couldn't see Mike's curled lips, or how his grip on the steering wheel tightened. He couldn't imagine how Mike's vision had tunnelled so that all he was aware of was the little yellow man in front of him. Like deer in the headlights, the dog and the dog man froze.

Mike stood on the gas and the truck nearly reared up in anticipation. He took off across the field, leaving ruts where the tires chewed grass and muck. Collin began to run, towards the far sidewalk first, then to the tennis courts. There was no chance. Mike's truck was right behind him, picking up speed until the muzzle was breathing down Collin's neck. In what seemed a mad dash to safety, Collin jumped and dove to the right. It was poor timing because the truck clipped his knees and threw him straight down. Mike felt the sickening jostle of going over Collin's legs, first with the front passenger's tire then the rear one.

Mike knew he wasn't dead and he considered getting out and finishing him off. He weighed whether it was more merciful to back up over him instead. Collin was screaming though. His dog was going mental. A light went on across the street. Any moment now someone would be peering out their window and spot him wheeling off of the field onto 37th Street. In his rearview, he could make out Collin's prone body, like a bump in the mud. He saw the mop, sopping wet with her tail between her legs, come to lick her master's wounds. Horror struck Mike as he realized that Collin would have to live. This fear catapulted him forward.

When he reached the main road, Mike drove quickly and deliberately away from the park. He swerved through puddles to clean off his tires. Once he was a safe distance from the scene, he pulled into a vacant lot and checked for any damage. There was a spot of missing paint on the fender and a chip where Mike could see yellow fibres from Collin's coat. He plucked the duck feathers out and rubbed at the surface with his thumb. If there had once been blood, he'd been absolved of it.

Mike had to remind himself to breathe. He had to remember his mission. Peach needed him now. He could no longer hide from his needs either. He would no longer let himself be haunted just because he'd killed his mother. She was gone and it was good she'd died. No, what haunted him was the thought of Peach, alone in the world like him. Mike would be everything and more for her. He wanted her body, but he wanted her soul too. He wasn't delusional; he knew she needed him just as much as he needed her. He would go to her. He would take care of her.

Fate had other plans it seemed. Just as Mike pulled up near Peach's townhouse and turned off his engine, he saw her scrambling out into the rain.

Habit

She locked up hurriedly and ran to her little green Toyota. Even in the downpour, Mike could see she was crying. *Word travels fast, then.* He had no doubt about where she was headed. He gave her time to pull out and make the left turn. For a moment he considered busting a window in her house and lying in wait. She might come back with Angie and that would be easier on all three of them. But Mike didn't want to wait any longer. What needed to be done now, could be done at the hospital.

Peach was too late to see Collin before he went in for emergency surgery. His left leg was tattered from the knee down. Both bones were in splinters. The doctor couldn't promise they'd let him keep it. The other leg was better, bruised, but not broken. He was lucky it had been cradled in a marshy patch of grass. He had minor scrapes on his hands, and a lump on his head, but otherwise he was certain to recover.

This news was overshadowed by the hideous fact that some lunatic had tried to take Collin down. Some fucker had deliberately driven through that dog park in an attempt to end his life. Peach paced the hospital hallways in a fury. Disgusted by the idea that someone could want to inflict this kind of damage, she wanted to kill something. Her hands responded by balling into fists. She eyed the second-rate paintings that lined the walls. Taking a breath, Peach lowered her heart rate and deliberately left the building. It was still pissing outside, but she stood under the awning. Worry splashed up at her. She wanted to call Angie to come wait with her, but Angie was dealing with something much larger right now: her husband's disappearing act.

It was chance that made her look up to see the devil himself striding away from the EMS panel door. He crossed the parking lot on her left, without noticing her. She guessed he'd been picking something up from work. At least she could put Angie's mind at ease and tell her she found the bastard.

"Mike!" she called.

Mike stopped and looked around through the rain before spotting her. Then he smiled and gave a little wave. When she motioned for him to come, he jogged out of the deluge and stood close to her under the awning. He looked like shit. There were scratches on the left side of his face and he smelled like cigarettes. Peach was in no mood to chastise him though. In fact, she thought a cigarette might be just what she needed right now too.

"How are you, Peach?"

"Not good, Michael. Not good at all. Collin's in surgery."

"What?" Mike searched her eyes. "What happened?"

"Someone hit him with their fucking truck. It was horrible. They drove right through a field and ran him down...like a..."

Dog.

Mike screwed up his face in concern and put his arm around her shoulders. She wrapped her arms around his middle and gave an outraged sob. Mike took the moment to press her head gently onto his shoulder. She felt so good. She smelled so good. Her curls were damp and downtrodden. Mike wanted to brush them out of her eyes and tell her it was going to be okay. But it was not going to be okay. Not in the way he wanted. Collin would survive. Superman would return. Mike just held her close, breathing her into him. If this were the only night they'd have, he'd have to make sure it lasted. After a moment, Peach let go. A moment after that, so did Mike. He didn't want to. He wanted to shelter her like this forever.

"Peach... I'm so sorry." She didn't start crying again. Instead, she pulled the tears away from her eyes with the sides of her hands.

"Yeah, well," she sniffed, "they're going to get the fucker. The police are already canvassing the neighbourhood. Somebody saw something. They know he was in a truck. Pat and Brenda picked Collin up and he said that much before he passed out from the pain."

"Crazy," said Mike, just to keep her talking. He didn't want to discuss Collin's last conscious memories. He wanted to get out of the open. Peach looked like she wanted to crush something. "Do you...want to go get coffee?" He asked it softly, willing her to nod her head and walk to the truck with him. She smiled weakly.

"No. I—I want to be here when Collin wakes up. God knows when that'll be."

Mike nodded. Peach breathed back her tears.

"So, what about you, Mike? What're you doing here?" Mike shifted his weight imperceptibly onto his toes. He wondered how this would need to happen. Before he could answer her question, she said, "I see you're smoking again."

Habit

"Yeah..." Mike replied. He looked out to his truck then down at Peach. "It's the stress I guess. Angie and I..."

"I heard," said Peach neatly.

Mike lowered his gaze but stayed near to her. He called on sheepishness and slid his gloved hand inside his pocket. He could almost feel her roll her eyes.

Peach relented. "Look. To be honest, I'm not going to rat on you. Actually, I was hoping to bum a smoke from you."

Mike raised his eyebrows. For a while he could only gape.

Then she asked, "What?"

"Nothing." Mike glanced to where his truck stood in a pool of darkness. "I just never thought you'd ask."

"So, you do have them on you?"

Mike pointed across the parking lot. "In my truck."

Peach followed the line of his finger. She had to squint in the spotlight to find his Ford parked in the shadows beneath it.

"Did you at least bring an umbrella?"

"No," Mike breathed.

"Well, let's go sit inside then. They can't run us out for smoking in a vehicle on the other side of the parking lot." Mike smiled and started out. He didn't wait for her, but he didn't rush away either. Peach stayed beneath the awning to watch him go. His stride was straight, hurried only by the rain. Only half an hour ago, Angie had sounded afraid on the phone. She may be a nervous woman, but Cricket was no coward. What the fuck was going through her husband's head? Peach shook her head and took out her phone.

Mike hopped into his truck while she was still only halfway across the lot. He whistled low, un-pocketing his smokes and popping them into the centre console. A minute later, Peach opened the passenger door and climbed clumsily inside.

"Jesus, Michael. Do you really need a two tonne?" Mike laughed and started the engine. He blasted the heat and checked all around them, as Peach gracelessly settled herself beside him. It was a comfortable seat, she had to admit. She breathed in the warm air of the vehicle. It smelled like leather, not cigarettes. Peach leaned back and breathed in for a moment. *Collin wore a leather coat.* She closed her eyes. Then she felt his fingers on her hand. She found Mike looking back at her. There was pain in his eyes. He didn't speak, but he surprised Peach by softly taking her hand. She hoped he wasn't going to kiss it. He only lifted it off the centre console.

Mike unhooked the hatch between them. His eyes still on Peach's, he removed his hand from hers, but hoped she understood that he wasn't just getting her out of the way. All of this was for her, only her. Mike recovered his paraphernalia but gave her a look that asked if she was sure she wanted this. Peach rolled her eyes.

One slim white cigarette came away at Mike's touch. He held this out to her. Peach took the offering and when Mike had his own smoke in his mouth, he found a lighter in his pocket. He turned to light hers first. Peach leaned in, looking down her nose. The flame highlighted the rose tint of her curls, but Mike was focused on her freckles. How had he never noticed those before?

Peach met his gaze, and the flame flicked out. She inhaled softly and immediately held the dart away from her face. She shut her eyes too late as the listless smoke stung them. Mike rolled down her window just as she fumbled to find the switch.

"Thanks," she whispered, with her eyes shut tight against the burn. She laid her arm way out into the open air. Rain assaulted her and she pulled back reluctantly.

"I'm surprised you're not coughing," Mike said once he'd lit his own cigarette. He watched her out of the corner of his eye.

Peach gave a dismissive gesture. "Yeah, yeah. Call me a hypocrite. I bum them off of Rita sometimes. But I deserve this one." She put the cigarette up to her lips and pulled. She held it in and then let it out as she said, "On a fucking night like this."

"I wasn't going to call you out. Not on a night like this."

She saw the tender hidden look in his eyes before he could turn away again. He was hurting. She could feel it. She wondered if maybe Angie was pushing him against a wall. Funny how baggage had a habit of following you into any new relationship. Or maybe she'd been pushing the baby on him again...

Habit

Mike's fingers fidgeted on the console. Peach sighed softly and laid her hand on his in solidarity. Their eyes met once again and she let him know that he could tell her anything.

God, but she was gorgeous. Mike stayed quiet. After the moment passed, Peach's thoughts turned back to Collin and she looked out the window. She removed her hand unconsciously and took another drag.

Mike asked, "You're really worried, aren't you?"

The question doused her fire completely. When she looked at him next, Mike thought her lip trembled. It was the trick of the light because when she looked away she said under her breath, "That fucker." For one tempting moment, Mike thought she meant Collin. Then he nodded gravely to himself; it was settled then. All they would have was this night together.

To lighten the mood, he said, "Come on. Let's go for a drive. Nothing better than riding in a big, warm truck on a rainy night." He leaned into the space between them and added, "Smoking like chimneys."

Peach smiled apologetically. "Mike," it was a soft plea. "I can't." Only, Mike heard the way she said his name.

"Come on." He put the truck in gear. "He won't be out of surgery for hours with those legs. You said so yourself."

But Peach had said nothing about Collin's legs. Her eyes fluttered from the gear shift to Mike. Mike fixed a smile into place. Peach saw his lips move, but not his hand. Even he was surprised by the swiftness of the syringe. Peach only had time to raise her forearm in front of her face before the needle bit into her neck and delivered its dose of ketamine. Peach dropped her cigarette onto her lap. Whirls of smoke settled where they'd been disturbed. Her body settled into the seat. The accusation in her eyes melted away. Consciousness abandoned her. Mike picked up the smouldering butt before it could burn her. Before she'd closed her eyes, he kissed her. As Mike pulled out of the lot, he ditched the syringe. The cigarette flew from his fingertips into the gutter. Its ember eye closed against the rain.

When Peach awoke, her head was still swirling with hallucinations. She was being carried, she thought by Collin...or her father. She was very small and she could tell he was taking her up to bed. She'd been spying on the movie from the bottom step. Her father often found her there. Now he was lifting her in his arms and ferrying her back to her dreams.

Mike lay her soundly on top of the sheets and took his place in a little reading chair by her side. They were both soaked from the rain. Mike's hair was dripping. Peach was making a damp spot on the bed. Mike realized that when he'd removed her shoes, he forgot to take off her jacket. She would be uncomfortable. Peach moaned when he touched her. His breath caught. The room lay in quiet anticipation.

The sound of the zipper tickled Mike's spine. It revealed pink skin under a simple white camisole. Her breath was slow and steady. She looked so peaceful. He thought back to all the times he'd dreamt of her. She'd never seemed so peaceful. He was ashamed that he had thought of ravaging her like some bastard in the dark. Looking down at Peach, all Mike wanted was to share that peaceful place. He bent down and stroked her hair. Her lips were parted. Mike steadied his breathing and closed his eyes. He kissed her lightly at first. The coolness of her lips gave him pause. He opened his eyes to look at her again. There was a flicker, but her eyes stayed closed.

Mike lifted her small form and removed the jacket. Her lids were still shut over fluttering eyes. He kissed her again, urgently this time. He wanted to warm her up, wanted to wake her, wanted to give her a part of himself in that kiss. He explored her mouth. It was an island—an oasis in the sea. He'd been bobbing along for so fucking long, fighting against the crashing waves. Mike came up for air.

Peach felt one raindrop roll from his forehead to hers, and then another, with each one cooling her skin. Collin was kissing her goodnight before he put her to bed. Her phone buzzed from inside the television and Collin left to see who was calling.

The screen read, *Cricket*. Mike stared down at the little pet name. He remembered the story clearly. Peach had christened Angie with this when she'd finally left the man who'd abused her their whole marriage. When she'd finally called the cops on him, Jackson Forcier punched Angie into the ground. He flipped open his knife, knowing full well he would go to jail for it. Knowing that he would go straight to prison, still he'd carved into her face. Peach said that Angie had been like Jackson's conscience; he cut her because he couldn't face himself.

Mike could never understand that part of a man. When he could have left her alone and gotten away, he chose vengeance. Mike thought he would have fled, the way he had with Collin and the unnamed woman, but then again he hadn't fled his mother. He had no choice there. She left him no choice and if she were alive today, he'd kill her again.

The phone went still in his hand. He had loved Angie for that story. He had wanted to kill Forcier, but he'd loved Angie. Mike stood there, levitating that moment in his hand. He had loved Angie as an extension of Peach. Now he had Peach. He killed the phone and the screen went black. He realized he was being watched. Peach's lids were only half-open, but her brow knitted as he turned to her. Her lips worked soundlessly.

Mike set the phone carefully onto the dresser.

"You're awake," he said, moving to shut the bedroom door. The light from the hallway closed like a book across Peach's face. The man who was neither her father, nor her lover circled the bed and stood over her. His features doubled then shuddered, then settled into place again.

"Michael?" It came out slurred.

He was silhouetted by the light from the street, but she knew he was smiling. She recognized the houses outside and knew where she was, too. *Home safe* came to mind, but she could smell cigarettes. She tried to lift her head from the pillow. Mike brushed her fallen hair out of her face.

"I have a confession," he said.

Peach didn't ask him what it was. She focused on regaining her composure. She didn't know if she needed to escape or to listen closely. The last hour was a blur. Then she remembered, Collin was hurt.

Mike's warm but calloused hand was cupping her chin.

He said, "Ask me what my confession is."

Peach's hackles rose. His grip tightened on her chin, but she didn't have a response, she just said, "Mike?"

"I killed my mother, Peach."

"What?"

"My own mother." He let go of her face but ran his fingers through her hair again. "I killed her when I realized she was going to kill me if I didn't."

Peach tried to understand the significance. She tried to picture the scene.

"I thought she overdosed..."

Mike chuckled. "You remembered." He kissed her forehead. "In a way, she did. But, I just had to tell you the truth. I had to get it off my chest. You don't know how long I've been holding back."

"Does...Angie know?"

All expression dropped off Mike's face as if his mask had fallen. He considered the question but decided there was no threat. "It doesn't even matter if she finds out. It's over between Angie and I."

"Michael, you can't mean..." Peach tried to lift herself out of the grog.

Mike put his hands on her shoulders and guided her back down. "I love you, Peach. I've loved you since I met you. It's my last confession, I swear, but it's true. I may have killed before, but I will never kill again with you by my side."

Peach could only open her mouth in bewilderment. No words came out. Mike took it as a sign of permission. He kissed her again, this time crawling on top of her. A puff of air escaped her once his weight had settled onto her waist.

"You're hurting me." Peach writhed, but Mike pinned her arms to her with his thighs. She searched for his eyes. They glinted. "Michael!" Peach tried again to free her limbs, but her efforts never touched him.

He leaned close to her face and whispered, "I've waited a long time for this." It was so quiet that Peach almost didn't hear him. She stopped struggling. She would not ask him what *this* was. She would not play his game. She should have listened to her fucking instincts.

Mike kissed her, hard. His teeth knocked into hers. He didn't notice. His tongue played across her teeth as if to count them. He flattened her tongue with his own. She felt him stiffen against her stomach. Peach cried out, filling his mouth with hot air until he broke the kiss.

Panting, Peach renewed her efforts to free herself. She planted her hands and feet on the bed. In one swift movement she bucked her hips, harder even than she meant to, and looked over her left shoulder at the same time. Mike's right hand was too late to brace himself and the top of his head cracked into the headboard. She took the tiny opportunity to dive under him, onto the floor.

"Fuck," said Mike to her back as she crawled away. Mike recovered his feet before she could though. He scooped her up under her arms and tossed her back onto the bed. When she tried to stand again, Mike hurled a finger at her.

"You stay where you're fucking put." His voice was quiet, but his eyes thundered. That finger was a lightning bolt. Peach tried to ignore it. She tried to focus on his features, but the ketamine and adrenaline were messing with her senses. Her own eyes narrowed into molten embers. She trembled with the flame she tried to light inside herself.

Mike held her gaze as if it were cool to the touch. He pulled back his finger, cinching her into place. Peach held very still then. She did not let him see that she was looking for a weapon in her peripheries.

Turning from her, he said in a low whisper, "I'm sorry, Peach. I'm not here to scare you." He looked out the window and Peach's eyes flew to the door, to her phone, to the headphones on her side table. She didn't even have a lamp to strike him with or a pen to stab him. She turned back to see Mike still staring out at the rain. He clasped his left wrist behind him. He stood looking out of the window as if he were a king, losing some battle in the distance. "I came here because I wanted to be honest with you."

Peach ground her teeth. "When are you going to start being honest?"

He glanced over his shoulder at her. "As soon as I know I can trust you."

"Trust *me*? How the fuck am I supposed to trust *you*."

"You should be grateful. I've looked after you more than you can ever know." Holding his posture, he turned to face her again. He caught the horrified certainty slice through her like a guillotine. The blood drained from Peach's face when she pictured Collin in Mike's headlights. Mike went to her then. He would not lose her to shock. He pressed his knuckles into the bed on either side of her shoulders and kissed her furiously. Sputtering, she pushed his face away. This time she punched out his elbow and when he was bent off balance, Peach rolled away and tried to escape over the other side of the bed. He was on top of her instantly, flattening her face into the bed with the palm of his hand.

"I don't want to hurt you, Peach." He leaned close to her ear, "I never wanted to hurt you." His words were soft. His grip wasn't. All his weight was resting on her body. Her right arm was crushed under his leg and he was holding her left hand in his.

"You've already hurt me!" she screamed. "You're hurting me right now!" Mike took some of the pressure off her.

"I'm sorry." He laughed a little. "I don't know my own strength. But Peach," he removed his hand from hers and stroked her cheek and said, "I love you. You know that don't you? That's the big secret with Mike." He laughed. "That's all it ever was."

"What are you talking about?"

"I want us to be together." She could feel him grinding against her leg then. Fire raged through her.

"Fuck you," spat Peach into the comforter. She groped around with her free hand while Mike pushed her hair to the side and used his tongue like a worm in her ear. His lips sucked at the skin on her neck like a leech. Peach tried to scream, but he forced her face into the blanket. He was crushing her whole body, while scrambling to get her pants off. Peach fought like hell. She kicked and twisted and freed one of her arms, but still Mike nearly had her naked. He went curiously still then. He let out a fatal groan and just lay paralyzed as if he'd been shot. Something like warm blood wet Peach's bare thigh. She stole a glance at the door. It was still closed. Mike shifted his weight.

"You fucking..." Mike tried to compose himself. "You're just like the rest." His caustic breath was next to her ear. He ground the wet spot into her leg. Peach let out a gasp as she realized what he'd done. She screamed in outrage, but Mike buried her face into the mattress, muffling her. Still screaming, she tried to escape but he forced her shoulder down with his elbow. "Shut the fuck up and hold still while I figure out what to do with you."

Peach did not comply. When her breath ran out, she fought to take in another and she screamed again. Mike pushed a pillow over her head. *Let her tire herself out.* If she thought this was the end, she was wrong. He hadn't had time to really think things through. He needed to prepare himself for the siege. Eventually she would let him in. She would still melt for him. He just had to stop that screaming first. The hand on top of the pillow pressed harder until she jerked for breath. She nearly headbutted him trying to lift her chin, but Mike shoved her face into the bed and leaned more weight onto the hand that held her. With her last strength, she floundered to escape. The screams faded along with her consciousness.

Mike removed his hand and let go of the breath he'd been holding. He moved back afraid he'd suffocated her. When he saw Peach's back expand and contract, he relaxed and kissed her warm shoulders. She'd be back soon enough. He needed respite. He didn't think her neighbours heard her scream, but he took off her sock and bunched it up into her mouth just in case she woke up and screamed again. He had wanted to trust her. Now he'd have to tie her up. Before he could crawl off to go look for some duct tape, Peach surfaced with a vengeance. She burst onto her hands and knees and elbowed him hard in the groin.

"Fuck!" Mike clutched himself with one hand. With the other, he closed Peach's hair in his fist and arched her, screaming, onto her back before she could get the gag out of her mouth. Her muted cry of pain did nothing to him. He just held her there by her golden locks and held himself until the bull's horn could be extracted from his balls. Meanwhile, Peach rehearsed through the pain.

"Okay," she begged.

"What's that? You've got something in your mouth."

"Okay," she mumbled again. "Mercy."

He didn't relinquish her. Bent unnaturally as it was, her back ached, but not as much as the top of her head. She thought he'd rip her hair out. His eyes cut into hers. She went still. She went quiet. When he was satisfied that she was finished screaming, he removed the balled up sock. Mike kept his other hand in her hair.

"Are you going to play nice?" he asked as he fumbled with her breasts, daring her to bluff. She kept her eyes on his and stirred only enough to position the cord in her right hand. Mike bore into her. Then he traced two fingers up her throat and parted her lips. Her teeth felt tender; she opened them against those prying fingers.

His glare was still sharp, but Peach forced herself to look at him. He dipped his fingers down her throat. She choked but held fast. He blocked her airway. Peach coughed but didn't blink. When Mike moved to kiss her again, her eyelids fluttered and Mike finally closed his.

Peach whipped her headphone cord around his throat and met it with her other hand. Feeling the touch to the nape of his neck, Mike backed off. Peach stayed with him. She pushed off her knees. His hand still held her hair, but now the momentum cantered Mike backwards. Still holding the cable with both hands, Peach crossed her fists and pressed all her weight into his throat. She straddled him awkwardly as he fell to his back on the floor. With a roar, she twisted away the last bit of slack in the line. The cord stretched white, cutting into both Mike's skin and Peach's. Peach shook with fury, willing Mike's eyes to roll. The cord snapped and Peach leapt off of Mike in the same instant.

Gasping and pulling up her pants, she beat him to the door. She wrenched it open while he staggered to his feet. He was two paces behind in the hallway, but he closed the gap on the stairs. Precisely as Mike was bowling Peach down to the ground level, the front door opened.

Peach's head hit the tile floor just as the intruder caught sight of the struggle. Neither Peach nor Mike heard the door over the crack of Peach's skull. Neither saw who approached them. Fireflies swarmed Peach's vision. The pain made her dizzy. Mike landed on top of her again and now he wrapped his hands around her throat. In his ire, he pressed hard enough to cut off her carotid artery along with her airway. Peach clawed Mike. She tried to pry his fingers off. Mike throttled her. Peach's ears rang from the swinging head injury. Her vision lagged from the lack of oxygen. She kicked her feet against the stair to try to lever him off, but her vision was darkening. There was a shadow. Peach felt the release on her neck when she heard the clap of clay against Mike's head. His fingers released, but his forehead hit her nose on its way down and she blacked out.

Angie looked down at the two bodies and then at her own hands. She flinched and dropped the heavy vase she'd used to kill her husband. She hadn't meant to kill him. She certainly hadn't meant for Peach to die. The vase only cracked into two pieces when it struck the tile. But the clatter was deafening. Angie hesitated a moment more before tentatively touching her fingers to Mike's neck. There was a pulse, fast and furious, but she realized it could only be her own. Her blood was in her ears. It was the only sensation she was aware of.

When Peach made a noise, Angie carefully rolled Mike's body off her. She looked at him uneasily. He was breathing. She could sense it now. Her eyes darted between him and her friend. They both had bloodied faces. The back of Peach's head was wet when Angie went to lift it. Peach groaned at the pain and tried to ward Angie off. Her feeble strength made Angie scared. Mike's sudden spasm made her scream.

She cradled Peach's head to her chest and pulled her carefully away, as if dragging her out of shark-infested waters. Peach's head lolled back and her body went limp in Angie's arms. She stopped her retreat to look down at her friend. Mike rolled, gurgling and blinking, onto his knees. Angie tried to tug Peach all the way out of his reach then. He noticed the movement and she watched his eyes focusing in on her. It was like looking down the barrel of a gun.

Mike saw the woman he loved being torn from him. He felt nauseous at the sight. He tried to speak, but only blood came out. Then he locked eyes with his wife. This bitch had smashed him over the head. Mike tried to calm himself, but then he noticed how lifeless Peach looked. Terror kicked his heart into overdrive when he saw the head wound. As it seemed to take all of Angie's strength to try to stand with Peach in her arms, Mike was worried about Peach's skull.

"Stop!" Mike lunged for Angie's ankle and pulled it out from under her. She went down and tried to shelter her friend's fall with her own body as best as she could. It cost her the wrist that she landed on. The clean snap ricocheted off the walls and it was Angie's turn to scream. Mike dragged Peach out of her trembling arms.

"No!" Angie cried. When Mike felt Peach's dead weight, he was certain she was gone. Angie had knocked him unconscious and now it was too late. He couldn't save her. Peach was dead and his world was spinning. He could feel Angie trying to steal her out from under him.

"Fuck off," Mike slurred, pulling Peach into himself. Angie backed away instinctively, but Mike's attention was on Peach. He was softer now, reverting to his first aid instincts, tilting her head back and listening for breath. For the moment Peach looked safe in his embrace. He was laying her down gently, assessing her wounds as if he hadn't inflicted them. Someone had crunched her nose. It was leaking red. Mike touched the back of her head deftly, but his body swayed. He almost fell on top of Peach when he tried to take off his shirt.

"What are you doing?" cried Angie, rushing to catch him.

"Have to save her." Mike was heavy in Angie's arms. She wanted to smack him and tell him not to touch her. He steadied himself and pushed his shirt up under Peach's head. Angie realized she couldn't hurt him, not without risking Peach. Instead, she pulled out her phone, careful not to reinjure her broken wrist, and started dialing 911. Mike snapped when he saw the phone in her hand.

"Don't you fucking do it." Angie avoided him like a mouse refusing to make eye contact with a cat. "If you call the cops... I'll kill you."

Still looking down, Angie said very quietly, "I'm calling an ambulance."

Mike snarled, "Give me that phone, Angela. I can take care of this myself." When she didn't move, Mike barked, "Do you want her to die? Give me the fucking phone!" Angie knew she couldn't comply, but he was like a bear with a fresh kill. She wanted to run, wanted to hide. When he reached for the phone, she flinched back. Mike struck her with a backhand that flung the phone out of her grip.

Angie folded over from the force and almost landed on her broken wrist. Pain shot through her as she hit her shoulder instead. She watched the cellphone skitter across the tile floor.

Mike growled, "It's over. You're nothing. If you say anything about this to the cops or to anyone, I'll slit your throat. Now back the fuck off."

The pain Angie felt was not from the blow, nor the break. She'd had worse. The pain was from the words like darts thrown into her gut. Mike wasn't saving Peach. He was saving her for himself. Angie looked between him and the phone, but he was no longer concerned with her existence. He was checking Peach's breathing again, with his ear bowed to her mouth. In his madness, he didn't even register Angie as a threat. He thought he was finished with her. She'd leave because he'd told her to.

She didn't. Instead, she reached behind her very slowly. She found what she was looking for and without drawing his attention to her, Angie swung one fractured piece of the vase across his face. Mike's body was thrown headfirst to the floor. The sharp edge of the vase lacerated his forehead and bit into his skull. Blood streamed into his eyes and his gulping mouth. He blinked blindly through the sheet of blood and tried to push himself off of the ground. His arms failed him and he lay there, crumpled and gasping.

Mike had never felt pain like this. It was short-circuiting his thoughts. Everything came out clipped. He had to help the woman he loved, but his wife was trying to kill him. He tried again to stand. Red seeped into his eye so that he saw two bloody women, one he could save if only he could kill the

Habit

other. Mike howled and heaved himself up. Another burst of pain, this time to the temple, pinned him to the ground. Now he saw nothing. He heard nothing over his own horrible drowning sounds. His eyes searched for something through the blood, but all he could see was a void. He reached out in one last attempt to save himself. There was no purchase to gain, no shore to wash up upon. The corners of his blood-soaked vision went black. Mike closed his eyes to the darkness.

Angie watched the light leave his eyes and then tears clouded her own vision. Misery was a cloak around her shoulders. She wanted to curl up and die beside her husband and her best friend. But Angie would not let herself lie down. She knelt over Peach and put her fingers to her pulse the way she'd done with Mike. This time she was calm, but she didn't feel anything. She gasped and put her cheek next to Peach's mouth, the way she'd seen Mike do. She could hear nothing, feel nothing. She didn't see Peach's chest rise again. Angie fell back, spluttering in terror, and dove for her phone.

The interview room felt more like a morgue. Alone within the cold, brick walls, Angie thought she should be laid out on the metal table instead of just slumped over it. Her head was bowed and her black hair hung in strings down her face. With difficulty, she kept her eyes from darting across the dark reflective window in the door, but she couldn't keep her hands from shaking. Even set in its cast, her right wrist was throbbing. Angie felt like her interrogators were standing right outside the door. She wasn't sure how long she'd been waiting here alone after failing to answer their questions. She was condemned to this six by six room until her lawyer showed up.

Mike was dead. He'd been photographed and printed and then zipped up in a body bag after EMS arrived. Meanwhile, at the hospital, the nurses helped Angie wash her face and hands before her x-ray. Still, she could smell his blood in her hair. She still heard the wheeze of his last breath snaking out of his body. Nobody gave her any news about Peach. But when Angie closed her eyes, she could still see the vase connecting with Mike's head, and Mike's head colliding with Peach's. Mike had headbutted her into quietus, but that was Angie's fault too. She shuddered at the thought and then looked up at the window.

Her reflection was a hulking, hollow-eyed thing, marred with the pink scar tissue on one side of her face, and a mottled bruise on the other. Two husbands. Two lessons. She didn't fight back and look what she got. She fought back and look what she got. Angie stretched her arms out on the table and rested her head down between them. She let loose a groan that came from deep in her belly. She had only wanted to stop him, but she hadn't called out. She had lashed out. Now Mike was gone and she was guilty even if it was self-defence.

After she was first brought down here, she instinctively asked for a phone call. She'd thought about calling a lawyer, but she didn't know a lawyer. She didn't want to have to need a lawyer. This was all a mistake. Staring down at the station's phone, she could think of only one person who might care to help her.

Officer Amanda Reid listened very carefully to what Angie was saying and when they'd hung up, she called the homicide detective and asked to assist with the interview. While Angie made her statement, Officer Reid had taken extensive notes. The detective, Peter Minhas, had listened without stirring. His expression never changed. When the story was over, Angie tasted sweat on her upper lip and her body felt feverish. Reid and Minhas waited until they were sure Angie was finished speaking and she was under control. She'd broken down more than once during the process.

Then, because the detective still hadn't said a word, Reid took the lead and said, "Mrs. Perry, I have some questions for you, just to make sure I understood everything."

Angie swallowed her composure back down. "Okay."

"You say you went over to Pamela Müller's house, but she sent you a text about seeing your husband at the hospital?"

"I... I went because she told me one thing, but he told me over the phone that he was out for dinner. He also said I couldn't join him, which I thought was weird."

"Do you always eat together?" asked Reid.

"No, but I could tell he wasn't in a restaurant. He was in his truck. Then I didn't hear from him for a long time and the next thing I know, I got the text from Peach... It scared me. I asked her why they were at the hospital."

"You said they work there together."

"Well, yeah. I mean, Peach is Mike's sierra."

"His what?"

Habit

"Sorry. His supervisor. But neither of them was supposed to be working last night." Reid made a note to check cellphone records and schedules.

"Okay, so your husband was at the hospital with his supervisor and you were worried that one of them was what—injured?" Angie couldn't lie, she hadn't really believed either of them was hurt. She thought only that Peach shouldn't be alone with Mike.

"I don't know what I was afraid of, maybe that Mike was lying to me because he'd been following her. Like I said, he's been acting weird around her, he's been weird in general..."

I noticed, thought Reid, acknowledging her own memories of the late Michael Perry.

"Did you know he was planning to hurt Ms. Müller?"

"No. But I know what I saw in that house." Angie was crying again. For a long time, she sat with her eyes pressed to the palms of her hands. The police analyzed her reaction very differently. To Detective Minhas, this was frustration from being questioned, it was not an involuntary reaction to trauma. To Officer Reid, it was a natural response to some horrible flashback. In truth, it was neither. Angie was simply exhausted. After this day, all she wanted was to curl up in a ball. She would not. Angie collected herself and said with finality, "It was lucky that I got there when I did."

"Why did you go there, Mrs. Perry?" It was Detective Minhas. He scanned the slow, calculated way his suspect raised her eyes to his.

Angie said cautiously, "I—I was scared. Peach *always* texts me back. We've known each other since before cellphones existed—back then you had to be where you said you were. Peach would have texted me back unless Mike was..." Angie wanted someone else to finish her sentence, but no one did. "Unless Mike was keeping her away from her phone."

"What did you do next?" asked Minhas.

"I waited an hour, but Mike never returned. Then I left my apartment. I knew that if I was wrong...well they'd be safe if they were at the hospital, right? I just wanted to make sure they weren't in trouble at the house." Amanda Reid stopped taking notes and folded her hands on the table.

"Okay Mrs. Perry," she said. "I think I understand. I just have a few more questions. We've already explained that none of this information is confidential, but I wanted to remind you of that. You don't have to say anything else to us without your lawyer."

Angie hesitated. Her voice was hoarse when she said, "I understand."

"And you wish to continue?"

After an agonizing moment, Angie said, "Yes."

"Okay, Mrs. Perry. You said *they* would be safe at the hospital and you wanted to be sure *they* weren't in trouble at the house. But you told us that you were afraid for Pamela—Peach's—safety. Why didn't you call the police before going to her house alone?"

"I...didn't want to overreact." Angie was kneading her hands. "I'm sorry I didn't call. I could have used the help." She looked between their faces, seeking confirmation. Reid looked like she wanted to comfort her, but Minhas was made of stone. Angie poured into his dark eyes, trying to make him understand. Failing that, she blurted out, "Mike was strangling her when I got to that house!" It was shrill. Angie sunk back down in her chair, trying to fold up into herself.

Reid looked to Minhas. Minhas said, "Mrs. Perry, we found what we suspect is your husband's DNA on Ms. Müller's person." Angie frowned.

"There was a lot of blood."

"Not blood." He lowered his voice respectively, "Semen. Is it possible they were having an affair?"

"I," Angie's throat was closing as she spoke. "I don't understand."

"It's simple," said Minhas, leaning in menacingly. "When she texted you to say she was at the hospital with your husband, Ms. Müller was giving you an alibi for him." The detective expected to get a reaction from Angie. It didn't come. "What she didn't realize was that he'd already lied to you..."

The insinuation slid down Angie's spine. "You think they were sleeping together."

"Do you?"

Angie didn't have an answer. She folded her arms and focused on her own quickening breath. Wasn't that the jealousy she'd swallowed on Thanksgiving, along with the fear she'd felt in her gut while they were all

Habit

playing Pictionary together? Hadn't Peach defended Mike when Angie poured her heart out?

"Mrs. Perry?" asked Officer Reid earnestly, "is that why you've been sleeping on the couch?" Angie gave the other woman a look of total despair. A simple no did not suffice. She could hear in the other woman's voice that she wanted to believe her when Angie said she'd been sleeping on the couch because Mike had mistreated her, but there was nothing she could add that didn't sound insincere. She couldn't talk about the dissatisfying sex, the distance, the depression. Even to Angie's ears, Mike sounded like a man who'd let go. Angie must look like the woman who wouldn't let him.

"Peach would tell you this is all a mistake if only..."

"I'm sorry, Mrs. Perry, but you're right." Reid opened her hands in surrender. "Without Ms. Müller's testimony to back you up, you are still under investigation for murder."

"And attempted murder." Minhas added.

The interview was over when Angie finally sealed her fate and asked for a lawyer. Alone in the soundproof room, under the scrutiny of the security camera, she examined her face in the glass again. Her vision clouded over. The walls closed in.

In an office down the hall, Minhas and Reid watched Angela Perry whimper on a computer screen. The detective wasn't sure what to make of her. He'd found her husband's semen on the other woman, and she hardly reacted to the news. She might have known. She might be a jealous wife come for revenge. She was big enough; she could easily outmatch her husband in a fight. But somehow in the confines of that basement room, she looked small and fragile.

Reid had a gut feeling about this woman, one that her partner understood but the detective did not. She was pondering on the facts when she heard a man's purposeful footsteps approaching the office.

Minhas called over, "Officer Harly, you're back."

"I am." Ben handed his partner one of the three coffees he was carrying on a tray. He gave a cup to Minhas and took the last one for himself. "What did I miss?"

"Not much," said Minhas, swearing under his breath when hot coffee sloshed onto his hand. "The crime scene painted a pretty vague picture. The upstairs bedroom had fingerprints and hair from at least three people."

"Mrs. Perry?"

"Nothing definitive yet... The bed looked slept in, but no other DNA was recovered. There was a broken pair of headphones that could have made the lines on Mr. Perry's throat, but the coroner confirmed it was the blow to the side of his head that likely killed him."

Reid interjected, "Angela said he struck her *after* she hit him."

"True." Minhas shrugged. "She has the bruise...but she also says her husband was trying to save Ms. Müller at one point..."

"Except he wouldn't let her call for help." Reid looked to Harly to see if he found any of this believable. Harly squinted in at the woman on the screen. Reid continued, "He struck her when she pulled out her phone."

"So she says." Minhas was not convinced.

Reid crossed her arms, cradling her coffee to her chest. All three of them had their eyes on the lone woman. They had been around and around Angie's statement already. Nothing was conclusive.

The detective learned a long time ago not to give a suspect the benefit of the doubt. They could smell when you were on their side and they'd say anything to make you see things from their perspective. A battered wife is one thing. A kidnapping another. A husband killed, and his lover on death's door...well, that spoke for itself. Still, the younger officer wanted to let Angela Perry go home.

"We searched her vehicle and the apartment and there was nothing to suggest she means to leave town." Minhas considered it but shook his head.

"Look Reid, she's confessed to killing him, yet she claims it was self-defence. She says she didn't mean to hurt Müller, but she admits that it's her fault she's in a coma."

"Because her husband headbutted her when Angela hit him."

"So she says. But you forget that Peach was also strangled. And before you argue, I don't care what Mrs. Perry says, the investigators agree that her hands are large enough to have made the marks on Müller's neck." Reid was quiet, and Minhas went on, "It's not likely Mrs. Perry is going home anytime soon. If that lawyer ever shows, he can request her release. Until then, she'll have to stay under custody. So, Harly, what's the word? Has Ms. Müller risen from the dead yet?"

"Unfortunately, no." Officer Harly took a long, life-giving sip of coffee before he continued, "I did have a conversation with her boyfriend though."

"He was visiting her in the hospital?"

"He was in the bed beside hers. Apparently, he was run down by a truck in Queen Elisabeth not even two hours before Angela Perry called Reid."

There was silence while the detective took that in.

"Any witnesses?" asked Officer Reid with hope in her voice.

"No, but the boyfriend remembers it was a truck, and there were tire marks found on the grass."

Minhas scoffed. "What kind of coincidence..."

"I don't think it was," replied Harly.

"You got a theory?"

"No, that's your job. All I've got is an investigator who matched those tracks to Perry's truck." He paused for another drink. "His truck was parked outside Pamela Müller's home last night. Now it's being combed over."

Minhas shook his head, "If you don't find anything in there we'll be back to square one."

"I understand that sir, that's why we're also checking through his phone records. I'll be personally following up with the mental health check called in by the guy's therapist this morning."

Detective Minhas' eyes widened over the rim of his coffee. He took a minute to digest what he was hearing. "So, Perry really might have gone off the deep end?" He didn't believe his own words. "First he attacks the boyfriend, then Müller?"

"Only Mrs. Perry shows up just in time," agreed Reid. *Like she said.*

Minhas shifted his weight. "What set him off?" He was weary from looking over the bloody crime scene photos and tired of interrogating the wife. Her lawyer was forty minutes late, and now Minhas was second guessing himself just standing around looking in at her. Reid noticed him patting himself down.

"Are you going for a smoke, detective?" she asked incredulously. Minhas found his pack and moved towards the door with a self-deprecating smile.

"I could use one too," mentioned Harly, following behind him.

Reid stared at her partner, but he only shrugged.

"Come on, there are worse habits."

Habit

Made in the USA
Monee, IL
04 November 2024

69377370R00121